"So…was reporti
imagined it would

They'd reached the bottom floor. The elevator doors opened and they made their way to the exit. Somehow Travis still managed to look like he'd just stepped off the pages of GQ.

"I thought those who can't, can at least talk about it," he said. "Turns out it's harder than people like you make it look."

"You did fine," Summer said in an attempt to be polite.

"I was terrible," he replied. She couldn't really argue with his self-assessment. She almost felt bad for him… until he opened the door for her and took note of the very dry parking lot, adding, "I don't know, Weather Girl, I think you might be losing your touch."

Summer couldn't hold back her grin as the thunder rumbled overhead. She opened her umbrella and stepped outside. The skies let go, raindrops sending tiny dust clouds into the air when they hit the pavement. "What was that?" she asked from under the protection of her big red umbrella. She cupped her ear with her free hand. "I can't hear you over the rain and thunder."

"Aren't you going to offer to walk me to my car?" he shouted as she backed away from him.

"I think you might be losing your touch, Ladykiller," she said, picking up the pace. "Good night!"

It wasn't as good as spotting a tornado, but watching Travis Lockwood get soaked to the bone as he ran to his fancy black sports car kind of made Summer's day.

Dear Reader,

Inspired by a friend's love of storm-chasing shows, I wrote this story centered around a woman who loves two things: her family and the weather. Family is forever. Weather is predictable. Love, on the other hand, isn't. There's no way to tell when it's coming or how long it's going to stick around. Not to mention it can be more dangerous than a tornado when your heart is on the line.

I absolutely loved bringing the characters of *The Weather Girl* to life. So much so that I often wonder what Summer would think of the weather reports I see on television. Summer and Travis had to ride out some storms to get to their happy ending, but you don't get a rainbow without a little rain!

I hope you enjoy the story and maybe fall in love with the weather girl, too! Come visit me at www.amyvastine.blogspot.com.

Amy Vastine

HARLEQUIN HEARTWARMING

Amy Vastine

The Weather Girl

Recycling programs
for this product may
not exist in your area.

ISBN-13: 978-0-373-36661-3

THE WEATHER GIRL

Copyright © 2014 by Amy Vastine

Printed in U.S.A.

H HARLEQUIN®
™ www.Harlequin.com

AMY VASTINE

has been plotting stories in her head for as long as she can remember. It's been a dream come true that people wanted to read them once she wrote them down. She lives outside Chicago with her high school sweetheart turned husband, three children and puppy dog. She loves to connect with readers on her Facebook author page, www.facebook.com/amyvastineauthor, and Twitter, @vastine7.

To my mom, who always believed in me.
Words cannot express how much I appreciate
and love you.

CHAPTER ONE

"It's another scorcher out there, Abilene. All across the Big Country, we're looking at upper nineties today and throughout the rest of the week. There's no relief from this drought in sight."

Summer shut off the radio and shook her head. Had no one ever heard of lower troposphere instability? Once again, the responsibility to set everyone straight fell solidly on her shoulders.

Storm waited patiently at the bottom of the stairs. She gave him a pat on his big, block head. "You can tell it's going to rain today. Can't you, boy?" The giant black Lab wagged his tail and barked once in agreement. When she was growing up, Summer's daddy always told her animals had a sixth sense about weather. It often made her wonder if she was born with some genetic abnormality that made her more like her trusted pet than the rest of the human race.

She sprinkled a little fish food in Isaac's tank and bid Storm farewell, snagging her umbrella on the way out the door. She'd need it today, despite what the weatherman on the radio said. Summer Raines always knew when it was going to rain, no matter what the computer models predicted or how cloudless the sky looked. She could feel it.

KLVA WAS BUZZING with an unusual energy when Summer arrived at the station. The new sports anchor had started today and everyone was giddy about it. The men were grouped together, enthusiastically reminiscing about game-changing plays and state championships. The women giggled and postured. Hair was big and clothes were tight today. The new guy was somewhat of a legend in these parts, born and raised in Sweetwater, and he played ball for Texas. The man's broadcasting experience was all on the other side of the microphone. He had held countless press conferences, only not as the press. Nobody else seemed to care his résumé consisted of nothing but football stats. For whatever reason, he was a big deal. A very big deal.

Ken Collins, the station director, believed this addition to the news team was going to give KLVA's ratings a major boost. Summer tried to focus on the positive. The former sports guy had been forced into early retirement. Bud Lawson gave her the creeps. His suits smelled like cigarettes and cheese and he thought it was completely appropriate to tell Summer he'd fantasized about her in a Dallas Cowboys cheerleading outfit. Even more disturbing, he'd attempted to pat her behind more than once. Summer spent a ridiculous amount of time and energy making sure her back was never turned to Bud.

Ken came to a dead stop in front of Summer and the umbrella resting against her desk. "When did you say it was going to rain? Richard didn't say that this morning. He said sunny and ninety. No rain. I washed my car on the way here."

She shrugged and Ken threw his hands up. "I only got the feeling before leaving the house," she explained. "Computer models say I'm wrong, but I'm pretty sure the winds are shifting."

"Great," he said with a huff. "Can you text

me the next time you get a feeling after the morning forecast? Please?"

"Will do, boss." Summer smiled as he shouted that they'd all better be ready for the staff meeting in ten minutes. Not everyone believed in Summer's abilities, but Ken and the leather interior of his convertible had learned the hard way that she often knew more than the average meteorologist.

"What are you wearing?" Rachel Crow came zooming across the newsroom, headed straight for Summer's desk. She was the station's most popular news anchor, beautiful and polished. On the air, she had the sweetest Southern disposition. Behind the scenes, however, she was a bit more…tenacious.

Summer looked down at her favorite silk top. It reminded her of Texas bluebonnets and matched the color of her eyes. "Clothes?"

Rachel was not amused. "What color are you wearing?"

"Blue."

"Yes! Yes, you're wearing blue!" Rachel tucked her auburn hair behind her ears as she looked around to make sure no one could overhear. "Do you know what color the Chicago Bears are?"

Summer didn't even know who the Chicago Bears *were*. "Blue?" she guessed.

"Blue," Rachel repeated solemnly. "Did you think about that when you got dressed this morning? Today, of all days?" Summer would have felt guilty if she had any clue what Rachel was talking about.

"I guess I wasn't thinking."

"Obviously."

"Hopefully you'll be able to forgive me."

"It's not my forgiveness you should be seeking, sugar. Not mine." Rachel shook her head and walked back to her desk.

Summer didn't have the time to worry about why the color blue and Chicago and bears were somehow the root of all evil today. She opened an email from her parents' friend Ryan Kimball about a tropical depression off the coast of Haiti that had turned into a tropical storm overnight. Ryan produced a storm-chasing show on the Discovery Channel that she watched religiously. He sent her the best pictures to post on KLVA's weather site since he was still out there, living the life her parents had lived until their untimely passing. He emailed her often, reminding her that storm chasing was in her blood, and she was kidding herself if she thought she could stay away forever.

"Looking up new ways to make sunny and ninety sound interesting?" a voice asked over Summer's shoulder. She spun in her seat and found her nemesis and fellow meteorologist, Richard Mitchell, appearing disheveled. He had removed his Dillard's Big and Tall suit coat, and his tie hung loosely around his neck. Richard was a large man who always seemed to be suffering in the Texas heat. The sweat stains on the armpits of his shirt made Summer cringe.

"I was checking on that tropical storm off the coast of—"

He cut in before she could finish. "I'm pretty sure the good people of Abilene couldn't care less about a tropical storm in the middle of nowhere. Unless, of course, you plan on telling them it's headed this way."

Richard's dislike of Summer was completely unjustified, if you asked her. She had earned the five and ten o'clock spots fair and square. She did her job well and people just plain liked her better than him. KLVA jumped to number two, ratingswise, when Summer switched from mornings to evenings.

"Well, as a matter of fact…" She glanced down at her bright red umbrella.

Richard's beady eyes widened. "There's no storm headed our way, Summer," he hissed. "If you go on the air and report that, you'll make a fool of yourself and this station!"

She glared at him. "There's only one fool in our department, and it's not me. Don't worry, I'll take full credit for my prediction and let our viewers know you thought differently."

Richard's face was redder than a July tomato. He pointed a thick, stubby finger at her. "You… You better watch yourself!" She laughed as he stomped off. "And don't you dare mention my name!" He shouted his idle threat over his shoulder. Richard could hate her all he wanted, but he knew if she thought it was going to rain, it most definitely would.

Ken came out of his office and called for everyone's attention. "All right, as most of you know, we have a new member to welcome to the KLVA team. Travis, come on over here."

Summer rolled her chair a little to the left to catch a glimpse of this supposed god among men. He emerged from the huddle of guys who had been reliving his glory days when she walked in. Travis was young, about Summer's age. His sandy blond hair sat on his head like a mop. The boy needed a haircut, but he wore a suit better than anyone else in the newsroom, perhaps in all of Texas. His broad shoulders and long legs made him a star on the field; his pearly white teeth and adorable dimples made him shine off-field. Her colleagues' big hair and tight clothes made sense now. Travis was a lady-killer.

Ken patted him on the back and squeezed his mammoth shoulder. "I am more than proud to officially introduce Travis Lockwood, our new evening sports anchor." More clapping, hooting and hollering took place.

Summer would admit he was cute, but this kind of welcome was unheard of around here. There was work to be done. She couldn't stop herself from opening The Weather Channel's website for a quick peck at the national map while Ken blathered on and on about Travis. She'd just clicked on a headline about how the drought was affecting the butterfly population when she heard her name.

"Right, Summer? I'm sure you can make that work."

Ken was looking at her expectantly. "Can

you repeat that, Ken? It's hard to hear y'all over here with the fan going." She pointed at the large oscillating fan blowing on Richard a few cubicles over.

"I said we're going to take thirty seconds from the weather segment and give it to Travis for the first couple weeks. Give him some time to really connect with the audience." Ken turned his attention back to Travis. "They're gonna love you, son."

Thirty seconds? Summer barely had enough time as it was to fit in everything she wanted to cover. She'd spent hours trimming here and there so she could add a segment she liked to call "Today in Weather History." She'd been gathering interesting weather facts for weeks. They could not take thirty seconds from her and give them to some stupid, former football player.

"I can't give you thirty seconds," she said over the din. The room immediately fell silent. All eyes were on Summer.

"What's that?" Ken's smile disappeared and his right eyebrow twitched. He didn't like being told no.

Summer cleared her throat and dug down deep for the courage she'd inherited from her parents. "I've been working on this special segment, and I need all the time I've been allotted. I don't have thirty seconds to give to sports."

Ken put his hands on his hips and looked down at his feet. Summer could see him wrestling with himself to stay polite. He raised his head and met Summer's stare. "That's all well and good, but your special segment is going to take a backseat to Travis right now. Everyone needs to be flexible here."

"Well, it seems to me, I'm the only one being asked to bend. Sports already gets a minute more than weather. It's not fair."

Ken laughed and scratched his head. "Life's not fair, Summer. Didn't your mama ever teach you that? My decision is final."

The entire newsroom looked back at Summer, waiting for her to do something stupid, like argue with him. But she kept her mouth shut, Ken ended the meeting and everyone went back to work. Everyone except Summer. She needed time to stew, her anger and frustration heating her body from the inside out.

Her sulk was quickly interrupted by one Mr. Lockwood. "I don't think we've been properly introduced. Travis Lockwood." His outstretched hand waited for hers. Summer glared at it before her manners got the best of her and she extended her hand.

"Summer Raines." She left off her usual "pleasure to meet you." She was madder than a wet hen but was determined to maintain her composure.

"Summer Raines, the weather girl," he said with a chuckle. "That's a good one. Who came up with that name?"

"My parents," she replied flatly, turning her attention back to the suffering butterfly population. "And my title is meteorologist. Not weather girl."

He had the nerve to appear abashed. "Sorry. No disrespect intended. Weather girl just fits better. You're cute, it's cute. Meteorologist sounds old and decrepit. More like…" He tipped his head in the direction of the noisy fan. "…that guy."

Summer refused to laugh, even if he was funny. She was also going to ignore that he'd called her cute. "All right, well, some of us need to get back to work on cutting thirty seconds from our report."

"I'm real sorry about that. I am. I don't want to step on any toes. Ken has high hopes

for me, but I'm a team player. I promise you."
He sat on the edge of her desk, oblivious of
the cold shoulder she was attempting to give
him.

She looked over at him. Those dimples
were almost too much. It didn't help that he
smelled good, like sunshine and soap. Besides the messy hair, he was the epitome of
the all-American guy. A big, strong man with
a chiseled jaw and a six-pack under his white
dress shirt. He probably had a cheerleader at
home and two more on the side. Summer was
going to steer clear. Men like him were nothing but trouble. Then she looked into his eyes.
They were the color of the sky just before it
rained. His mouth smiled, but his eyes carried his storm. Whatever the trouble was, she
suddenly felt guilty for being unkind.

She sighed. "It's fine. It's not your fault.
My issue is with Ken."

Travis brightened instantly. "Good. I'm
glad there aren't any hard feelings between
us."

Nope, no hard feelings. No feelings at all.
He could go be cute and charming somewhere else. But he didn't move. He sat there,
staring at her. His attention made her ner-

vous. When Summer got nervous, her brain did unusual things. "Did you know that even though most of the country has been dealing with excessive heat and drought conditions, Anchorage had its coldest July on record?"

Instead of wandering away confused and annoyed the way everyone else did when she spouted random facts, Travis leaned forward, looking interested. "Really? That's weird, huh?"

"Travis!" Rachel sashayed over, hand on hip and lipstick newly applied. "Now, don't you worry your pretty little head about Summer. She's the only one in Abilene who cares more about weather than football. Want me to give you a private tour of the studio before we go on the air?"

"Sure." Travis stood up and turned his attention back to the weather girl. "Looking forward to working with you, Summer."

She nodded. "I'm sure it's going to be great."

Rachel pursed her lips and scrunched up her nose. *Be nice,* she mouthed silently from behind Travis. The two of them left Summer alone with her discontented thoughts.

Had she really just let Travis the Time

Stealer make her nervous? Did he really think he could turn on the charm and hope all would be forgiven? No way. Summer was going to find a way to reclaim her thirty seconds. One way or another, she would get her "This Day in Weather History" segment. Travis and Ken could count on that.

BY THE TIME the five o'clock news rolled around, dusty gray clouds had moved in over Abilene and the rest of Big Country. Even though none of the computer models were predicting rain, Summer was going to promise some. During the commercial before her report, Travis walked by the green screen.

"Do y'all say break a leg or something before you go on?"

"Um, no. No one says that," Summer replied, trying not to laugh. The sound assistant adjusted her mic while Pete, one of the engineering techs, made sure the lighting was right.

"Well, good luck, then, Weather Girl." Travis started to walk toward the news desk but stopped. "You should wear blue every day."

Her mouth dropped open. "Huh?"

"It looks nice. Makes your eyes stand out."

He pointed at her face as though she'd forgotten where her eyes were located. "You have amazing eyes."

Summer was momentarily speechless. She looked over at a scowling Rachel, who practically had smoke blowing out her ears. "Funny. I was actually encouraged not to wear blue today. It kills bears in Chicago or something."

Rachel pinched the bridge of her nose and shook her head. Travis's brow furrowed. "The color blue kills bears? For real?"

"I think. Maybe not. I heard that somewhere, but that person was probably wrong because why in the world would blue have anything to do with bears? I mean, that makes no sense, right? I'm sure bears like blue," Summer rambled. How she wished she'd remained speechless. Her nerves took over. "Did you know that even though Chicago is called the Windy City, it doesn't even rank in the top ten windiest cities in the U.S.?"

"Really?"

"Really. Blue Hill, Massachusetts, is actually the windiest city."

"Blue Hill?" Travis smiled. "Are you messin' with me?"

"I never mess around about the weather."

"Ten seconds," the director called out. "Places, everyone."

Summer shook her head, trying to clear it of all this nonsense brought on by the man who needed an extra thirty seconds. She closed her eyes and pictured an F5 tornado blowing through town and taking Richard, Ken, Rachel and Travis with it. Once all the troublemakers in her life were swept away by her imaginary tornado, Summer felt back in control. She opened her eyes just as the light above the camera turned on.

Summer cut the national outlook out of her segment and somehow managed to fit her entire forecast into the little time she'd been given.

"Everyone, including the National Weather Service, says we shouldn't expect precipitation anytime soon. But, believe it or not, I say the rain will fall tonight across most of West Central Texas," she said, ending her report over at the news desk.

"Well, if Summer Raines says we're going to get some unexpected showers, I'll be grabbing my umbrella on the way out tonight, for sure." Rachel shot a big, fake smile into the camera. No one would believe she was staring daggers at Summer a few minutes ago.

"I do so appreciate your faith in me, Rachel," Summer returned sweetly.

The control room switched to Camera 2 so Rachel and Brian could introduce Travis. Summer hung around to watch, something she'd never done when Bud was on the air. Travis was nervous and it showed. Sweat made his moppy hair stick to his forehead. He fluctuated between speaking too fast and not fast enough. Maybe he was one of those athletes who'd been pushed through school without having to actually learn things, like how to read. That or the words on the Teleprompter were written in Chinese. He saved himself a little when he bantered with Rachel and Brian. He was better unscripted.

By the ten o'clock newscast, someone must have given him a few pointers. He managed to maintain a stable rate of speech, though it was still too fast. He ad-libbed more and wiped the sweat off his forehead during the highlight clips.

The viewers—and their colleagues—would probably still love him. People cut guys like Travis more slack than they deserved. If he ever figured out how to read, Summer would have to kiss her thirty seconds goodbye for good. She hung out in the Stormwatch Room, avoiding being seen in the newsroom sulking. She checked up on the storm in the Atlantic that had picked up enough speed to be classified as a hurricane. It would die out at sea, though. This day in weather history, Hurricane Nadine raged and whipped across the water. It maxed out at wind speeds of eighty-five miles per hour. No one in Abilene would ever know about it because all they cared about were Travis Lockwood's thoughts on the Dallas Cowboys' preseason.

The lights were low in the newsroom when Summer finally dared to show her face. All the producers and writers had gone home for the night. Ken's office was lit up behind drawn shades. He was likely congratulating himself with a glass of his secret whiskey he only broke out on special occasions. Still feeling defeated, Summer shut down her computer and picked up her bag and umbrella.

"You heading home?"

She jumped. Travis was leaning against the wall across from the elevators, somehow still managing to look as if he just stepped off the pages of *GQ*.

"It's about that time, I guess." She fiddled with her umbrella, spinning it on its pointy tip.

"You really can tell when it's going to rain? Even when the computers say differently?"

"What do computers really know?" Summer shot back. "Sometimes I think people have forgotten how to trust those feelings we all get. That tickle on the back of your neck right before something bad happens. The knot in your gut when something's not right. The way your heart tells you to stay or go."

The elevator arrived and the doors opened. Travis pushed off the wall and followed Summer inside. "Hearts can be fickle. Hard to trust," he said. His eyes stayed focused on the numbers above the door as they lit up.

"True." Summer's heart had played a trick or two on her before. "But usually we aren't listening close enough."

Travis nodded. That storm inside him had done some damage, that much was clear.

"So, was reporting about sports all you imagined it would be?" she asked as they reached the bottom floor. The doors opened and they made their way to the exit.

"I thought those who can't play can at least talk about it. Turns out it's harder than people like you make it look."

"You did fine," she said, to be polite.

"I was terrible."

Summer couldn't argue with his self-assessment. She almost felt bad for him until he held open the door for her and took note of the very dry parking lot.

"I don't know, Weather Girl. I think you might be losing your touch."

Summer couldn't hold back her grin as the thunder rumbled overhead. She opened her big red umbrella and stepped outside. The skies let go, raindrops sending tiny dust clouds into the air where they hit the pavement. "What was that?" she asked. She cupped her ear with her free hand. "I can't hear you over the rain and thunder."

"Aren't you going to offer to walk me to my car?" he shouted as she slowly backed away.

"I think you might be losing your touch, Lady-killer." She picked up the pace. "Good night!"

It wasn't a tornado, but watching Travis

Lockwood get soaked to the bone as he ran to his fancy black sports car kind of made Summer's day.

CHAPTER TWO

TRAVIS WAS HALFWAY out the door for his morning run when his phone rang. It was his mother, and he knew better than to ignore the call.

"Hey, Mom. Did you watch last night?"

"Did I watch last night? Of course I did! You were so great." Her definition of "great" must have been skewed by motherly devotion. "Your aunt Kelly called me right away to say you looked so handsome. And I just got off the phone with your brother. He thought you did super. Well, except he disagrees with your opinion of the Cowboys' defense, but you know Conner. He's decided the Texans are the only team in the state worth watching this year."

"What did Dad have to say?" Travis feared the answer but asked anyway. His father's opinion was never affected by silly emotion.

His mother paused. Not a good sign. "You

know your father. He was so tired last night and was asleep before the news came on. I recorded it, though. I'll make sure he watches."

His dad hadn't even bothered to watch. Travis was used to hearing his father's long list of things he needed to work on before the next game, but complete apathy was something he hadn't expected. Postgame criticism never hurt this badly. Was this what he had to look forward to? Disappointment masked as indifference?

Travis was having a hard enough time dealing with his own disappointment. His football career was over before it had truly had a chance to begin. One and a half seasons; that was all he got before a Chicago Bears linebacker sacked him and reinjured his shoulder. Playing football was all he knew. Since he was six years old, Travis had worked endless hours to be the best quarterback to come out of Texas. His father had been his coach until he was twelve. Then his parents hired the first private quarterback coach. The expectations were high and the pressure increased exponentially over time. Outside of football, his dad apparently had no expectations of him.

"Listen, Mom. I was about to head out for

a run before work. I'll call you in a couple of days, all right?"

"Sounds good. Don't worry about your dad, honey. Training camp started and he's in mourning, I guess. But he'll come around. You'll see. We love you, Travis. You know that."

"I know. Love you, too. Gotta run." He hung up and pushed his earbuds in, turning up the music good and loud. Travis never doubted his mother's love. The woman had doted on him his entire life regardless of how he did on the field. His father's love always felt more conditional. When the doctors informed them Travis's shoulder injury was career-ending, he had seen the look on his father's face. All the work, all the time, all the money he'd put into Travis was wasted. All his father's hopes and dreams died that day.

Mourning. His dad was mourning more than training camp.

Travis tried to clear his mind as he ran. He welcomed the burn in his legs and the ache in his chest as he hit the six-mile mark. The air was still a little thick from the rain last night, though there was no sign of it on the pavement. Travis shook his head at the memory of the girl with the red umbrella running to her car. Summer Raines. That girl was unusual, to say the least.

Women loved Travis. Back in high school and college, they lined up to get nothing more than a minute of his time.And his year and a half in the NFL? He could have dated a different woman every week.

He didn't do that, though. He had one girlfriend in high school, went out with a couple of girls in college and found himself a pretty lady who wanted to marry him during his first year with the Dolphins. But Brooke went running for the hills as soon as she found out Travis Lockwood wasn't going to be the next Dan Marino.

Fickle hearts. Stupid, fickle hearts.

Losing his career was tough. Losing faith in the person he thought was his true love was devastating. Travis's life had been on a nice, straight path, then all of a sudden it took a very sharp right. Then a left, before he spun out. Now he didn't know which direction he was headed. He was alone and unsure if that was the way it should be. After Brooke took his ring and stomped on his heart, trust would never come easily to him again.

Six months after his last football game, Travis picked up the pieces of his broken heart and his busted shoulder and returned to Sweetwater to start over. He was still loved throughout West Central Texas even if he couldn't play ball anymore. Everybody knew who he was and still thought he was worth something. Ken Collins thought he was worth something. He called Travis up and asked if he wanted to use that communications degree he'd earned. Sportscasting wasn't Travis's dream job, but hell, neither was football. Football had simply been his only option. When he couldn't play anymore, reporting on it seemed like a decent alternative—at least until Travis could figure out what he really wanted to do with his life.

The problem with reporting seemed to be that he wasn't very good at it. It was probably for the best that his dad hadn't watched him fail. It was only a matter of time before he disappointed Ken the way he'd let his dad down. Travis needed to work harder if he didn't want to end up unemployed again. Everyone at the station had welcomed him with open arms. Well, almost everyone. Summer Raines wasn't impressed. She didn't know who he was or what he had accomplished in his life. She didn't seem to know or care much about football at all. The weather girl was dedicated to her craft—period.

Travis sped up, sweat dripping down his forehead. He wiped it out of his eyes with the back of his hand. He was in the zone now, his body working like a well-oiled machine. No one who saw him running would suspect he was damaged beyond repair. Of course, out here there was no one trying to throw him down on the ground, looking to completely destroy his weakened shoulder. He was in great physical shape, just not for the one thing he thought he was born to do.

He pushed himself harder than usual. Rachel would likely give him some on-air pointers. She came off as more than willing to mentor the newcomer. So unlike the weather girl, who was excellent at her job but didn't seem to be much of a team player. Both women were experienced reporters. He also couldn't deny they were attractive. Rachel had a face that was made for television—a friendly smile, high cheekbones and porcelain skin. Summer had long blond hair with a little curl and the prettiest eyes he had ever seen.

As he sprinted back toward his house, he thought about how the last thing he needed was to give someone else a chance to break what was left of his heart. Rachel had been incredibly kind to him on his first day, but her intentions were familiarly questionable. She was too impressed with who Travis had been. Summer didn't like him. She had made that clear, and maybe that was what made her a safe mentor. He'd never get caught in the rain unprepared, and there was no chance they'd ever fall in love. It was a win-win for him, and it'd been a long time since Travis had won at anything.

"YOU REMEMBER PLAYING Wylie your senior year? My son was tight end. Maybe you remember him— Sean Harper? Number 80. He was a junior. Made all-conference his senior year."

Travis had played in thousands of football games. He remembered lots of opponents. He knew all the quarterbacks, several linemen, a handful of linebackers. Tight ends? Not so many. But the portly man with the bright green tie sitting beside him looked so desperate for Travis to recall his son, he lied.

"Sean Harper from Wylie." He paused as though he was trying to place him. "Oh yeah, tight end. He was a helluva player. Where'd he go after high school?"

Mr. Harper was beaming. "He went to A&M. Didn't play ball. Graduates this spring with a degree in accounting."

"You must be very proud."

"He's got a bright future ahead of him. His mom and I couldn't be prouder." Mr. Harper smiled and went back to his lunch. Bright future. Travis remembered what it felt like to have one of those. Suddenly, his shoulder ached and his stomach hurt. He tried to get in a couple bites before someone else asked him a football-related question, reminding him once again that his future wasn't looking nearly as good as Sean Harper's.

Making an appearance for the station at the Abilene Rotary Club luncheon sounded like a dream until Travis realized how little eating would actually be involved. After helping to present a service award to a gangly, pimply-faced teenager, he'd been bombarded with a million questions. The small banquet hall was filled with many of Abilene's finest, people who cared enough to give back to their community. Businessmen and businesswomen, local leaders, regular citizens who found purpose in promoting goodwill through their fellowship. Travis was surrounded by very nice people. Very nice people who wanted to talk to the fallen hero of West Central Texas. Each time he lifted his fork to his mouth, he was thwarted by another question.

"What channel do you work for again?" a woman with silver hair asked from across the table.

"He's over at Channel 6 with Rachel Crow and that weather girl who always knows when it's going to rain," Mr. Harper replied, allowing Travis to indulge in his first bite of the chicken that had been cooling on his plate.

"Oh, Summer Raines." The woman smiled. "I love her."

"You have to tell us," another gentleman in a dark blue blazer said, his eyes crinkling in the corners. "Is it true she has magic powers? Can she really predict when it's going to rain, or is it a gimmick?"

Travis's mouth was full of some of the best mashed potatoes he'd had in a long time. He swallowed them quickly as all eyes turned on him. It was strange to talk about something

other than his football past—or lack of a football future. Summer Raines had offered him
a reprieve, and she wasn't even here. "Well,
I haven't been working there long enough to
be sure, but I don't think it's magic. She's just
real good at her job."

"Rumor is she's a witch," one of the
younger women at the table whispered.
"That's why she's so connected with nature.
Wicca, they call it."

Travis snorted. Were these people serious? Travis didn't know the woman well,
but she sure wasn't a witch. "I don't think
she's a witch. She takes the weather seriously.
Spends a lot of time looking at things online.
Maps and radars, you know. Weather stuff."
He had no idea what he was talking about.
The other diners stared as though they could
tell.

"She's the only one I trust. She's always
right," the gray-haired woman said, breaking the silence.

The man beside her agreed. "Never been
wrong in all the time I've watched."

Travis was impressed. He drank some iced
tea and finished his lunch while the table continued to discuss the storms Summer had pre-

dicted. The weather girl was quite the legend in her own right. If he could learn from her, Travis might be able to pull this sportscasting thing off.

THE NEWSROOM WAS quieter today. Yesterday everyone had bombarded Travis with their memories of games they had watched him play over the years. One of the producers had been following Travis's career since he was in Pee Wee. Today, people were still friendly, but not as in-his-face. There was only one face he wanted to get in front of, and she was already at her desk, on her computer.

"Good afternoon, Weather Girl."

Her annoyance at that nickname was obvious. Her naturally pink cheeks flushed red and made him smile. She hated him and he loved it.

"Mr. Lockwood, good to see you were able to dry off after last night," she quipped.

Travis's laugh was deep. How he'd missed laughing for real and not for show. "I plan on telling Ken it's entirely your fault if I catch a cold."

"I don't control the weather, I just predict it." She turned her attention back to her monitor. Her soft-looking curls fell down like a curtain, shielding her face from him. He wanted to reach out and push them behind her ear so he could see those cheeks, those eyes. Her eyes really were amazing. They were big and blue like the Texas sky.

He sat on the edge of her desk. She flipped her hair off her shoulder and side-eyed him, saying nothing. He picked up the framed photo of a young couple and a curly-haired, little girl in front of something that looked like a souped-up tank. She snatched it out of his hands and set it back in its place. "Is there something you need? Maybe you're looking to unload thirty seconds from your segment? Or are you just here to bother me?"

"I was the special guest at the Abilene Rotary Club's luncheon today. They think you have magic powers. Said you've never been wrong about when it's going to rain." He left out the part where they wondered if she was a witch.

"No magic powers," she said, trying to look disinterested.

"That's what I said. I told them it was nothing but luck, and odds were you'd get it wrong one of these days."

Summer stopped what she was doing and turned her whole body in his direction. "Did you, now?"

Finally, he had her full attention. He smiled. Most ladies loved the dimples, but they only seemed to fuel Summer's fire. "I mean, if it's not magic, what else could it be?"

"You were a football player before this, correct?"

He liked how she had to ask, as if she wasn't completely sure. "Yes, ma'am."

"Does that not require any intuition at all? Or do you just learn how to play and that's it? Anybody with any athletic ability can do it?"

Again, she made him laugh. "Anyone can play. But to be good, you need to read more than a playbook."

"Exactly," she said with a smile and a wave of her hand. "I read more than the radar. I can't explain how it works, I just feel it. I'm sure there are things you can't teach someone about football. They just know it or they don't."

"Well, that's probably true. My mom swears I was born wearing a helmet. I probably know more about football than I want to." That was the truth. He had slept, eaten, drunk and breathed football his entire life. "Anytime you want to learn something about the game, I'd be happy to teach you."

She froze, her pretty pink lips parted. He'd hit the nerve he was looking for. Football held about as much of her interest as watching paint dry held his. She turned forward and shook her head. "I don't want to learn about football."

"Maybe you could teach me about predicting the rain, then?" Travis knew all about defensive strategy. She could block his pass all afternoon, but he wasn't going to stop trying for that touchdown.

She shook her head again. "You don't want to hear about weather forecasting."

"I do. I swear."

"Go away, Mr. Lockwood."

"You're leaving me no choice," he warned. "I'm gonna have to tell everyone at the Rotary Club it's magic."

Summer dropped her face into her hands and groaned in frustration. She was too much fun. It took so little to get her riled up. Sitting back up, she swiveled her chair in his direction and narrowed her eyes. "What do you want to know? That it dates back to 650

B.C.? Or how the Babylonians tried to make guesses based on things like cloud formations and other atmospheric phenomena?" He saw something in her eyes flicker. She truly lived for this stuff. "I mean, can you imagine? How accurate could they have been back then? If they did ever get it right, I think those people were simply more in tune with nature. Genetically, as a species, we—"

She stopped and snapped her mouth shut. Travis was entranced; he wanted her to continue. To have someone actually talk to him about something other than what he did when he was in a uniform was refreshing. "What? We what?"

Summer looked up at him, searching. She stood abruptly. "I'm not going to talk about weather only to have you laugh about it later with everyone else in the newsroom," she snapped. Before he could respond, she took off for the one place he couldn't follow—the dreaded ladies' room.

"Don't mind her." Travis spun around to find Rachel twirling a strand of hair. "She's a little socially inept. I think she's one of those savants. The kind of person who knows a whole bunch about one thing in particular but lacks social graces."

If she thought speaking of a coworker that way was somehow becoming, she was wrong. Summer's fear that he'd mock her made complete sense now. One thing he'd learned about women over the years was that the ones who tore down the others deserved his respect the least. Brooke had been a woman-basher, always pointing out the faults in the women she called friends. Travis had no time for that in his life anymore.

"Have you seen Ken? I need to check in with him."

Rachel's forehead creased. She was clearly shocked by his disregard for her comments about the weather girl. "He's probably in his office," she said, regaining her composure.

Travis nodded and took off. He figured there was only one way to earn Summer's trust and therefore her help. He had to convince Ken that Summer needed her thirty seconds back.

CHAPTER THREE

THE MORNING SUN was no more forgiving than the one that beat down any other time of day in September. Summer fanned herself with the church bulletin.

"Excellent sermon today, pastor," her grandfather said, shaking Pastor John's hand.

"Thank you, David. I meant to ask Summer if we should be praying for more rain or not. You got us a little bit earlier in the week, but it wasn't enough."

Summer loved that people thought she had some sort of control over the rain because she forecasted it. Predicting and causing were unfortunately two very different things, but meteorologists got blamed for weather conditions regardless. "Never hurts to pray," she replied.

"Isn't that the truth?" The pastor smiled kindly. "We'll see you next Sunday, Miss Raines."

Summer followed her grandparents back to the house. They always walked to church unless the weather prevented it. Some people were born for this heat. David and Sarah Raines were two of those people.

"So, tell me about this new sportscaster y'all got over there at Channel 6 now." Summer's grandmother hooked arms with her and patted her hand. "I thought he was kind of cute."

Summer's eyes rolled behind her sunglasses. Travis was annoyingly cute and ridiculously humble. He was also the reason Summer had to talk faster during her report. Her blood boiled. She fanned herself a little faster.

"He's barely capable of doing what he's being paid to do, Mimi. I'm sure we stole a few viewers away from Channel 4 last week, but I'm not so sure they're going to come back for more."

"I think if he were on Channel 4, I'd switch over after you were done so I could see him." Mimi winked and tugged on her arm. The woman always had a devilish look in her eyes—eyes that were the same blue as Summer's. People always told her she looked like her grandmother. Mimi's blond hair was a tad lighter but had the same gentle curl, although no one would ever know it because she always wore it in a long braid that fell down her back.

"You hear that, Big D?" Summer leaned forward to get her gentle giant of a grandfather's attention. He walked without a care on Mimi's other side. "You okay with her ogling the new sports guy every night?"

He shook his head at their nonsense. "She can look all she wants. She knows she's stuck with this old man until the good Lord takes me away. Then she can get herself an upgrade."

Mimi's sigh was loud and exaggerated. "Knowing how stubborn your granddad is, he'll probably outlive me and be the lucky one who gets to trade up."

Summer laughed. "That's probably best. They don't make men like they used to. I don't think you could upgrade if you were given the chance."

Big D reached behind his wife and placed his hand on his granddaughter's back. "You're a good girl, Summer."

Sundays were always the same—church

and lunch with her grandparents, followed by a quiet evening at home…alone. Summer didn't mind being by herself, but she enjoyed the first part of the day much more than the second. She loved working in the garden with Mimi or sharing the newspaper with Big D. Her grandparents were so different from her parents. They loved their simple life. They believed in putting down roots. They'd both lived in Abilene their entire lives. Before he retired, her grandfather had taught environmental science at the Christian university in town for over thirty years while her grandmother stayed home and raised three children. Summer's father was the youngest and the only boy. Gavin Raines was more like a leaf in the wind rather than a tree rooted in the ground.

"Don't think I didn't notice how you deflected the conversation away from the sports guy," Mimi said later as they put the finishing touches on an apple pie.

Summer smashed her lips together. She was not going to spill any of the feelings she was having about Travis. No matter how perceptive her grandmother thought she was being, there was nothing to tell. There was never going to be anything between Summer and the ex-football player who couldn't read a Teleprompter to save his life. His presence at the station ruined her chances of doing more than reporting the highs and lows for the week. All Summer wanted was to share her passion for Mother Nature. Was that too much to ask?

She opened the oven and put the pie in before setting the timer. "Did you know that in ten minutes, a hurricane can release more energy than all the world's nuclear weapons combined?"

"Well, well." Mimi rubbed her hands together with a gleeful look in her eye. "There must be a really good story about this boy if I'm gettin' weather facts."

"There was a hurricane near Haiti earlier this week. I find hurricanes quite fascinating," Summer said in her defense.

"I think you find something else more fascinating than you want to admit."

"He took thirty seconds of my weather report away. I find nothing the least bit fascinating about him *or* football. Football, football, football! Do people in Texas not know there are other things happening in the world besides football?"

Mimi bit her tongue, trying not to infuriate her already irrational granddaughter. Summer had moved to Abilene when she was sixteen and never quite acclimated to the Texas way of life. Being raised by hard-core storm chasers probably hadn't helped. "Oh, sweetheart, it's not his fault that football reigns supreme around these parts. You can't hold the general public's preferences against him."

Summer sat back down at the kitchen table, flustered. She hated that it was so easy for him. He waltzed into the studio and all the viewers were going to love him no matter what. She didn't love him. She didn't even like him. She barely tolerated him. "He also calls me Weather Girl. Says it sounds cute."

Mimi had to cover her mouth to stop her laughter from sending Summer into a real fit. "He thinks *you're* cute, doesn't he?"

Summer crossed her arms as she narrowed her eyes at the old woman. "If it weren't for the apple pie, I would so be going home right now."

Big D walked into the kitchen wondering if he needed to call for an ambulance. His wife was laughing so hard, her face was bright red. Mimi got up, wiping her eyes and shaking her head. She shooed them both out so she could get lunch ready.

"She still giving you a hard time about that quarterback?" Big D asked. He'd always had a soft spot for his granddaughter, but it got bigger after her parents died. Summer knew it and never took advantage. It was nice having Big D looking out for her, even when he only had to protect her from nosy grandmothers.

"She just wants me to get married before she dies. I figure the longer I drag it out, the longer she'll stick around. Maybe I'll wait until she's a hundred."

He looked up at the ceiling pleadingly. "Lord, help me."

"Be nice," Summer warned.

"She wants you to be happy, darlin'. That's all she wants."

She wanted them to be happy, too. When her dad died, so did a little piece of them. Summer's presence helped, healed some of the wounds. Still, one thing she'd learned in the hard years since her parents' deaths—people don't get over burying a child. Mimi was having a good day today, but next week was the anniversary of her son and daughter-in-law's deaths. As feisty as the old woman in the other room was, she still suffered from a broken heart. The dark days were coming. Summer could feel it.

"I am happy." Big D gave her a knowing look from his oversize recliner. "Most of the time," she added.

"I never thought you'd stick around here. Not that I mind, of course. I just thought you'd be more like your daddy, I guess."

Summer had two reasons why she stuck around, and they were both in this house. Part of her yearned to be in the thick of things, studying weather phenomena on location instead of reporting about them from the safety of a television studio. Nevertheless, she knew her grandmother wanted nothing more than for her to marry someone with roots in Texas and raise a family that would fill the dining room table every Sunday. Summer wasn't looking for some guy to settle down with because she wasn't sure she wanted to settle down. Sometimes she hoped there was a man out there who was going to blow into town and sweep her off her feet, take her away and show her the adventure of a lifetime. That was a secret she'd never dare tell.

"I'm good, Big D. Don't you waste one more minute worrying about me."

He sat forward and patted her knee with a weathered but gentle hand. "I could say the same thing to you, sweetheart."

SUMMER SPENT ALL of Sunday night thinking about what her grandfather had said. She thought about it again while she waited for her turn to speak to a bunch of kids at one of the local libraries Monday afternoon. It also crossed her mind when she arrived at the station later and opened an email from Ryan.

I have big news when I see you. You won't be able to say no this time. Your career as a boring, Texas weather girl is over.

Ryan was crazy. Wasn't he? Being a meteorologist was the perfect job for her. Summer got paid to talk about the weather five days a week. What more could she ask for?

Adventure.

The truth was, the thrill of a storm chase was like nothing else she had ever known.

She tried to appease the wild child inside her with rock climbing, hiking, even skydiving. Nothing came close. Summer loved the weather, but did she love being the—

"Weather Girl." Travis was all smiles as he sat on the corner of her desk. "Did you have a good weekend?"

"I had a great weekend," Summer said, taking a good look at him. His hair was shorter, a lot shorter. It made him look older, less like a boy and more like a man. "It looks like someone attacked your head with some clippers."

Looking sheepish, he rubbed his clean-shaven jaw with his knuckles. "I got a haircut," he said, stating the obvious. "My aunt Kelly's neighbor's book club apparently thought it was too long. Kelly agreed and called my mother, who called me and said she wasn't going to bake any red velvet cupcakes when I came to visit if I didn't get it cut."

"She drives a hard bargain."

"You have no idea. Her cupcakes make me cry," he whispered.

"Interesting," Summer said, not interested in the least.

"I'll ask her to bake you some. She likes you." He cringed and closed his eyes. His cheeks turned pink. "I mean she watches you and likes you, you know, as a weather girl."

If anyone knew about sticking her foot in her mouth, it was Summer. "If it makes you feel any better, my grandmother thinks you're cute," she confessed to ease his embarrassment.

"She does?" His eyes were bright like the clouds had lifted. "And would you say you consider your grandmother a wise woman?"

"Oh, Mimi is completely off her rocker. I mean, she is more than a few cards short of a full deck. Bonkers. Mad as a hatter. Crazy as a—"

"Okay, okay!" Travis put his fingers on her lips. "I get it."

Summer's heart skipped a beat, then flew into overdrive. Before she could process this unexpected physical reaction, Travis pulled his hand away and shoved it deep in his pants pocket.

"Did you know that the highest temperature ever recorded was 136 degrees Fahrenheit in Azizia, Libya?" she blurted out. "Can you imagine?"

His Adam's apple bobbed up and down. "That's crazy hot."

"Summer, Travis. Can you two come here a minute?" Ken called from the doorway of his office, breaking the tension.

Travis stood up and smiled. "I talked to him about giving your thirty seconds back."

Her thirty seconds. Summer made a mad dash to Ken's door. She could barely contain her excitement as she took a seat and waited for the two men to settle in. Maybe Travis wasn't so bad after all.

"I want to run through your upcoming appearances. You guys know about the Balloon Festival in a couple weeks?"

"I'm running in the 10K, so I'll be there all day," Summer announced anxiously. She wanted him to get to the part about her thirty seconds.

"You run?" Travis asked, seeming surprised. Summer nodded and bit her tongue. Was it really that shocking? Was he unaware of the fact that women could run? Did she not look like a runner?

"Well, you two don't need to be there until three o'clock. Brian and Rachel will be kicking off the event in the morning. You'll need to be there after the balloon launch. I'm sending some head shots for Travis to autograph. I think we could get a lot of traffic."

Abilene hosted an annual hot-air balloon festival to raise money for local charities. It attracted tens of thousands of people as well as local and national media attention. KLVA sent reporters to cover the event and held a meet and greet with some of the station's personalities. Above and beyond Rachel and their anchor, Brian, Travis was certain to be a big draw this year. Summer loved the Balloon Fest, but she dreaded having to spend the afternoon dealing with the football god and his disciples. This obsession with a man who threw a ball to other men made absolutely no sense to her.

Ken was momentarily distracted by an email alert. He slid his reading glasses off the top of his head and onto his face. He took his sweet time reading the message and typing a response.

"I run," Travis whispered.

"That's super," Summer whispered back. Did he want a medal? Did he not get enough attention for his previous career? Clearly he needed recognition for being able to run, as well.

"Okay." Ken turned away from the computer. "There's also the Rodeo Parade next month. You'll both need to be available for that, too."

"No problem," they said at the same time.

"Perfect. Then I've only got one other thing." Ken sat back, took his glasses off and set them on his desk. "Travis came to talk to me earlier about giving the thirty seconds back to weather."

"I appreciate that," Summer said, meaning it wholeheartedly.

"He and I discussed it, and I think I came up with the greatest idea," Ken continued.

Summer's smile faltered a bit. Ken had come up with an idea? Wasn't the idea giving weather back its thirty seconds?

"So, picture this," Ken said, holding his hands up as if he were framing the scene. "Instead of weather getting an extra thirty seconds each night, we add a whole special segment once a week."

Summer almost leaped out of her seat. A segment? A special segment? Her grandmother was right. Travis was cute. He was unbelievably cute. He was maybe the cutest guy she had ever met. "I am so glad you changed your mind," she said in a rush. "Like I told you a few weeks ago, I've been working on this weather history—"

Ken held up his hand to stop her. "Summer, Summer, hold on there. Let me finish."

The knot in her stomach told her something was wrong. Something was very wrong. She stole a glance in Travis's direction. He was rubbing the back of his neck, and his tension only added to her worry.

"Travis is going to bring a lot of viewers to the station, but he needs some—" Ken smiled at Travis apologetically before turning back to Summer "—polishing if we want to keep the viewers from switching back to Channel 4. You're a natural when it comes to reporting. You two are both young, attractive people. I've seen you banter in the newsroom. I like it. I like it a lot. I like it so much, I want to combine weather and sports during football season." His steepled fingers slid together to join his two hands.

Summer felt the heat rising up her chest. This was not what she wanted to hear.

"We send you two to do special on-location reports. Summer tells everybody how hot it is on the field and Travis talks about how hot the action is. He'll learn a thing or two from you. The viewers will eat you two up. It's brilliant. We'll do a couple of the high-school games to warm you up. Local games here in Abilene, Sweetwater's homecoming and then I want to send you down to Austin. Travis's alma mater. Summer in a Longhorns T-shirt. It's gonna be magic."

There were no words. No words for what Summer was feeling. She was being asked to report the weather at a football game. At several football games. No "This Day in Weather History." No escape from the nightmare that had begun when Travis Lockwood stepped into the newsroom.

"So, what do you think? You love it?" Ken looked back and forth between them with a huge, ugly smile.

Travis cleared his throat. Twice. "Ah, I think I'm game if Summer's game. I mean, as I said earlier, I want to prove myself— prove you didn't made a mistake hiring me."

Summer was having an out-of-body experience. She was no longer sitting in the chair. She hovered above everyone, looking down at the disastrous scene. Ken was all too pleased with himself, and when he came up with ideas like this, there was no stopping him. Nothing she said would make a difference, but she tried anyway.

"A Texas game means you want us to work on the weekend. Richard's not going to like that. He thinks things are unfair already. If I take the weekends, too, no telling what kind of fit he'll throw." Her voice shook slightly as she fought to keep herself together.

"I don't really care what Richard will and won't like. We're talking one Saturday. Most of these segments will be local high-school games on Friday nights. Maybe we'll send you to Dallas for a Cowboys game." Ken's focus went back to Travis. "You think you could work your connections to get us some one-on-ones? Maybe you and Romo? Travis! This is the best idea I've ever had!"

The walls began to close in on Summer. She needed to get out. She needed to leave the building. Without saying a word, she bolted from the office, past the elevators and straight to the stairwell. Her footsteps echoed as she made her way down.

"Summer!"

Her name didn't even register until she had pushed open the heavy door into the lobby.

She couldn't face Travis right now. Oh, the things she might say if she opened her mouth. This was his fault. If he hadn't come to work at Channel 6, she wouldn't be dealing with these changes. She certainly wouldn't have to go to football games every week. Weather would be nothing but a second thought on those days.

Fueled by her frustration, Summer exited through the building's revolving doors. The afternoon sun momentarily blinded her, and in her frantic need to get away, she bumped into a passerby. Shielding her eyes, she apologized to the man and kept moving with no destination in mind. Maybe Ryan was right. Maybe what Summer needed was an escape from it all. Why did she want to be a stupid weather girl anyway?

A hand wrapped around her arm, and Travis tugged her to a stop. "Summer, please. Don't be mad."

"Don't be mad?" Her anger rose. "First you take thirty seconds. Now you talk Ken into getting your own special segment? And I have to be dragged along with you?"

"I didn't ask him for anything," he said, letting her go and sounding exasperated. "All

I'm trying to do is find a way to do this job and do it well."

"Do it well? You can't even read the prompter!" If she was going to tell him how she felt, she was going to let all the ugly out. "You come in here with no experience, no résumé, nothing! You got this job because of who you were, not who you are. You smile and you charm everyone, but I know you're a fraud. You're nothing but a big fraud who took my thirty seconds. I've been asking Ken for a special weather segment for months and he gives the time to you instead. I shouldn't be mad? What should I be exactly?"

There was no boyish grin, no twinkling eyes. Travis looked pissed and not afraid to show it. He stepped forward, and Summer's back pressed against the warm brick behind her. He caged her in with his arms. His rock-hard body barcly an inch from hers made it hard to concentrate. "I didn't take your stupid thirty seconds. They were given to me. I didn't ask for them. I didn't plot to ruin your life. I simply took the job I was offered. And maybe I don't have any experience, but I'm willing to learn. Maybe I am a fraud, but I'm not your punching bag."

Summer felt as if her chest was going to break open from the pounding of her heart. She opened her mouth to say something but could think of nothing. He was right. She was blaming him for things that weren't really under his control.

Travis stepped back and ran his fingers through his too-short-to-tug hair. "I don't know what I'm doing or why I'm doing it. But you don't know me." He laughed without humor. "Here I thought that was a good thing," he said more to himself than her. He looked her in the eye, casting no doubt on his sincerity. "I tried to give you your time back. I asked Ken to do that, but he came up with this instead. I'm sorry football offends you so much. I'm sorry I offend you so much. Be mad. I don't really care."

With that, he stormed back inside, leaving Summer breathing heavily and filled with regret. She had cast him as the villain for no other reason than to make herself the victim. Summer was mad all right—mad at herself.

CHAPTER FOUR

TRAVIS WAS NO stranger to hard work. He was never one to back down from a challenge or to give up without a fight. He'd been fortunate that his talent on the football field made things easier for him. For every loss there were ten wins. Travis wasn't afraid of losing, though. There was only one thing he truly feared—failure. Failing wasn't the same as losing. Losing was temporary. Failing meant there was no coming back. His football career was a failure. He would not meet the goals his father had set for him or the ones he had set for himself. And according to the Weather Girl, his career in sportscasting was destined to end in failure, as well.

She'd called him a fraud, which was true. He didn't know the first thing about reporting. He tried faking it, but that wasn't working as well as he'd hoped. Summer also wanted to blame him for all her problems. As if having to attend a football game once a week was the worst problem in the world to have. She needed to get over herself. The world didn't revolve around the weather *or* football. Travis had learned that the hard way. As much as he enjoyed their harmless banter, he wouldn't accept her wrath. It was one thing to be uninterested. It was another to be mean.

Summer could be as mad as she wanted. He didn't care anymore—not about the length of her weather report, and not about her. From now on if he needed someone to tell him what a loser he was, he'd call his father. He also didn't need Summer pointing out he wasn't good enough. He had an ex-fiancée who had made that clear when she left him. Summer's opinion didn't matter.

Travis pinched the bridge of his nose and closed his eyes. Maybe Ken was right. Maybe going to these football games would help him. Obviously he needed the ego boost more than he thought. He'd be able to forget all about his current shortcomings by living it up in Austin or Dallas for a weekend.

Of course, what Ken didn't know was that Travis had no pull in the NFL anymore. He was damaged goods. People around these parts still worshipped the ground he walked on, but in the big leagues, he was nothing. It was embarrassing to think he'd have to sit down with Tony Romo and ask him questions about playing ball.

Travis had met the Dallas QB once when he was still in Austin. Back then, the expectations for him were high and there wasn't a team in the league that wasn't looking at their quarterback situation and wondering if they could get their hands on Travis. Romo was friendly enough, but he knew someday Travis was going to be real competition. Travis loved that, the unspoken anxiety he created in opponents. Nowadays, the only opponent he had was a sassy weather girl who wanted her stupid thirty seconds back, and she had proved too tough for him.

"Is there a storm headed our way that Summer didn't bother to tell us about?" Rachel voice startled him. She ran a finger along the top of Travis's desk and her blouse was open one button too low to be professional. Rachel, unlike Summer, had no issues with making things personal between the two of them.

Travis shook his head and leaned back in his chair. "She's getting some fresh air. Ken gave her a bit of bad news."

"She's moving to weekends?" Rachel certainly loved gossip. Travis shook his head. "He's cutting some of her appearances?" Travis shook his head again. "He's letting her go?"

"No, no. Nothing like that," Travis assured her. "She has to go to football games with me. That's all."

Something flashed in Rachel's eyes—displeasure, he thought. "Now, why in the world would Ken be sending Summer out to football games with you? That girl doesn't know a thing about football!"

"He's got it in his head that we have some sort of chemistry. I'd agree if oil and water somehow reacted to each other. But I think the only thing we do is push each other away."

Rachel tapped her painted fingernails on his desktop as she glared at Ken's office door. "You and Summer? Is he saying you two have better chemistry than Brian and me?"

"I don't think so."

"Is he saying you and I don't have chemistry?"

"Your name didn't really come up," Travis said, not understanding what she was getting at.

She paled and put a hand over her heart, looking horror-struck. "He's saying I don't have chemistry with anyone?"

"I can't really say what he thinks about your chemistry because like I said, you didn't come up in the conversation."

Rachel's hands were balled into fists at her sides as she stalked over to Ken's door. "Well, if he thinks he's going to groom that blond weather freak to take me out, he's got another think coming."

"What in the world are you talking about?" Travis shouted. He had no idea what was going on anymore.

Rachel pushed open the door without knocking and slammed it shut behind her. The women at KLVA were all certifiable. Just as that thought crossed his mind, in walked Summer. Those bluebell eyes met his and were brimming with something other than the anger and disgust that had been present a few minutes ago. She headed straight for Ken's office, knocking politely. Rachel flung open the door, almost knocking Summer over.

She pointed an angry finger at the bewildered weather girl. "Don't think I'm not on to you, Rain Princess. I know what you're up to. I know."

Travis watched as Rachel stomped off, knocking into one of the production assistants and snapping at the woman to get out of her way. Summer looked over at him, trying to make sense of what had happened. All he could do was shrug. He had no idea what was in the water today. Still slightly shaken, she stepped into Ken's office and closed the door behind her.

Try as he might, Travis couldn't keep himself from checking constantly for Summer to emerge. Although he couldn't make out exactly what was being said, Ken's voice was loud and scolding. When Summer finally opened the door, her expression gave away nothing. No telling what had gone on in there. She slowly walked toward Travis's desk. Her hair was pulled over one shoulder and he could tell she was nervous.

"I was wrong to take my frustration out on you. I'm sorry," she said like a child who had been told to apologize but didn't really mean it. She began to turn away.

"Hold up." Travis rose to his feet. He was a good foot and a half taller than her, and his size caused her to take a step back. "Obviously Ken told you you're stuck with me." She didn't deny it but arched an impressive eyebrow. "I get that you think I don't deserve to work here, but what is it about me that makes you so angry, huh? Does your boyfriend watch too much football on Sundays? Maybe your brother's team got beat by Sweetwater back in the day?"

"I don't have a brother or a boyfriend. Not that it's any of your business," she grumbled.

"I wasn't trying to pry."

"Listen, my weather time matters to me. You were given my time." There was another flash of resentment in her eyes. "I'm also allergic to people who are looking to make fun of me."

When had he ever mocked her? He had been nothing but nice to her even though she was the only person at the station who refused to jump on the welcome wagon. "I would never make fun of you for being passionate about something you love."

She regarded him with her head tilted slightly. "Is this your dream job? Is this what you want to do for the rest of your life?"

"I don't know."

"Maybe you should figure that out because sharing what I know about the weather is what I want to do with mine." She retreated to her desk. All hope of her helping him become a more polished sportscaster evaporated. Travis dropped back into his chair. His indecision made him feel ridiculous. He wasn't a child. He was a man who should know what he wanted out of life. Sadly, he did not.

TRAVIS WAS HARD-PRESSED to get any tips on improving his on-air performance. Summer Raines managed to be as elusive as... well, summer rain in Texas for the rest of the week. Travis and Summer's work-related appearances kept them from connecting before newscasts. She was all-business and disappeared as soon as she finished giving her forecast. It was probably for the best. If they didn't interact, she wouldn't have the chance to make him feel guilty.

Determined not to fail, Travis spent all his free time memorizing his reports. The less he had to rely on the Teleprompter, the better. His nerves still got the best of him now and again. He fumbled through the end of Friday's five o'clock report. It wasn't a complete disaster, but still not good enough. He resolved to hide in his car and practice during the break until it was flawless.

He was surprised to find Rachel waiting for him by his desk when he stopped to grab his keys. "Great job at five, Travis. You're really going to be a big draw." She put her hand on his arm and not so subtly squeezed his biceps. She must have liked what she felt because she let out an appreciative hum. "You've been an excellent addition to the team."

Travis took a step back. He was far from excellent. He wasn't even good yet. Over Rachel's shoulder, he spotted Summer on her way to the elevators. She looked at him, then Rachel, before averting her eyes and ducking her head. She pushed the button on the wall and stared at the little arrows above the doors. As unpleasant as an elevator ride with the Weather Girl seemed, it was definitely the lesser of two evils at this point.

Smiling graciously, Travis thanked Rachel and attempted to escape. She stepped in his way. "Did you bring dinner or would you like to join me for something to eat?"

"That's sweet of you, but—" he started.

"Great!" Rachel slipped her arm under his.

"I know this lovely place close by. The owners are big fans of mine. We'll be treated like royalty." She winked and led him to her desk to get her purse as Summer disappeared into the elevator alone.

Intercepted.

Thanks to Rachel's love of attention, their dinner took forever. She posed for pictures with other diners and made Travis sign autographs. In the end, they didn't get back to the station until it was nearly time to go on the air. Travis spent a few minutes hiding in the bathroom, practicing his report. It certainly wasn't going to be flawless. He'd be lucky if it lived up to his mediocre performance at five.

When he went to drop his notes on his desk before heading into the studio, Brian and Summer were standing nearby. "Come out for a couple drinks, Summer. It won't kill you," he heard Brian say.

Brian Sanchez was a decent guy and a likable anchorman. He had one of those faces that made you trust everything he had to say. So far, he hadn't given Travis any reason to believe that wasn't the case. Brian was also the unofficial social director at the station. He organized poker games and managed the station's softball team. He planned office picnics and Christmas parties. Tonight, he'd invited people out for drinks after work. Rachel had mentioned it at dinner—multiple times.

Instead of accepting his offer, Summer cleared her throat. "Did you know that the average snowflake is made up of 180 billion molecules of water?" she asked.

Travis shook his head at her response. Did she have any idea how lucky she was that her nerves didn't affect her work? He stood up as Brian continued to press. "Do not try to freak me out with your weather facts. You're coming with us. No backing out." Spotting Travis, he pulled him into the conversation. "You're coming, right Travis?"

Travis held up his hands. "Don't use me as bait. If she hears I'm coming, she won't show for sure."

"Your presence has no effect on my decision to go or not," Summer quickly retorted.

"There you have it!" Brian smacked Travis on the back. "It's settled. You're both coming." He smiled as he took off to catch one of the writers who needed some harassing about going out, as well.

Summer looked less than thrilled at the

prospect of drinks with her coworkers. "You don't have to go," Travis said, trying to give her an out.

"Maybe I want to go," she replied stubbornly.

"Then you should go."

"Maybe I will."

"Great."

"Great."

"I guess I'll see you there."

"I guess so." Summer's shoulder brushed against his arm as she slipped past him. As refreshing as her disinterest was, Travis was beginning to think it wouldn't be so bad if she could at least tolerate him.

The ten o'clock newscast didn't improve his mood. Travis's segment was passable at best. Ken was going to fire him if he didn't find a way to loosen up. Even though the Rangers looked as though they were headed for their third championship in the American League, rattling off baseball stats just wasn't his thing. He sat at his desk, wondering if being a football player was all he was ever going to be good at.

"Who's ready to celebrate Travis's first full week?" Rachel said from behind him. Travis turned around to find not only Rachel, but also Brian and a few of the guys from the control room ready to go. The writers and the evening producer were standing by the elevators with two of the women from marketing who'd finished work hours ago.

The large group headed down the street to a small bar with a pool table and good country music. As expected, the conversations centered on Travis, football or a combination of both. He found himself regurgitating the same stories he'd been telling all week long. Most wanted to know about Miami and what it was like to play in certain stadiums. Some wanted to talk about winning the Big 12 Championship game against Nebraska. Others focused on the high-school teams and what Travis thought of them. Rachel was clingy and her perfume made his nose itch.

The only decent conversation he had all night was with Summer, of all people. He overheard her telling one of the production assistants about some hurricane activity in the Caribbean and he joined in, sharing his storm experiences last year in Miami. Unfortunately, other people didn't find weather as interesting as he and Summer did, and it wasn't long before the focus shifted to Travis and football. Like it always did. No matter how hard he tried to not let it. As soon as that happened, Summer disappeared.

He found her talking to a young man in a black cowboy hat a little while later. His jeans and flannel shirt were a dead giveaway that he didn't work for the station. Unfortunately, he had a nephew who played for the local high school, and he wanted to know what Travis thought about the competition in 4A. Summer moved on pretty quickly.

Travis ordered one more drink from the bartender, who was quick to admit he had been a big Travis Lockwood fan. The old man kindly offered up his condolences regarding the shoulder injury. The pity was always hard to swallow. Travis could see it in people's eyes before it even came out of their mouths. Everyone was sorry his dream hadn't been fully realized. Sometimes Travis wanted to ask them how they knew what his dreams were. Maybe football had nothing to do with his dreams.

After enduring one more conversation about UT's prospects for a championship, Travis decided to call it a night. He slipped out, only to find the Weather Girl standing outside the door, digging through her enormous red bag.

"Here I've been waiting all evening to find out what the Babylonians had genetically that we don't and you're out here trying to sneak away without saying good-night," he said.

"Good night, Travis." She pulled her keys out and held them up, victorious.

"You hate me so much you won't even tell me, huh?"

Summer exhaled loudly. "I don't hate you. My grandma taught me hating someone is nothing but a big waste of time. Time that could be spent planting a garden or cleaning my room."

"I think your grandma was trying to get you to do your chores."

One side of her mouth quirked up as she headed for the parking lot. "Probably. She's tricky like that."

Travis followed. "You're killing me here. Why won't you tell me?"

"What do you want from me, exactly?"

Travis sighed and decided to be totally honest with her. "Someone to talk to who doesn't want to rehash every play I ever made on the football field. Someone who won't sit across from me hoping I'm going to take her home or kiss her good-night."

"Don't ever try to kiss me." The fierceness in her voice left no room for doubt. "That will get you a slap across the face, mister."

He held his hands up in surrender. "No kissing. Yes, ma'am. But I really do want to know about the Babylonians."

She clicked the button to unlock her car and pulled the door open. "I think the Babylonians could feel the rain coming like I do. My dad told me once that humans probably evolved so that we didn't need to be that sensitive to certain things. We had better shelter, tracked seasons formally, developed tools like barometers and Doppler radar. We didn't need to feel it anymore. Maybe I'm the last of the supersensitive humans."

When she talked about the weather, she came to life. There was something about the look in her eye when she shared that kind of information. It was a spark that flashed inside her, a light that he wanted to make brighter. "I think I get it. I might need you to be my date to the next Rotary meeting to explain it to them, though."

Summer flushed. "Did you know that we've been experiencing above-average temps for the last forty days in a row?"

"It's definitely hot around here. Not as hot as that place in Libya you were talking about, but still very hot."

She stared at him for a minute and he worried he hadn't gotten the country right. He could have sworn she said Libya.

Climbing into her car, she gave him one more curious look. "Good night, Travis."

"Good night, Summer." He watched her drive away. She didn't hate him. She didn't like him, either, but maybe she was coming close to tolerating him.

CHAPTER FIVE

SUMMER KNEW THINGS weren't going to go the way she wanted this week. It was destined to be a terrible, no good week. Between the changes at work and the date on the calendar, there was no way she was going to come out unscathed. Mimi stopped getting out of bed starting on Wednesday. Claimed to be feeling under the weather. A broken heart was not an ailment you could fix by picking something up at the drugstore, so Summer tried all her other tricks. She came over to help plant some bulbs for next spring, offered to paint the powder room Mimi had been complaining about a couple weeks ago, even asked for a cooking lesson. Nothing Summer did raised Mimi's spirits much. By Saturday, Big D had given up trying and told Summer she should do the same. He figured she'd get out of bed on Sunday, no point in pushing her any more than they already had.

Sunday was the tenth anniversary of her

parents' deaths and they always went to the cemetery for a small memorial. Mimi and Big D visited throughout the year, but the anniversary was the only time Summer went. It bugged her a little that her parents were buried in Texas. She imagined two free spirits like them would have wanted their ashes spread out over the sea, where their remains would continue the journey around the world for the rest of time.

Of course, they hadn't been expecting to die so young, and there was no will, no burial wishes written down. Mimi wanted them close and Summer's other grandparents were out of the picture. They had basically disowned their Miss Georgia Peach daughter when she'd come home from college telling them she'd met a boy who wanted her to chase dangerous storms with him all across the country.

Despite Big D's advice, Summer showed up at her grandparents' on Saturday anyway. It was better than sitting at home, wondering why Travis Lockwood cared so much about what she thought, or what Ryan was going to tell her when he showed up in Abilene tomorrow. She kissed her grandfather hello and made sure he had lunch before knocking on the bedroom door.

"Can I come in?" Summer asked, pushing the door open a crack. The room was dark, the shades pulled down and the curtains drawn.

"I'm not feelin' well. You might want to keep your distance," Mimi said softly.

Couldn't catch a broken heart, either, so Summer stepped inside. Mimi looked so small, all curled up on her bed under the quilt she'd stitched with her own hands. She had her back to the door and didn't move when Summer's footsteps made the wood floors creak. Summer ran her hand over one of the clusters of quilted stars. Mimi often joked she didn't need to camp; she slept under the stars every night. She had sewn one with a similar Seven Sisters pattern for Summer when she moved out.

Without asking, Summer climbed into the bed and wrapped herself around her grandmother from behind. She pressed her cheek against the back of Mimi's shoulder. "Did you now that when lightning strikes sandy soil, this kind of glass forms? People have actually found tubes of glass in the sand after thunderstorms."

"Lightning glass, huh?" the old woman replied.

"Yep. Kinda looks like a charred, hollow tree branch. I want some."

"Touchable lightning."

Summer smiled. "I knew you'd know why I thought it was cool. Being able to hold lightning in your hand? I'd feel like Zeus."

"Touch all the lightning glass you want, but stay away from the electrical kind, please." Mimi gave Summer's hand a pat.

"Yes, ma'am." They lay together in the dark and quiet, giving and taking comfort that couldn't be expressed any other way. "Want to come to the store with me to pick up what we need for lunch tomorrow? Ryan texted me. He said he and Kelly would be here when we get done with church."

"It's a testament to the kind of people your parents were, him coming here every year to remember them. He's never stopped being your daddy's best friend."

Summer squeezed her grandmother tightly. "Daddy had the best of everything. The best friends, the best wife, the best parents."

Mimi sniffled. "The best daughter," she added.

A few more minutes passed in silence. Sometimes Mimi came out from under the dark clouds on her own. Other times she needed Summer to show her the way. Summer rolled off the bed and went to the windows, throwing open the curtains. "Come to the store with me."

Mimi didn't argue or make excuses. Without any fuss, she sat up and hooked her legs over the side of the bed. As she ran her fingers through the tangles in her long blond hair, her all-cried-out eyes looked over at Summer. "I thank the good Lord every day that you weren't in the car that night."

Summer's parents had traveled with her all over North America when she was a child. They were the ones running toward a storm when everyone else was running away. They were scientists and adventurers who lived every day to the fullest, and woke up every morning with the purpose of discovering something new. It seemed like some sort of sad joke that two people who chased deadly storms would be done in by a drunk driver on the way home from their anniversary dinner, but that was the reality. One simple date night ended in a horrific tragedy that left Summer orphaned at sixteen.

She'd shamefully cursed God many times after the accident. It wasn't until she was an adult that she realized how blessed she really was. God took her parents but saw to it that she had her grandparents and they had her. The lump in Summer's throat made it impossible to respond to Mimi's comment. She simply nodded and gave her grandmother a few minutes to get ready. Maybe they both needed to get out of the house and focus on other things.

SUNDAY STARTED LIKE every other Sunday, with church and a leisurely walk home. The late morning sun was unforgiving today— temperatures were expected to reach into the nineties. The neighbors were all inside, enjoying their air-conditioning. Outdoor work had to be done just before sunrise or in the hour before sunset. The heat didn't allow for much more. Big D pulled out his handkerchief and wiped the sweat from the back of his neck. The collar of his white dress shirt was soaked.

"You sure you haven't been feeling any rain comin'?" he asked his granddaughter. "What I wouldn't give for some rain."

"Nope. Nothing."

"Sure your rain feelings aren't being distracted by some other feelings lately? Like the ones I think you have for that sports fella," Mimi chimed in with waggling eyebrows. She was unusually spirited given the date.

Summer nudged her with an elbow. How in the world had Travis found his way into their conversation? "There are no feelings. Rain or otherwise."

"You know, the more I watch him, the more I like him. I can't imagine what it must be like to be around him in person. He's one good-lookin' young man. Even Big D said he thought you two would be cute together."

"I'm fairly certain I never used the word *cute*," the old man interjected. "And leave the girl alone. Pestering her isn't going to get you what you want. Knowing Summer, she'll do the exact opposite of what you want just to spite you."

Summer laughed. He knew her all too well. Her grandmother had this way of riling up the rebellious sixteen-year-old inside her, the one she never dared to be when she really was a teenager. Travis was exactly what Mimi wanted for Summer—someone with roots in the area, with good genes and a pleasant disposition. Someone she could settle down with here in Texas until they were old and gray like Mimi and Big D. Only Summer didn't want to settle. Someday she was going to leave this place. Someday she would live a life of adventure.

"Travis Lockwood and I are completely incompatible. When you see it snow in July, you'll see me and that man get together."

"Careful, now, you know better than all of us that it snows somewhere in July," Mimi said with a smirk. As much as Summer hated being teased, it was worth it to see her grandmother smiling. She'd endure anything to keep Mimi in this mood, today of all days.

A cherry-red rental car was idling in the Raineses' driveway when they turned down their quiet street. Ryan came jogging down the sidewalk to greet them with hugs and hellos. Seeing Ryan again was like reuniting with a long-lost family member. He looked the same as he had the last time she'd seen him. Ryan had an actor's build—short but fit. What he lacked in height, he made up for in charisma and charm. He dressed as if he were auditioning for the role of Indiana Jones, minus the bullwhip. The man loved his khaki and his fedora. Wire-rimmed glasses were a new addition to the ensemble. They were an unfortunate side effect of old age, he complained. Summer rolled her eyes at that. His hair was a little grayer, but he still looked very much like the man she knew as a child.

His wife, Kelly, was the complete opposite of the woman Summer's mother had been. Grace Raines was born and raised to be a Southern belle. She grew up surrounded by wealth and privilege in Savannah. She went to college for the sole purpose of meeting a husband, or so her parents thought. Grace secretly had a passion for science and nature. When she met Gavin in an environmental science class freshman year, it was love at first sight. They were each other's missing half.

Kelly, on the other hand, was a Yankee through and through. Business-minded and independent. Ryan had met her when he started working for the Discovery Channel. She was an executive, working out of their

Maryland headquarters. It wasn't love at first sight, but a relationship that grew over time.

As different as she was from Grace, Summer liked Kelly. She was smart and savvy, and always knew what to say and when to say it. That was something Summer never felt she could pull off. Knowing the average rainfall in San Francisco was anything but practical when you lived in Texas.

"When did you guys paint the house?" Kelly asked as they made their way up the walkway to the front porch. She already looked uncomfortable in the Texas heat. Her brown hair was pulled into a high ponytail and her cheeks were flushed. "We were looking for a white house and drove up to this green beauty."

"Summer and I took that on last fall. We decided just because it was built in 1920 didn't mean it needed to look like it," Big D answered.

Ryan ruffled Summer's hair as he had when she was a child. "Well, aren't you the good little granddaughter?" She swatted his hand away. She was a good granddaughter, but she was also a twenty-six-year-old woman who had spent a long time getting her hair right this morning.

Inside the bungalow, Mimi brought out a pitcher of lemonade and glasses filled with ice. Big D switched on the ceiling fan and sat down in his faded blue chair. Ryan had loved Gavin Raines like a brother and had nothing but respect and affection for the man's family. Summer appreciated that he'd never lost touch after her parents died. She also loved listening to him talk. He could tell a story that made her feel as if she were there. The tales he told about storms she herself had witnessed were even more spectacular. Her memory never did them justice.

Ryan and his television crew had been busy documenting the string of tornadoes that had ravaged much of Tornado Alley and some Southern states over the summer. "We spent two weeks in Joplin trying to help. The damage an EF5 can do—" Ryan shook his head. "—you can't imagine. We could have spent two years there and still had work to do."

"Six F5 tornadoes in one year. That has to be a record," Big D said.

"Nope. There were seven in 1974," Summer said, beating Ryan to the punch.

Ryan smiled. "You don't even have to think about it, do you? It just pops into your head."

Summer shrugged. Sometimes it was that easy. Mimi called it another one of her gifts. Certain things she read or saw got filed away in her brain. Then, when she needed them, they appeared. Of course, there were also those times when facts jumped out of their files randomly. It was times like that her gift seemed more like a curse.

After lunch, Big D and Kelly offered to help Mimi clean up so Summer and Ryan could catch up in private. Ryan listened patiently about the latest drama at work. When she finished her tirade about the ridiculousness of Texas football, he asked her to join him outside. "Let's go check out that paint job."

The front porch wrapped around the west side of the house. Brick-based pillars supported the hangover roof that provided the shade Summer and Ryan were enjoying. Mimi had set two stone urns filled with sweet-smelling pink, purple and white alyssum on either side of the front door. Ryan took a seat in one of the rocking chairs, gesturing for Summer to take the other.

"So…" he started.

"So." Summer rocked her chair back and forth in an attempt to ease her nerves. She knew he didn't want to hear about the house. Ryan had something up his sleeve, and she wanted to know what it was almost as much as she didn't.

"Tell me something," he said. "When you hear my stories, how do they make you feel?"

Truth be told, they made her jealous. Jealous she didn't have stories like that to tell. She decided not to lie, but not to tell the whole truth, either. "I love your stories. You tell them well."

"What if I could offer you the chance to tell your own stories?" He watched the curiosity almost kill her, then relented. "I'm starting a new show. It's going to feature someone with a pure passion for storms past and present. Someone who isn't afraid to chase a tornado or explore a polar ice cap. I need someone who knows more about weather history than all of my researchers combined. I need you, Summer. I want you to star in your very own weather show."

Summer was speechless. This was it. The kind of adventure she dreamed about. Her gut told her to say yes, but her heart made her pause. There was no way this job would allow her to live in Abilene. Leaving Mimi and Big D was something she couldn't do. Not right now. The timing was all wrong.

"It sounds amazing, it does. It's just that my life is here. Mimi and Big D—"

"—seem like they're doing great. Mimi looks better than I've seen her in a long time."

Ryan knew how hard Mimi had taken her son's death. He was well aware of the depths of her depression. Summer hesitated. "She's doing really well, but—"

"But you think if you left, she'd what? Fall apart again?"

"No." Summer wasn't that arrogant. She knew Mimi was stronger than that, even after the episodes this past week. Summer's presence wasn't exactly necessary. Still, she felt better knowing she could watch over her grandparents. They weren't getting any younger and she felt a responsibility to both of them. "She'd be fine. I just… I like it here."

Ryan dropped his chin and gave her the look that said he knew better. She'd just spent the past twenty minutes complaining about work. There was no way he was going to believe she had a perfect life. "Think about how you'd never have to worry about losing thirty seconds again. Never have to go to any football games. The whole show would be yours. I'm telling you, Summer, I can't imagine anyone more perfect for this job than the daughter of Gavin and Gracie Raines."

She couldn't deny that the idea was more than appealing. The thought of seeing the storms she only got to read about was enough to make her ask him to take her away with him tonight.

"We start filming in a couple months," Ryan said. "Give me a chance to woo you a little bit. I won't accept any answer other than yes until the end of next month. Promise me you'll think about it."

Summer nodded. Even if she did turn him down, something told her this job was all she'd be able to think about anyway.

"Y'all ready to head over to the cemetery?" Big D popped his head out the front door. Summer wondered how much he had overheard. The look in his eyes told her it was more than she would have liked.

EVERYONE RODE TOGETHER out to Gavin and Grace's final resting place. Summer hated the cemetery, but when her aunts stopped coming a few years ago, she saw how much it hurt Mimi. She'd heard her grandmother telling Big D she felt they didn't want to honor their brother's memory. Summer knew then she'd be making the trip once a year for the rest of her life.

The Garden of Memories was a lovely place with the greenest grass in all of West Central Texas. A fountain of blue, sparkling water marked the entrance to the main grounds. Summer often thought they were trying to pass this place off as some sort of resort. A resort for the dead didn't seem all that appealing to her.

Summer believed in God and heaven. She believed people had souls and their earthly bodies were only a temporary home. Her parents weren't here in Abilene. They were living above the storms, chasing them on the other side. She wondered what they thought about this job Ryan was offering her. Knowing them, they'd want her to take it. Lord knew they would have.

Summer's parents were buried next to a marble angel sculpture. Her big white head tilted so that her vacant eyes looked down at them. The angel gave Mimi some peace of mind, so Summer ignored the way it creeped her out.

Ryan put his arm around her and gave her shoulder a squeeze. His knowing smile helped her relax a little. He knew this wasn't her favorite thing to do. Sometimes she wondered if his reasons for coming every year had more to do with her than paying his respects to the dead. Whatever his reasons were, she was grateful for his presence.

The five of them gathered around the two graves that shared one headstone. Summer always thought her parents would approve of that much. Mimi bent down and cleared some leaves from the base. The air smelled like the grass had been mown recently. Mimi ran her fingers over Gavin's name carved into the granite. Watching her made the tiny ache in Summer's chest grow. She looked at her feet and shifted her focus to the grass cuttings stuck to her shoes until the pain subsided.

"Ten years. How is it possible that so much time has gone by?" Mimi murmured, taking Big D's hand and standing back up. "I can still remember Gavin playing with his sisters in the sprinklers or riding his bike up and down our street, showing me all his fancy tricks."

"Fancy tricks that usually ended up with you needin' to bandage some part of his body," Big D added.

Summer smiled. The only part about this day she liked was hearing stories about her dad, seeing pieces of him that were from a time before she existed.

"The man was brilliant and daring but not very coordinated," Ryan said with a laugh.

"Grace was definitely the one with all the…well, grace," Mimi said.

That Summer did remember. When she was little, she thought her mother was a princess. Grace didn't wear fancy clothes or walk around in high-heeled shoes, but her elegance shone in the way she carried herself. Her kindness mixed with a quiet strength made her seem regal.

"They were perfect for each other." Ryan's hand found its way back onto Summer's shoulder. "Two people doing what they were born to do and loving every minute of it. We should all be so lucky to find that in our lives. People we love and risks worth taking."

Summer was thankful for her sunglasses as

she blinked back tears. What were you supposed to do when you had to choose between
the people you loved and those worthwhile
risks? Not many people lucked out the way
her parents had.

There were a few more stories to be told
before Big D led them all in a prayer. Mimi
kissed her fingers and touched the headstone.
The two couples turned back toward the parking lot. Summer's feet stayed planted, her
eyes fixed on the names Gavin and Grace.
She was never much for sharing at these
things. She usually listened to everyone else's
stories and said a silent prayer that her parents were happy where they were. Today she
felt as though she needed to say something
to them. Alone.

"You comin'?" Big D asked, holding his
free hand out for her.

"Can I have a minute? I'll meet y'all back
at the car."

"Take as much time as you need, sweetheart." He smiled and turned back toward
the path and the giant angel staring at them.

She waited until they were all far enough
away to have her say. "Well, you two, I'm
sure you know what Ryan said to me today.

You also know why I didn't say yes." The wind picked up and blew her hair around. She wrestled with it until the loose strands were securely tucked behind her ears. "I just want you to know that I promised to take care of Mimi and Big D and I plan on keeping that promise. I mean, who knows if things would work out if I went off and did this crazy show? It could be off the air in a few months and I'd be out of a job. I like to know what's coming and there's just no telling with this wild idea Ryan's got. Right?"

Summer knew she was trying to convince herself more than them. It wasn't as though they could voice their opinion anyway. She started to leave but stopped. "I miss you guys. All the time. I love you," she said, lifting her hand and waving goodbye to the headstone. She hoped that was an acceptable way to end a conversation with the dead. As she passed the angel she mumbled an amen just in case.

CHAPTER SIX

TRAVIS FINISHED HIS run in record time. His morning workouts were all he had to block out the negativity constantly whirling in his head. Besides struggling at work, he had heard through the grapevine that his ex had moved in with some Miami basketball player. How quickly Brooke had become an expert in making Travis feel completely insignificant.

West Central Texas still loved him, but the novelty of his presence at the station was destined to wear off sooner than later. All he was looking for was a little guidance, but his father was ignoring him. Not that the old man could coach him in broadcasting. But maybe he could tell Travis if he should give it up and pursue something else. If he told him what that something else should be, that would be helpful, too.

Ken's special assignment had made things a little easier. Talking about football at a football game felt much more natural than being behind a news desk. He and Summer had survived their first Friday night game together, and it was evident the woman was from another planet. She knew nothing about football. She claimed she went to high school in Abilene, even claimed to remember some of the guys who played when she was in school, but she had no clue what a first down was or how many points a touchdown was worth.

Summer didn't know one single rule of the game, but she could tell him the average snowfall in British Columbia. She was an anomaly, for sure. An anomaly with eyes framed by the longest lashes, who challenged high-school cheerleaders to a handspring competition during halftime.

After a shower and another unanswered phone call to his dad, Travis's plan was to spend the morning making this house his home instead of some temporary living space. The modest two-bedroom cottage was nothing compared to his villa in Miami, but he didn't want to invest too much in a place that might not be permanent.

There were plenty of pictures to hang and boxes to unpack before he had to make an appearance at the Balloon Festival. But just as he hammered in the first nail, a knock at the door startled him.

"Ouch!" Travis shoved his hammered thumb in his mouth as if that would soothe the pain.

"You have to save me." Conner Lockwood pushed his way into his little brother's house without waiting for an invitation.

"Conner, buddy, good to see you. Please come in," Travis said to the empty front porch.

"Do you know what it's like to live in a house with a human less than three months old? It's torture. She cries. All the time. She poops. All the time. She wants nothing to do with me! In fact, I think she hates me. All she wants is Heidi."

Travis had to stop him right there. He shut the door and joined his brother in the living room. "You have a beautiful wife and an adorable baby girl. Am I really supposed to feel bad for you?"

Conner had already made himself comfortable on the black leather couch, stretched out as if it were some kind of therapy session. "I told Heidi you called me and needed someone to help move some furniture. Please let me stay here. Please," he whined.

Travis took pity on him and let him stay. His brother was a good example of what life after football was for most. He played ball at LSU but wasn't destined to go any further than that. He met Heidi at school and married her as soon as they graduated. They moved back to Texas, and Conner went to work for their dad's insurance company, opening an office in Abilene.

Conner lived a modest life and still wore his state championship ring. Like many former Texas high-school football players, he talked about that time in his life as if it was the glory days. Travis hated to think like that. He didn't want to feel as though his best years had come and gone. He wanted to believe there was more.

Conner helped hang some pictures and move some furniture around so he wasn't completely lying to his wife. "Best thing about Brooke breaking off the engagement? You got to keep all your stuff." Conner picked up the remote for the large flat-screen TV that hung on the wall. "I'm pretty sure that if

Heidi ever leaves me, she'll take everything with her."

"Ah yes, the upside to having the woman you thought you were in love with dump you. Thanks for pointing that out and for bringing her up. I appreciate that." Travis handed him a beer and took a sip of his own before sitting down.

"Brother, you are so better off. Like I said, better you saw her true colors before you made the full commitment."

As if saying "I do" would have made him feel more committed. He'd planned on spending the rest of his life with Brooke. He'd imagined growing old with her. Of course, things would have been worse if they had gotten married. Travis knew he had avoided making the biggest mistake of his life now that Brooke's true intentions were revealed, but it still stung to be rejected, to be told you weren't good enough because you weren't a quarterback anymore.

Conner's phone beeped, eliciting a pathetic groan from him. He pulled it out of his pocket and checked the screen. "Give me a reason I need to hang out here longer. Quick."

"Sorry, I have to go to Red Bud Park for

the Balloon Festival and sign autographs. I can't hide you all day."

"Balloon Festival and autographs?"

"Hot-air balloons. They fly a whole bunch of them for charity or something. And yes, people still want my autograph," Travis said sourly.

"Of course people want your autograph. You're Travis Lockwood. I bet the girls still throw themselves at you." There was a hint of jealousy in his tone.

Travis let it slide, knowing it was never easy for Conner to be the older brother of the Sweetwater superstar quarterback. Things had been always easier for Travis growing up. Everyone lavished attention and praise on him, while Conner was often overlooked. When they were younger, there was some resentment on Conner's part. Their father invested much more time, energy and money into Travis. But as they got older, Conner found it in his heart to be more supportive than envious. He had always been there for his younger brother, cheering him on and sharing in his spoils. He was a good man who was struggling in this new role of being a father.

"Maybe my car isn't working and I need you to drive me over there," Travis offered.

An appreciative smile spread across Conner's face as he texted Heidi. The two men headed over to Red Bud Park in Conner's car, in case anyone saw them. The field was littered with almost a dozen hot-air balloons ready for takeoff. Several were red, white and blue, and there was even a balloon shaped like a cupcake. Local businesses from all over the Big Country had booths lined up at the edges of the grass. The smell of good ol'-fashioned Texas barbecue filled the air. Kids ran around, clinging tightly to their purple cotton candy or cherry-red snow cones.

Shannon, an intern from the station, was standing next to the KLVA van when Travis and Conner arrived. "You made it just in time to see them launch," she said as Travis approached.

"Where's Summer?" He swore that wasn't going to be his first question, but it popped out anyway.

Shannon smiled. "Oh, you'll see."

A loud air horn sounded, signaling the fliers for takeoff. Within minutes, the sky was filled with a myriad of colored balloons. Travis took out his camera and got a few shots of the incredible sight.

"You still like to take pictures, huh?" Conner asked, holding up his camera phone to capture the moment.

"It's become a hobby, I guess. How about I just send you some copies of mine?" Travis said, pushing Conner's phone down. There was no way a camera phone would do the view justice. Once he was satisfied with his shots, he turned his attention back to Shannon. "Where'd you say Summer was again?"

Shannon pointed up at the balloons. "Watch the big purple one."

The balloon was about a hundred feet in the air while the others had floated much higher. The KLVA cameramen were planted underneath it as if they were waiting for someone to jump out. Travis used his camera to zoom in on the basket. Sure enough, he caught sight of a blond ponytail. The next thing he knew, Summer was opening the basket as though she was going to jump.

"What the hell is she doing?" Heart racing, he wondered why there wasn't someone up there telling her that was unsafe.

"Just watch," Shannon said. Then Summer

launched herself from the basket, swan-diving as if she were going to land in a swimming pool. But there was no swimming pool. There was nothing. No net, nothing to save her from a fall that high. That was when he noticed the cord attached to her leg. Down she went, until the bungee cord stretched and pulled her back up, again and again, to the delight of the crowd.

Travis, mouth agape, stared at her dangling body until he began to laugh. He laughed so hard he nearly cried. She felt the rain coming, but she didn't feel fear. She was completely fearless. Summer Raines was full of surprises.

"SAME TIME NEXT year?" Travis heard the man escorting Summer back to the van ask.

"You know it, Hank," Summer said, giving his tall, wiry frame a hug. Hank looked like a younger version of Travis's high-school chemistry teacher, Mr. Thomas, which was pretty much the complete opposite of Travis.

"Thanks for the heads-up about the rain. Last thing I want to do is wrestle with that balloon in a downpour." Hank pushed his sunglasses up his nose. Summer had predicted there would be isolated showers this afternoon, but the sun was shining as it had been all day. Travis figured the rain was on its way, though. He knew better than to question Summer's "feelings."

"Always happy to help." Her face was flushed. That must have been some adrenaline rush. Travis wondered what it would feel like to touch her, to feel her blood flowing through her veins, her skin tingling. Hank looked as though he wanted to feel what she was feeling, too. Hank gave Summer a sheepish wave before taking off.

"Look who made it back to earth in one piece," Travis said. Astonishingly, Summer smiled and her cheeks flushed a deeper red.

"Look who remembered he had an appearance." She took her spot next to him in their booth. Ken had sent a stack of promo pictures for Travis to sign. By the look of the line, he was going to be there all night.

His eyes narrowed. "Hey, now, I was totally on time. Of course, if I knew I could jump out of a balloon, I would have shown up a few minutes earlier."

"You wanna go?" She started to get up.

Travis grabbed her arm and pulled her back in her seat. "Maybe next time."

There was no tingling, but he defintely felt something when they touched. Summer swallowed hard and stared at his hand as if it were a bear trap wrapped around her arm. Her skin was warm and soft, but he let go before she felt the need to yank her arm away. They had managed to get along for an entire week—he didn't want to ruin that streak by giving her the wrong impression. He had sworn he wasn't interested in anything other than friendship. Touching was most likely against the friendship rules.

"Bull crap." Conner coughed into his fist behind them, causing Summer to glance over her shoulder.

Travis prayed his brother would not embarrass him. "Don't make me call your wife and tell her what really went on today," he warned.

"You wouldn't," Conner gasped.

"Friend of yours?" Summer asked.

"Related, unfortunately."

"Conner Lockwood." He stuck out his hand and Summer shook it firmly.

"Summer Raines. Nice to meet you."

He didn't let go of her hand right away, kissing the back of it like some sort of gentleman. "The pleasure is all mine because you, pretty lady, are insane. The way you took a nosedive." Conner shook his head in awe. "That was crazy."

"Leave her alone," Travis said, scrawling his name on another picture of himself. "The only crazy person here is me—for letting you tag along."

"Boy, can you feel the love?" Conner said to Summer, ignoring his brother completely. "He acts like he's the only interesting person around here. Did you know that I played for LSU the year we won—"

Travis interrupted, "She doesn't care about football. You're boring her and you've just met. Nice work."

"Doesn't care about football?" Conner's eyes widened in shock, as if he'd been told she wasn't from this planet. "He's kidding, right?"

Summer shrugged. "I'm into more extreme sports. Sorry."

Travis chuckled as Conner's jaw dropped. He really didn't have to worry about her holding her own.

"More extreme? You're kidding." Conner turned to Travis. "She has to be kidding. Tell me she's kidding." He looked Summer up and down. "You're not from around here, are you?"

"Texans and their football. I'll never understand."

"Is that a no?"

"Not originally from around here, no."

"You're lucky. We've kicked Texans out of the state for lesser crimes."

Summer laughed. Of *course* she liked Conner. He was one of the good guys. Travis spent the rest of the afternoon signing everything put in front of him and smiling for every photo. There were plenty of lovely ladies in line, but the little kids were on the receiving end of most of his attention. He signed so many footballs he lost count.

After Heidi called for the third time, and Conner ran out of excuses, he tapped Travis on the shoulder. "I'll be moving in with you if I don't head home. Any way someone can give you a lift?" He not so nonchalantly glanced in Summer's direction.

"I can drop you off," Summer offered.

Travis bit back his frustration. It was a nice

gesture, even if he was certain she was only offering because Conner had asked. "You sure?"

"Or I could," Shannon chimed in.

Summer stiffened as if challenged, then smiled at the intern. "I got it. It's really no big deal."

"It's no big deal for me, either. I have nothing to do after this. I can drive Travis home."

"I think I already said I got it."

"I'm just saying, I'm sure you're busy—"

"I'm not."

"Well, I'm sure you're busier than I am."

Conner began to laugh and both women stopped arguing. He patted Travis on the back. "Some things never change, do they, little brother?" Turning to leave, he gave Summer and Shannon a wave. "Nice to meet you ladies."

The look on Summer's face said she was about to spout off every high temperature ever recorded. Her discomfort made Travis feel worse. It was obvious to him that she'd only offered because Conner was asking, not because she was interested in Travis. Shannon, on the other hand, was one of the women still enamored with who he had been. "I'm sure

I can grab a ride with the guys in the van," he suggested.

"Had I known driving you home was going to be such an issue—" Summer began.

"I'll go with you," he jumped in. At this point, not accepting her offer would be more offensive than anything else he could do. "Thank you."

When the signing finally came to an end, Travis and Summer wished Shannon and the crew a good evening. Clouds had moved in and the wind picked up, sending discarded fliers and garbage tumbling across the field. The energy in the air felt different, heavier, and Travis's skin tingled. He smiled at his observation. The Weather Girl was rubbing off on him.

She was too busy to notice.

Summer held her closed red umbrella in one hand and dug through her big bag of tricks with the other.

"So you know when it's going to rain and you like to throw yourself out of hot-air balloons. What else do you do?"

"Wouldn't you like to know?" she said, her mouth twisting in frustration as her keys continued to elude her. She shook the bag in an attempt to locate them by their jingle.

"I really would like to know," he said, perhaps too curious for his own good. Summer shook her head and continued hunting for the elusive car keys. "Have you always been like this?"

"Like what? Completely incapable of finding my stupid keys?"

He liked the way she could be so self-deprecating. Brooke had never wanted to admit she was anything but flawless. "Fearless," he said, taking the umbrella from her so she could use both hands to rummage through her bag. He wished he could get that feeling back. The one that made him believe he could do anything he set his mind to. Lately, that other f-word—failure—was haunting him.

Summer laughed. "If you bungee-jump and have no fear, there's something wrong with you. It's that little bit of fear that makes it fun." She found the keys and unlocked her car.

Travis opened his door and moved the passenger seat back to accommodate his long legs. "That's probably true. Being afraid is what makes overcoming something that much more rewarding, right?"

"Exactly." She started up the car and switched on the wipers. Travis was about to question that decision when big, fat raindrops began hitting the windshield. She was freakishly good at her job.

"So maybe the real question is, what else are you afraid of, Weather Girl?"

Summer squeezed her lips together before stealing a glance in his direction. "I'm *afraid* you broke Shannon's heart by not choosing her to drive you home. I've never seen someone so disappointed."

"Nice deflection." That probably wasn't the first thing that had popped into her head, but he was sure it was all he was going to get. "Shannon's a good kid."

"Good kid, huh? She's not that much younger than you are."

"Maybe. She just reminds me of the girls I knew in college."

Summer's eyes were glued to the road. "Did you know Texas averages a hundred and twenty-six tornadoes a year?"

Travis rubbed his neck and looked out his window at the suddenly ominous gray sky.

He wondered if she knew something she wasn't telling him. "Wow, is that the most?"

"Yeah, we have more than twice as many as Oklahoma." She sped up the wipers and tightened her grip on the steering wheel. "But we're also the second biggest state, so the data is a little skewed."

"I've lived in Texas all my life and never seen one."

"Well, your life is far from over."

"This is true. Something to look forward to, I guess." He paused for a beat. Looking forward to something would be nice. He wasn't so sure he should be hoping for a tornado, though. "I think that's what I'm the most afraid of," he said. "I don't want my life to be over. There's still got to be something out there for me. I don't want to miss it, you know?"

Her eyes slid to his. "Then you have to use that fear to push yourself to take risks you normally wouldn't. You never know what could happen."

He could fail. He could fail and fail again. The fear of it nearly paralyzed him. He was so used to living in a world where the only decisions he had to make were the ones on the football field. His path was always brightly lit and filled with one way signs. Now the world was filled with endless possibilities, and he didn't have a clue what signs he should be looking for. Except the one pointing home. He came back to West Central Texas because it was the least scary place to start.

Travis directed Summer to his cottage but didn't jump out right away when they arrived. The rain had picked up and it pounded on the car so loudly it didn't feel awkward to sit in silence for a minute. "Thanks for the lift. I owe you one."

"No trouble, really." Summer shrugged. She reached back and grabbed her umbrella. "Here, use this. You can give it back to me on Monday."

"You sure?"

"I can park in my garage. You need it more than me. I wouldn't want to be responsible for you getting sick, now, would I?"

"The way things have been going, I might need a reason to call in sick."

Summer shook her head. "You have to stop trying so hard. When you overthink things, the words get all jumbled. Try pretending you're telling the crew what happened in the world of sports instead of reporting it to all of Big Country. It's as simple as having a conversation with some guys at the bar."

"That's some good advice. Thank you."

"Who knows, ESPN could come calling, and I'd get my thirty seconds back."

Travis's laugh felt good coming out. "Well, we all know how much you want those thirty seconds." Wishing her good-night, he popped open the umbrella and stepped into the rain. Summer lingered until he got his front door open, then backed out of his driveway after he waved. He shook off the excess water from the umbrella and set it by the door to dry. Flicking on some lights, he made his way to the couch and lay down, throwing an arm over his eyes.

Summer was beautiful and interesting, but being around her made Travis feel mighty inferior. ESPN would never knock on his door, but he'd give her suggestion a go. Travis was used to carrying the team, not being the weakest link. Not that Summer intended to make him feel that way. She was who she was. She was excellent at her job. She bungee-jumped out of hot-air balloons. She believed in taking risks. Her only weakness was her inability to find her keys to save her life.

Travis wanted to take some risks, too. He wanted to face fear and beat it. If only he could decide what risk to take.

CHAPTER SEVEN

RICHARD WAS IN a particularly bad mood when Summer arrived at the station on a cloudless Tuesday. He had his fan on high even though the air-conditioning was set at a comfortable sixty-eight degrees. His thinning brown hair, peppered with gray, was damp at his temples.

Richard didn't get into broadcasting meteorology because of his looks. It was his knowledge that had won him his job some twenty-plus years ago. He loved to talk about things like jet streams and isobars, which tended to do nothing but confuse people. Summer thought part of his dislike for her stemmed from the fact that she knew more about weather than he did. It was his "thing" to know the science of meteorology. Summer came in and knew more, remembered more without having to look it up and presented it in a way that didn't make people feel stupid.

Today, he hated her because Ken had some

big ideas. Ideas that made Summer the head and face of the Channel 6 Weather Team. Ideas that made Richard attack Ken in the middle of the newsroom.

"I've been chief meteorologist for ten years! This is a demotion!" Richard raged.

"First of all, you were never given that title by the station," Ken argued. "Second, nothing has changed. You still do weekday mornings. I could put you on weekends. That would be a demotion."

Richard's fist pounded on the desktop. "She's a joke, Ken! She thinks she can feel the rain coming and tells the viewers that. They think she's crazy. I've had people tell me so at appearances."

Summer chose not to share what people said about him at *her* appearances. None of it was flattering. She decided it was best to rise above it and keep her mouth shut. This was Ken's battle anyway.

"Then they must love crazy because our ratings are the highest they've been in years. Summer and Travis are going to be the stars of our new marketing campaign, like it or not."

"Do Rachel and Brian know that?" Richard

continued, the vein in his forehead bulging. "I thought they were the faces of Channel 6. You really know how to stab your veterans in the back, Ken. Good work."

"Rachel and Brian are team players. Team players get to stay. You don't want to be a team player? There's the door." Ken pointed to the elevators, trying not to lose his cool. Nobody challenged Ken out in the open. He could handle a confrontation in his office, but in front of his staff he was much less tolerant.

Summer wasn't going to hold her breath for Richard to quit. He knew KLVA was the end of the road for him. There wasn't a station in all of Texas that was going to pick him up at his age. Fresh-faced newbies were joining the workforce every day. Richard was old-school. *Old* being the key word.

"I'm not going anywhere until you fire me. And I dare you to fire me." His false bravado was not impressive. He had a family to take care of—two boys in college and a daughter getting married next summer. Being out of work wasn't something Richard could afford.

"Don't tempt me!" Ken shouted as he headed back to his office, finished with this pointless argument.

Summer stood next to the fan, shaking her head. "It's just a title and some stupid billboards. It doesn't mean anything."

Richard scowled at her. "Get the hell away from my desk, you stupid witch."

"Whoa, that's no way to talk to a lady." Travis magically appeared at Summer's side. He spoke calmly, but the twitch in his jaw gave away his mounting anger. "Maybe you should go outside and get some air. You're looking a little caged-in."

Richard had obviously lost his mind. He got up in Travis's face. "You're no better than her, Lockwood! All you are is a pretty-faced…loser!"

Before Summer could tell them both to keep their testosterone in check, Travis tackled Richard. The two men began to scuffle on the newsroom floor. Appalled, Summer grabbed Travis's arm and tried to pry him off Richard, who had absolutely no chance in a fight against a man half his age and in better shape than he'd ever been in his entire life.

Travis got up and pointed a finger at the big man on the floor. "Talk to me or her like that again and…" He stopped as if a switch had flipped inside him and he realized what he was doing. Everyone in the newsroom was staring. Then the whispers began. Travis looked around at all the shocked and frightened faces, stopping on Summer's. His eyes were so dark and sad. The storm inside him blew over, but the damage had been done. After a second or two, he took off. Summer followed.

"Are you crazy?" she asked, grabbing the back of his jacket and pulling him to a stop. This wasn't the easygoing Travis she had spent the afternoon with last weekend, the one who Mimi would marry her off to if she had any real say in who Summer married. This Travis had clenched fists and his chest heaved with labored breaths.

He spun around to face her as his anger bubbled to the surface. "That guy needs an attitude adjustment," he said gruffly.

Summer stood her ground even though she could feel her whole body shaking. "I don't know how they do things in the NFL, but here, we don't settle disputes by tackling people in the newsroom."

"He shouldn't talk to you like that."

"I don't need defending." She wasn't the damsel-in-distress type. Trouble with Richard was nothing new. She'd been handling it way before Travis got here, and she'd be dealing with it long after he was gone. "Richard hates me. He'll always hate me. Beating him up isn't going to change that."

"Well, he should watch who he calls a loser." His fist hit the wall and rattled the pictures that hung in the narrow hallway. This time when he took off, Summer let him go. Evidently, the fight wasn't about her after all.

THE FIVE O'CLOCK newscast began like any other. Summer put on her mic. She checked the monitor to make sure her hair looked all right. She picked up her clicker for the green screen. Nothing too exciting to report tonight. West Central Texas was experiencing normal weather patterns. She planned to talk a little bit about the unseasonably cooler temps up North, just to spice things up.

Travis took his spot to Rachel's right. Thankfully, his baby-blue tie helped make his eyes more blue than gray under the studio lights, but the tension in his shoulders and the frown on his face made it clear he was still bothered.

The studio director counted down and Rachel introduced the weather segment. Summer wished her viewership a good evening. She clicked the button so people at home would see the national map with the current temps in various big cities. Another click and the map of West Central Texas popped up. She clicked it again, expecting the screen to change to a broader view with weather-in-motion radar. Instead, the graphic with the high temperatures for the day appeared on the monitor.

She played it off, carrying on as if there was nothing wrong. Until she clicked again and the five-day outlook appeared. Her heart rate sped up. She tried to go back, she skipped ahead, she apologized for the technical difficulties. She tried to deliver her report without the visuals, giving up on the screen behind her altogether.

"We'll hope you get everything worked out by ten," Rachel said as Summer's segment came to an end. "You should be better prepared by then, right?"

Somehow Summer kept smiling even as she imagined poking Rachel in the eye. "I'm sure the technical team will figure out what the glitch is."

Summer stormed into the control room, looking for Ken. "I'm going to give you one guess as to who messed with my graphics." Someone had most definitely messed with her graphics. And she was ready to shove his fan right down his throat.

"You don't know that."

Summer put her hands on her hips. "Someone had to go in and switch them around. Who else would want to disrupt my forecast besides Richard?"

Ken tried to appease her. "I'll look into it."

"You'll look into it?"

"We've had enough drama around here for one day, don't you think? I will look into it. Maybe it was a computer glitch."

"It wasn't a glitch. Someone had to go in and—"

"I'll look into it, Summer. What more do you want me to say?" Ken asked, losing his patience. She was going to have to accept that was all he could do. Not that Richard was going to admit to his deceit. Or maybe he would. Maybe he'd get off on gloating. Ken would have to take some sort of action then.

Travis found her a couple hours later in the Stormwatch Room, guarding her graphics. From the look of him, the softer, gentler Travis was back. He dropped a bag from the deli across the street on the desk. "Someone said you didn't get dinner. I brought this as a peace offering. I feel like maybe this was all my fault. Like fighting with him pushed poor Richard over the edge."

"Well, Ken doesn't think Richard had anything to do with it. But part of me wishes I hadn't broken up that fight earlier today." Summer took a peek in the bag. Inside, there was a sandwich and a bag of chips. Her stomach growled.

"I have to say, you handled yourself on the air better than I would have. You were a total pro."

His compliment didn't soothe her injured ego as much as she would have liked. "I almost tackled Rachel after she insinuated I was unprepared."

Travis laughed until she turned her glare on him. "I'm sorry. I was picturing you tackling Rachel. I shouldn't laugh. I know it had to be horrifying.'

Summer sighed. "I don't understand what Richard's so mad about. It's a couple billboards and some promos."

"Yeah, it's not like you were given thirty seconds of his reporting time. I mean, that would be a legitimate reason to hate someone," he said.

Touché.

"Hate's a waste of time, remember?" she said, pulling the sandwich out of the bag. "How can I hate someone who bought me dinner without being asked?"

Travis stood with his hands in his pockets. He wasn't wearing his suit coat and his tie was loosened just a bit. Even though he looked good, it was clear he wasn't a suit-and-tie kind of guy. "Like I said, I fueled the fire, I'm sure. And if I scared you earlier when I lost my temper, I'm sorry about that, too."

Carefully unwrapping the sandwich, Summer took a second to consider how his outburst made her feel. It had been somewhat scary to see him lose control like that. At the same time, it made her curious. Why would the opinion of someone like Richard matter so much to someone like Travis? "Apology accepted. Thanks for the sandwich."

Travis shrugged and started backing out the door. "Gotta make up for being the bad guy somehow."

THE TEN O'CLOCK report went off without a hitch. Summer was vigilant and took no chances. She checked and double-checked seconds before she went on. She didn't have high hopes that Ken would get Richard to confess. It flabbergasted her that he would be so petty. Did he really think that tampering with her graphics would make her quit? There were much better reasons to quit than this trouble.

Ryan's name stood out in her inbox as she checked her email one more time before heading out for the night. He was trying much harder than Richard was to get her to change jobs.

Imagine staring up at a million points of light in the sky from the comfort of your bed, or watching the mesmerizing northern lights dance above you before you fall asleep. Come work for me and there's a glass igloo in the Finnish Lapland with your name on it. They don't have those in Texas, do they?

Summer rubbed her tired eyes and closed the message. She couldn't deal with this now. Not when she was coming off a bad day at work. Leaning back in her chair, she glanced over her shoulder at Travis and Rachel. The flirtatious news anchor sat in Travis's chair and twirled a strand of hair around her finger. Did women really think stuff like that worked? From across the dimly lit newsroom, it was hard to tell if Travis was falling for it or not. He stood beside his desk and loosened his tie, politely nodding at whatever she was saying.

Rachel was irksome. Rachel and her perfectly plucked eyebrows. Her sparkling white teeth and generous…assets. She was a thirty-something ex-cheerleader who wanted nothing more than to sink her claws into someone like Travis. Young, handsome, virile. The last guy she dated had probably been collecting Social Security for a couple years. Rachel was obviously looking for fresher meat.

Summer tried to ignore them, but Rachel was speaking so loudly about how much she loved the idea of Travis starring in ads for the station. Unsurprisingly, she didn't mention anything about Summer, who went back to her computer and looked up information on glass igloos in Finland. Ryan's bait was too tempting, given the circumstances. Brian walked past her desk a few minutes later and wished her good-night.

"Have a good one," she replied with a weary smile. She shut down her desktop and grabbed her stuff. Rachel and Travis were laughing together, giving her a much-needed push out the door. "Good night, y'all," she said, getting Travis's attention.

"Summer, wait. Let me walk you to your car." Travis pulled his jacket out from behind Rachel.

She didn't need to be escorted to her car. It wasn't like Richard was going to be waiting in the parking lot to take her out. She was about to refuse when Rachel chimed in. "Pete can walk her to her car. Right, Pete?" Summer hadn't even noticed the tech engineer lurking in the shadows. Pete didn't look too keen on walking anywhere with Summer.

"I got it," Travis said. "Have a nice evening." He scurried to catch up to Summer.

The elevator arrived and Travis held it open so she could walk in first. The doors closed, and even though there were only two of them, the space felt smaller than usual.

"Did you know that in the winter months in the northernmost parts of Finland, the sun doesn't rise for fifty-one days?"

"I'm making you nervous, aren't I?" Travis asked, almost apologetic.

She shook her head, though the gesture was a lie. Lately there was this gentle pull when she was near him that was followed by a much bigger desire to run far away. He was more complicated than she'd first thought, and that made him interesting. She didn't need interesting men in her life. Especially not when Ryan was tempting her to fly the coop earlier than she'd planned.

They made it downstairs without any other weather facts escaping her lips. The parking lot was nearly empty. Some clouds had rolled in, but they didn't hold any rain. Summer hadn't felt rain since Sunday.

"Hopefully tomorrow will be a better day," Travis said as they approached her car.

Summer sighed and started searching the bottomless pit that was her purse. "If today is any indication of what I have to look forward to, I'm not sure I'm going to like being the face of the station."

"It's one heck of a face," he said. "One of the prettiest in Texas."

She froze for a moment, wondering if she'd heard him right. "If you're trying to get more weather facts out of me, it's not going to work."

He shook his head and grabbed her bag from her, reached in and pulled out her keys effortlessly. He didn't bother hiding his grin. "Good night, Weather Girl."

She snatched her keys from his hand, got in her car and drove home. Summer couldn't wait to get into bed and put this crazy day to rest. Storm greeted her at the door as if he'd been waiting for her for days. She took him out back and let him run around under a perfect crescent moon. Her head fell back as she gazed up at the twinkling stars set against the inky backdrop. Summer loved the endlessness of the Texas sky. It reminded her that there was so much more world out there for her to discover. People in Finland looked up at the same moon, but she couldn't help wondering if there would be different stars to wish on over there.

Back inside the house, she quickly changed out of her work clothes. Washing off the studio makeup helped her feel better. She stared at the reflection in the mirror. Somehow she'd become the face of Channel 6. Mimi was going to love that title. She ran her hands over her cheeks and thought about Travis and what he'd said. Did he really think she was pretty? Her eyes looked tired. Her bottom lip was too big compared to her top lip. The dusting of freckles across the bridge of her nose always made her feel like a kid, but that wasn't the way she'd felt when Travis looked at her tonight.

She turned up the air-conditioning so she could sleep under the covers comfortably. Giving her pillow a fluff, she lay down and stared up at the ceiling fan her grandfather had helped her install as it spun slowly. It usually did the trick in lulling her to sleep. Tonight her head was too full. Her thoughts were scattered. Finland. The Arctic Circle. Northern lights. Ryan sure knew how to entice her. Faraway places with seasons and snow. Mother Nature's brilliant light show. Texas did not have glass igloos. But Texas was her home. It had her grandparents. It had her dog and a job she was usually very good at. It also had Travis.

She laughed out loud as she flipped onto her side. She pulled the covers up under her chin. Was he a reason to stay or a reason to run away? She grabbed the other pillow and used it to cover her head. She'd told her parents she wasn't taking the job, but maybe they were trying to send her a message. Maybe it wasn't Richard who had messed with her graphics. Maybe it was divine intervention. Maybe it was a sign that television meteorology wasn't for her.

Or maybe Abilene had more to offer her than she thought. Travis was the first guy who didn't make a run for it every time she rambled on about the weather. He asked questions. He listened to her answers. Very few people humored her. Even fewer encouraged her to keep talking. Awkward silence was usually the only response to her weirdness. Travis didn't make her feel weird. He almost made her feel normal.

Normal was something Summer hadn't ever felt. Was that a sign? She tossed the pillow on the floor, restlessly flipping over to her other side. As normal as Travis made her feel, the man was a bigger unknown than the job Ryan was luring her into. Travis was dealing with a world of hurt, hurt that had nothing to do with his shoulder. He didn't have to say it, he was one of those people who tried to hide his vulnerability but couldn't stop his eyes from giving it away.

Summer rolled onto her stomach, smashing her face into her pillow. She hated not being able to predict the future. Not knowing meant things could go very wrong, like they had the night her parents died. She was such a hypocrite. She'd told Travis not to be trapped by fear, and that was exactly what was happening to her. Life needed to be worth living. If she stayed in Texas, she needed something more.

CHAPTER EIGHT

THE NEWSROOM WAS a maze of desks filled with producers, assignment editors, reporters and anchors. People were always on the phone, on their computers or consulting with one another about a story. When Travis pushed away from his desk and spun his chair a quarter turn to the left, he could watch the Weather Girl do all those things. She was usually staring at her monitor, probably researching some random weather fact like the average snowfall in Idaho. Summer knew the strangest things.

Travis was on the phone with his mother, who decided she needed to see him and meet his coworker before the football game on Friday. "I don't know, Mom. Can't I just introduce you to her at the game?"

"I promised to help sell tickets for the booster club's fifty/fifty raffle. I'll be working. You two will be working. Can't you both come over beforehand? I'm baking." The woman drove a hard bargain.

Travis leaned back and looked left. As if she knew he was watching, Summer turned her head to meet his stare. He watched as the heat crept up her neck, the skin flushing red. Her fingers glided up her throat as if she was trying to contain the blush.

"I'll ask her, but no promises." He continued watching Summer until the right side of her mouth curved up in a shy, stop-looking-at-me-like-that smile. Those soft pink lips of hers were something. He knew they were soft. He had touched them.

Travis slid back toward his desk and rested his forehead on his fist while his mom told him all about what his aunt Kelly had to say about the road construction between Sweetwater and Abilene. He wished traffic was his only issue with going home. "I'll let you get back to work," she said before hanging up. "We'll see you on Friday. Your dad's looking forward to seeing you. He misses you."

It took everything he had not to laugh out loud. His dad missed him? His dad could visit anytime he wanted. Travis lived the same forty minutes away that Conner did, and Travis knew he'd been to Conner's house plenty of times since the baby was born. Travis's phone worked just fine, too. His dad didn't miss him. His dad missed who he had been. He didn't have the time of day for this version of his son.

Travis didn't dare bring up the trouble with his dad. It was better his mom thought everything between them was fine. Travis had grown up in a house where he was taught not to worry his mother.

He hung up and scrubbed his face with his hands. This Friday was going to be torture. It was time for him to face all the people who'd supported him and his career all these years. He had to suffer through all their condolences, sympathetic looks and pats on the back. Best of all, Summer would be there to witness it, giving her more reason to think he was a loser.

His relationship with Summer was shaky at best. She hated football. She was unfazed by the dimples. All the things that made him so desirable to women in the past had no effect on her. There was no reason for her to agree to meet his mother. Still, Travis was a glutton for punishment. He got up and perched himself on the corner of her desk. She smelled like spring—fresh and flowery.

"So, we're going to the Sweetwater homecoming game this weekend." He picked up her paper clip holder, which she promptly took away from him and set back down. "Do you know what that means?"

Refusing to look at him, Summer sighed. "It means I need to bring earplugs to protect my hearing from the screaming fans and my abundance of indifference to make sure your head doesn't get too big."

"Ha-ha." Considering he was coming back a has-been, there was no danger of an overinflated head. "I don't think you have to worry about that."

"Oh, come on, the fair prince is returning to his kingdom," she said with a flourish of her hand.

Little did she know, his trip to Sweetwater was more like the return of the prodigal son. He had squandered his chances of fame and fortune and could only hope his father would forgive him. This was a bad idea. Inviting her to his parents' house was asking her to make things too personal between them. He'd tell his mom she couldn't make it. He'd do a brief introduction at the game and that would be that. "Never mind."

He headed back to his desk and pulled up his script for the five o'clock newscast. He tried putting some of the report in his own words to make it easier to regurgitate.

"So what does it mean?" Summer pressed. She folded her arms across her chest. "And don't say nothing."

Leaning back in his chair, his fingers nervously drummed on his thighs. "It means I'm going home, and maybe you'd ride with me instead of in the station van. We could stop by my parents' before the game. My mom's a big fan of yours." Her bluebird eyes widened a bit. "I told her I could probably get her some one-on-one time with you if she made cupcakes."

"Cupcakes? The red velvet ones?"

"Those are the ones," he said, managing a smile. It was humiliating to need a bribe.

She pondered his request for a second or two. "Did you know there was a tornado in Sweetwater back in 1986 that developed with little warning and caused almost fifteen million dollars in damages?" Her voice was a little higher than normal.

Travis figured that was better than a no. "My parents lived in Sweetwater back in '86.

My mom might be able to give you a first-hand account of that tornado."

Interest flickered in her eyes. "Don't tease me."

"No lie," he said, making a mental note to call his mother immediately and make sure she knew something about that storm before Friday.

"Summer!" Ken shouted across the news-room. He marched over to Travis's desk, his face red and his fingers tugging on the collar of his shirt as if his tie was too tight. "Why are you here and not at your appearance?"

"Someone from the school called me and said they had to cancel," she replied calmly.

"That's funny, because I just got a call from the principal of Hooper Elementary, asking why she had a gymnasium full of children and no meteorologist there to enlighten them about tornadoes."

Summer shook her head and flipped through the planner on her desk. "I swear, someone canceled. I didn't write down the name, but I know the woman said she was from Hooper."

"Why would they call you and not me?" Ken's tone put Travis on edge. He felt the urge to stand in between his livid boss and the Weather Girl. "When have you ever handled scheduling your own appearances? Everything goes through me, Summer. It always has."

Flustered and looking as if she wanted to share every fact she knew about tornadoes— or any weather phenomena, for that matter— Summer continued to defend herself. "I didn't think about it. I assumed they had someone transfer the call to me. We can reschedule. Whatever they want to do."

"They want you there thirty minutes ago. That's what they want. You represent this station. When you mess up, it makes us all look bad. Be where you are supposed to be when you're supposed to be there."

"But—"

"No excuses. I rebooked you for next week." Ken turned to go but stopped. "And this time, even if someone calls to cancel, I expect you to show up anyway, understand?"

Summer clamped her lips together and nodded. Ken went back to his office, slamming his door hard enough to quiet the whole newsroom for a second or two. Travis watched

Summer take a deep breath, forcing herself to remain in control.

"Boy, I think the boss man needs a day off," Travis said to lighten the mood.

"Someone called and canceled. I have never missed an appearance in the three years I've worked here." Summer bit her lip.

"Say it," Travis said. Her chin trembled. "Say it. You know you need to say it." Summer covered her face with her hands, shaking her head vigorously. "Summer…"

From behind her hands, she let it out. "Did you know Hurricane Katrina caused 108 billion dollars in damages and was responsible for 1,836 deaths? Or that the storm surge was twenty feet high and approximately ninety thousand square miles were affected?"

"It's incredible how much destruction one storm can cause," Travis said.

Summer dropped her hands and glanced down at him. She was so darn adorable he couldn't help wanting to make her feel better. Travis stood up and touched her shoulder. "You missed an appearance. It isn't like you destroyed the entire Gulf coast."

Summer gave him the smile he was looking for. She didn't need to say anything; the gratitude was clear in her eyes.

"So you'll come with me?" he asked, feeling a bit more confident than he did when this conversation first started.

"Let's see… I don't have to ride in the van, I get cupcakes and a firsthand account of the Sweetwater tornado." She seemed to pause for dramatic effect. "You got yourself a deal."

ALL OF SWEETWATER was properly geared up for the big Friday night homecoming game. Store windows throughout the downtown were decorated with fire-truck red and bright white paint. Signs lined the streets, wishing the Mustangs good luck and encouraging them to WIN, WIN, WIN. Several houses proudly displayed the names and numbers of the players who lived there. Football never failed to bring this community together.

The Lockwoods lived on a friendly street in the heart of Sweetwater just a few blocks from the high school. Travis fondly remembered playing games of two-hand touch in the street with Conner and the neighbor kids. Eight or so boys of varying ages would gather out there before getting called in for dinner.

It was the only time football was carefree for Travis. No pressure. His only worry had been getting out of the way of passing cars.

There were no boys playing ball or parents coming home from work today. The street was quiet as they climbed out of the car. Summer, on the other hand, had been quite talkative on the drive over. Besides the weather, she chatted about her dog and her grandparents. She continued to be evasive about her parents, but Travis sensed they weren't a topic for small talk.

A large shade tree in front of the house cast early-evening shadows on the path that led to the door. "Welcome to Casa Lockwood," he said, holding the door open for her as they entered the house. The smell of every possible bakery delight enveloped them. His mother must have spent the entire day making treats for her beloved son. Travis inhaled deeply.

"Anybody home?" he called out.

There was quite a racket in the kitchen, clanking pans and a buzzing timer.

"Oh, my baby boy is home!" His mom came flying out to greet her guests. She had an apple-red apron tied around her waist and her hair was done up in a sophisticated twist.

Olivia Lockwood looked good no matter the time or the place. She introduced herself to Summer and gave her a hug before quickly moving on to Travis, who she clung to for dear life.

There was little resemblance between mother and son, aside from the dimples. His mom was a petite, dark-haired former beauty queen. Everyone who knew them always noted how he and his mother shared the same smile, but everything else was clearly inherited from his father.

"Hi, Mama. Smells good in here."

Visibly overjoyed at the thought of feeding her son, his mom bounced on the balls of her feet. "Just wait till you see what I got for you to take back to Abilene."

One thing Travis truly loved about home was his mother's cooking. "Where's Dad?"

His mother's face fell for a second, but she quickly put her hostess smile back on. "Oh, you know him. He's slower than molasses. Came home from work and messed around in the backyard for twenty minutes. Now he's upstairs doing Lord knows what. I'll run up and get him."

Travis frowned. Avoid, avoid, avoid. It was

all his dad did lately. He didn't come to the phone when Travis called. He hadn't been to Abilene to see Travis's new place yet. He hadn't even responded to the few texts Travis had sent.

Travis and Summer moved farther into the house. Everything was beautifully arranged. The UT blanket Travis had given his mother for Christmas one year was perfectly folded and draped over her favorite chair by the fireplace. Framed photos of the first grandchild littered the mantel. All of Olivia's *Martha Stewart Living* magazines sat beside the chair in a basket. Travis's mother loved baskets. She had enough to hold just about everything in the entire house that needed holding.

"These pictures are beautiful," Summer said from behind him. She stared up at the wall of photographs framed on the wall opposite the fireplace.

"I can't believe she did this." He smiled, surprised his mother had chosen so many of his favorites. She'd framed the photos he'd taken of the Statue of Liberty at night, and the fog rolling in around the Golden Gate Bridge. There was the one of his grandmother's rose garden in full bloom, and the one of the giant bean in Millennium Park from his wintery trip to Chicago last year.

"Did you know this sculpture is really called *Cloud Gate?*" Summer asked, pointing to that last photo. "No one calls it that, but I think it's a much better name than *The Bean*." Her nose wrinkled and Travis's smile widened. Only Summer would know something like that.

"He's quite talented, isn't he?" His mother had snuck up on both of them.

"Who?" Summer asked.

"Travis. He's got a good eye for pretty things, don't you think?" His mother gave him a wink that made him wonder whether she was still talking about the photographs.

Summer looked a little stunned. "You took these?"

Travis shrugged. "Anybody can take pictures of things."

"I can't even take a picture of my dog without it turning out blurry," she replied, turning back to the photos.

He'd never put too much thought into how easy or difficult it was to capture a decent shot. Travis photographed things he thought were cool to look at when he traveled around the States. It was his way of remembering the places he'd been.

The buzzer went off in the kitchen. "Can I help you with anything, Mrs. Lockwood?" Summer asked.

"Oh, call me Olivia, dear." She took Summer by the hand and pulled her toward the kitchen. "You can help me box up some goodies for Coach Phillips. Travis, you go tell your father to get down here."

Travis begrudgingly obliged while Summer followed his mom into the kitchen. He didn't have to go all the way up—he bumped into his dad on the stairs.

"You made it," the elder Lockwood said, giving his son an awkward pat on the back. Something was up. His dad was smiling. It had been a while since Travis had seen that.

"Mom thought you got lost up there."

He stopped abruptly at the bottom landing and turned to face Travis, who was right on his heels. Father used to tower over son when Travis was a kid. Now, even though the boy was a man and he could look his dad in the eye, Travis still felt intimidated in his presence. They shared the same broad shoulders and stormy blue eyes. His dad was in good shape for his age, could probably bench-press the same weight as Travis if they made a game of it. There was no one more competitive than Sam Lockwood.

"I was on the phone." His dad's strong hand came down on Travis's bad shoulder. "I think I found the guy who's going to fix you," he said in a hushed tone. He smiled wider, then took off for the kitchen, where they could hear nothing but laughter and more clanging.

Travis grabbed his dad's arm and stopped him. "What's that supposed to mean?"

His dad leaned back to get a look inside the kitchen, and, satisfied no one was paying them any mind, he whispered, "I found a doctor, Trav. This guy has looked at all the reports and all the scans. He thinks he can go in—"

"Dad, I don't think—"

Clinging to the last of his hope, his father made his case. "I've talked to a lot of people, son. All of them say this guy works miracles. He believes we can get you back on the field in a year."

Travis's stomach ached, but no longer from hunger. He'd been waiting for his dad to offer up his opinion on what he should do next with his life, but he never thought it would be this. They had been to half a dozen doctors, who had in turn consulted with enough specialists to fill an entire hospital. All of them said Travis risked permanent nerve damage if he continued to play. There was nothing that could be done. Playing football was not an option, and he hated that he had to disappoint his father one more time. As if the past six months hadn't been enough.

"I'm retired. It's over," Travis said, watching his dad's eyes shift from hopeful back to disappointed. It was almost too much to bear.

"You won't even go consult with him? Hear him out?"

"I don't see the point of any more surgeries."

"So you give up, is that it?"

"I need a plan B, Dad." They'd had this conversation. After doctors number five and six. Travis needed closure. He couldn't hold on to old dreams. "I can't go back. You think I can play, knowing twenty doctors told me one hit could leave me with debilitating pain the rest of my life? Football is as mental as it is physical. I will not be the same player.

I won't be what any team needs. I won't be who you need me to be."

"You think I need you to be a sportscaster for a small-town news station?" His father's words stung worse than the pinched nerves in Travis's neck.

"I'm doing the only thing that was offered to me. If I could play, I would. I...I can't."

"Well, I had no idea I raised a quitter," his dad said bitterly, leaving Travis standing there thoroughly shamed.

From where he wallowed outside the kitchen, Travis could hear his father turn his frustration on his mother. "Good Lord, Olivia, are you having a bake sale? Who is going to eat all of this stuff?"

"Did you forget how much food your sons eat?" his mom shot back.

"I know how much our oldest eats, but for all I know the one out there gave up on eatin', too." His father's comment was another hit to Travis's crumbling defenses.

"What in the world are you talking about?" his mom asked. Travis couldn't understand how the disappointment didn't exist in her world. He wondered if his parents ever talked about him and what his father shared or didn't share.

"Nothing, Liv. Nothing," Travis heard his dad answer.

His mother jumped right into introducing Summer. Travis suddenly regretted bringing the Weather Girl. The last thing he wanted was for Summer to see how dysfunctional his family had become. He mustered up the courage to set foot into the kitchen and was taken aback by the abundance of baked goods. All of Travis's favorite cookies lay cooling on racks: chocolate chip, peanut butter, oatmeal brown sugar. Brownies, cupcakes and mini pies covered the island. Summer flashed him a smile. She was tying red and white ribbons on bags of treats. His mother must have given her the 1950s frilly and flowery apron she was wearing. Leave it to Summer to figure out how to fit right in just when Travis felt as if he didn't belong here anymore.

"Did someone say bake sale?" Travis asked as if that were his reason for looking and sounding so dejected.

"See?" his mother said to his father. "He hasn't lost his appetite. I know my son." She turned to him. "I made a few extras for the coaches and some of the boosters. But you can have whatever you want."

He wasn't as hungry as he had been when he arrived, but Travis wasn't about to turn down the red velvet goodness she placed in front of him. The cream cheese frosting was homemade and like nothing he'd ever tasted anywhere else. He wasn't lying when he told Summer his mother's cupcakes made him cry.

The two women made small talk while they packed up the goodies and watched the men devour what was still fair game. Conner, Heidi and baby Lily showed up, adding another dimension to the conversation. It was interesting to listen to Summer talk about normal "girl" things like the best place to buy shoes. Travis was sure she'd jump right in with a million questions about the Sweetwater tornado. He really needed to stop making assumptions when it came to her. She was always more than he expected.

"So, does the station mind you two dating? Don't they have rules over there?" Travis's father was the first one to stick his foot in his mouth.

Summer looked as mortified as Travis felt. The color drained from her face and her eyes flew to his with the accusation that he had somehow given his dad that impression.

They spoke at the same time. "We're not—"

Conner's grin showed how much he enjoyed Travis's torture. "Summer jumps out of hot-air balloons. She probably dates guys way more exciting than Travis."

Travis glared at his brother for the dig. "Mom wanted to meet her," he clarified. He looked at his mother, who was smiling as if she knew something he didn't.

"She's Summer Raines, the best weather girl West Texas has ever had. I always listen to you. That fool over at Channel 4 never gets it right. I swear, every time he says rain, it's sunny. Plus, you just seem so sweet. I was happy to hear Travis was traveling around with you, and I'm just gonna say it, because Travis's aunt Kelly called me the other day and everyone in her neighbor's book club agrees—you two are too cute together."

Travis was sure he was going to die right there. His mother had a way of embarrassing him that could win her awards, if they gave awards for those sorts of things.

"Did you know that the lowest recorded

temperature in U.S. history was almost eighty degrees below zero?" Summer said in a rush. Travis could see she wanted to stop there but couldn't. "There's a camp up in northern Alaska, along the Alaskan pipeline, that reported temps that low back in 1971."

"Well, that's fascinating." His mom smiled. Her manners were impeccable.

Sam froze, a cookie sticking out of his mouth. He broke off half and spoke around the part that was already in his mouth. "What the heck has that got to do with anything?"

Travis set down the chocolate-frosted brownie he was about to bite into and did his best to change the subject. "Summer was hoping you'd share what you remember about the '86 tornado."

His mother took his conversational baton and ran with it. She dived into a story that more than satisfied Summer's curiosity and steered away from any dating discussion. Travis had to wonder how many people his mom had spoken to this past week to come up with such a detailed and exciting tale. If she really had experienced all that, he was mad at her for holding out on him all these years. She went on and on about not having power or water for days, and couldn't get over that there were never any sirens. It was lucky for the town that only one person was killed.

"Sounding those alarms is so crucial, but predicting something like that is difficult. Sometimes the weather bureau only has a moment's notice," Summer said.

Sam rolled his eyes and made a beeline for the door. Travis followed him, feeling the need to confront his dad about being so rude. It was a decision he regretted almost immediately.

"I have to work with her. I'd appreciate it if you didn't make her feel uncomfortable."

His father spun around and Travis almost ran into him. They were nose to nose and the tension between them was palpable. "That's what you're going to become, isn't it?" his father asked, pointing back at the kitchen. "Someone who talks about life instead of living it. It's sad. It's so sad I can't bear to watch it happen. This isn't what I wanted for you."

Travis could feel the weight of his father's world come crashing down on top of him. A complete failure, that's what he was. There was nothing to say as his father turned and headed back upstairs.

CHAPTER NINE

SUMMER CONSIDERED HERSELF a dependable, hard-working person. Her follow-through in one particular area was severely lacking, however. Ken had asked Summer to mentor Travis, and so far she had offered him little advice. This needed to be rectified, especially considering all the trouble she'd been having at work lately. A little good karma couldn't hurt.

In an attempt to find some common ground, Summer had invited Travis to join her for her early-morning workout on Saturday to get the ball rolling. He'd been the one to point out that they were both runners.

The morning sun wasn't too punishing as they ran the bleachers at Elmer Gray Stadium. Summer used to tag along with Big D on weekends to run the track when he still worked for Abilene Christian University. Simply running a couple miles on a track was too easy for someone like Travis, though. Summer knew she needed to push him harder, so she had given him two choices: the bleachers or the running hills. He thought keeping up with a girl would be a piece of cake. He thought the bleachers were too tough for her. Little did he know he had once again underestimated this particular girl.

Summer beat him to the top on their final climb and waited for him to catch up. Each time his foot hit the step, the aluminum rattled and vibrated.

"I thought you said you ran," she said, hands on her hips and head cocked to the side.

Travis wiped his sweaty face and tried to catch his breath. "I do run. I run my neighborhood every day."

"Well, when I asked you to choose between this and the running hills, you're the one who said, and I quote, 'Former football player, Sunshine. I can run the bleachers in my sleep.'" Summer shook her head with a smile. "Might I suggest not running these in your sleep? I'd hate to see what would happen if you were unconscious, Sunshine."

"You." He pointed at her, still quite winded. "You are not human."

Summer laughed. Yesterday, she had thought the same thing about him. She shouldn't have been surprised that Travis Lockwood was a god in Sweetwater. When he was in his element, surrounded by the boys in their uniforms who listened to every word falling from his lips as if it were gospel, he looked as though he was born to lead. The man gave inspirational speeches like no other. Even Pastor John could learn a thing or two from him. Summer could see why he was a successful quarterback; he knew how to encourage, how to listen and how to command the attention of a crowd big or small.

It was so different from the man she had come to know. The one who seemed so unsure of himself, so insecure about his ability to do his job. She'd given him a hard time, but it was clear no one was harder on Travis than Travis himself.

Former teammates and coaches, on the other hand, had nothing but absolute respect for him. She could hear it in the way they spoke to him, about him. She saw it in the way they welcomed him home with arms wide open. His brother obviously had a great love for Travis. His talent on the field won many people over, but it was who, not what, Travis was that made those close to him adore him.

Olivia Lockwood had mentioned more than once how much her son meant to the people of Sweetwater. Many of them had been rooting for him his entire life. That should have been a blessing, but Summer could see how much it pained him, given his early retirement from football. Travis's injury impacted more than just him, and he seemed to carry the weight of that reality around constantly. Summer watched him practically apologize to everyone at that homecoming game for not living out their hopes and dreams.

Travis's lack of broadcasting experience had annoyed Summer when they first met, but the truth was this was probably the last thing he wanted to be doing. No one could tell Summer she couldn't study weather phenomena. Even if she didn't get paid for it, she could still *do* it. A seemingly healthy Travis didn't have that luxury. It made her feel guilty for being so mean. It also made her think she could help him focus on his strengths instead of his weaknesses. She'd asked him to bring his camera along, even if it seemed like a strange request for a workout.

THEY WALKED ACROSS the top of the bleachers for a cool down and then made their way back to ground level. Travis pulled a towel out of his gym bag and rubbed it over his head. "I'd be back in NFL shape in no time if I trained with you."

Summer bent down to stretch the overworked muscles in her legs that were sure to be sore tomorrow. In her effort to prove him wrong, she'd pushed herself harder than usual. She'd be paying for it later, but it was more than worth it.

"From the look of things, I think I might give you a heart attack. Good thing you're retired."

Travis let out a breathy laugh. "Tell my dad that."

Sam Lockwood was an interesting character. The physical similarities between father and son were stunning. Luckily for Travis, personalitywise, he was one hundred percent his mother. Summer thought the elder Mr. Lockwood was like a troubling weather front.

She noticed right away that his dark storm clouds loomed heavily over Travis.

"Dads can be tough. My mom was so much easier to talk to than my dad," she said, trying to empathize even though her father was basically her hero.

Travis sat down on the metal bleacher and leaned forward, his arms resting on his knees. "My mom is pretty great."

"She's amazing, and if I gain weight after finishing off that box of goodies she sent me home with, I'm blaming you, not her."

He smiled at the ground before looking up to catch her eye. "What happened to your parents? You only talk about them in the past tense."

Summer hadn't avoided the subject on purpose. She simply didn't like to focus on their deaths. Their lives were much more interesting. "They were killed in a car accident by a drunk driver."

"I'm so sorry," he said sincerely. "How long ago?"

"Ten years." She took a seat next to him, grabbing the full water bottle on the ground at his feet. "I was sixteen, homeschooled my whole life and used to doing what I love all day, every day."

"I can't imagine losing my parents so young."

Summer shrugged. At least she'd been old enough to remember them when they passed. She didn't have to rely on the memories of others. As she looked up at the blue sky, she knew her mom and dad were up there looking out for her. She was also beginning to believe they were helping Ryan convince her to take his job offer. His last email tempted her with pictures of penguins swimming in icy waters alongside someone in a kayak. The subject line read "No penguins in Texas!" He was right, of course. Not even the Abilene Zoo had penguins.

Thinking about leaving and traveling the world made Summer's head spin and her stomach hurt. Every time she thought she could be an adventurer right here in Texas, even without the penguins, Ryan would send a tantalizing email or Richard would be especially rude. Then Mimi would call about coming over on Sunday to help plant the fall hyacinth bulbs and Summer's faith in her decision to stay was firmly renewed.

Who would help with all that work if Summer was gone?

"I'm sorry for bringing it up," Travis said, putting his hand on her knee, clearly misunderstanding why she'd gotten lost in her head for a minute. The warmth of his palm gave her stomach a new reason to flip-flop.

She shook her head and told him not to apologize. Talking about her parents didn't depress her anymore. Dwelling on things you couldn't change was almost as pointless as hating someone. "Grab your stuff. Let's stretch on the grass."

The field was looking rough. The summer drought had not been kind, and since it wasn't a football field, it rarely got watered. The brown-tipped blades crunched under their feet. There were two groundskeepers working there today. One had been around for years and knew Summer. The other was a younger man with earbuds in. He ignored them as they walked by.

There was talk of tearing this track stadium down and building a football-only venue in its place. Some people didn't like that idea, but seeing as how football was a way of life around here, it seemed inevitable. Since meeting Travis, Summer was realizing more and more how football dominated in this town, this county and heck, the whole state.

"This isn't the football practice field, is it?" Travis asked as he kicked the dry ground.

There were football goalposts at each end of the field, but Summer had never known this place to be used for anything but track. "I think they practiced here a while back." She pointed to the south end of the stadium. "Then they got some fancy turf over on that field over there. I mean, would you be caught dead playing on this?"

Travis's face fell. "Don't suppose I would."

She sat down in the middle of the field and patted the ground next to her for him to join her. Summer didn't want to put him in a bad mood, but she couldn't avoid talking about football if she wanted to help him out. She lay back on the grass and looked up at the sky. It had gone from a pretty periwinkle when they first arrived to a late-morning baby blue. Puffy white clouds floated along without a care in the world.

Travis lay down, as well. They were as close as they could be without touching. They probably looked strange, lying in the middle of a burned-out field, but Summer didn't care. It was a gorgeous day and the bleacher run had taken its toll.

"Ever spend an afternoon looking up at the sky?" she asked, turning her head to find him looking at her and not at the clouds.

"A whole afternoon? That must be a weather girl thing." He laughed as he looked skyward.

"Meteorologist thing," she corrected, although she couldn't picture Richard spending the day looking at the sky.

"Have I been missing out on something?"

"Absolutely." The sky always reminded her that she was one small part of something much bigger. It was too easy to get caught up in her own drama. Sometimes she needed to remember that the world did not revolve around her. Maybe Travis needed reminding, too. "Do you miss playing football?"

He didn't answer right away. Travis was quiet, contemplative. "Sometimes."

"It must be hard not to be able to do what you love." She glanced back at him. This was the question that had been begging to be asked since she'd decided to make amends.

"I love football. I'll always love football,"

Travis said matter-of-factly. "But I don't know if I loved playing it."

Summer rolled on her side to face him at his unexpected answer. "Seriously? How can that be?"

His jaw tensed before he answered, "I don't know. Football was always an expectation, not really a dream. Does that make sense?"

Summer had been thinking long and hard about dreams and expectations lately. Dream jobs. Family expectations. "Well, what's your dream?" she asked, eager to know. Travis shrugged. Discouraged, Summer continued to press him. "There has to be something you're passionate about."

"Sure, I'm passionate about a lot of things. There's this place outside Sweetwater with the best pulled pork sandwiches you've ever tasted. And I have a lot of passion for Kenny Chesney. The man can sing a country song better than anyone."

She smacked his shoulder, causing him to sit up.

"Careful, now, I'm injured, remember?" He rubbed his shoulder as if it needed nursing. Summer knew better than to believe it wasn't for show.

"Be serious for a minute," she said, refocusing her attention on the cotton candy clouds. "I asked you once if working at the station was your dream job, and you said you didn't know. Has that changed?"

She watched his profile as he frowned.

"It's a job. I can't afford to be real picky."

"Why not?" she asked. "The way I see it, you've been given a chance to do anything you want with your life. Anything is possible. None of those expectations hold you back anymore. I would think that'd be a pretty exciting position to be in."

"That's one way to look at it, I guess," he said as if he'd never thought of it that way before.

"I noticed yesterday that you take lovely photographs." She tapped his camera bag with her foot. "I need some images for my daily weather photo segment, and today is perfect for capturing a little piece of the sky."

"You want me to take pictures for you?"

"Why else would I ask you to bring a camera?"

His eyes shifted to the clouds above them. "Should I be worried about these clouds? Are you setting me up to be rained on?"

"Cumulus clouds don't carry rain." She rolled her eyes. "And if it was going to rain, I would have made you bring my umbrella—which you seem to be holding hostage."

Travis hid his face with his hands. "Let's add remembering umbrellas to the ever-growing list of things I'm not very good at."

He was in worse shape than she thought. "Travis…if you want, I can help you with your news reports. You're a million times better than you were when you started. I wouldn't have to help very much." Summer sat up. "But you need to think bigger."

Moving his hands out of the way, he looked up at her. "Bigger?"

"I think you should give yourself a chance to be more than Travis Lockwood, Football Star."

"Ex-Football Star," he corrected, sitting up and taking his camera out of his bag.

He really bought into this idea that all he'd ever be was a broken football player. He seemed to want to be more, he just didn't realize he already was. She watched him fiddle with his camera and remove the lens cap. "Can I make an observation?"

"Observe away," he said, as if he didn't think he could stop her anyway.

"You have an insatiable curiosity. I see that in the pictures you take. I hear it in the questions you ask. Don't be trapped by your past. Anything is possible. Start dreaming." She nudged him with her elbow. "What about Travis Lockwood, Lion Tamer?"

The look on his face said she was crazy. "Are we really doing this?"

"Come on," she encouraged.

Travis shook his head but played along. "I hate cats. Big and small."

"All right, no cats." She hummed and thought. "What about Travis Lockwood, Restaurateur? No cats. All the barbecue you want. Reasonable and achievable."

"Much more doable," he said, adjusting the zoom lens and snapping a few pictures of those carefree clouds floating above them.

"Ever think about Travis Lockwood, Motivational Speaker?"

His camera came down and those eyebrows pinched together again. "Motivational speaker? Really? You think people want to hear me talk?"

"You were pretty inspirational to those

high-school boys. I think lots of people would listen to you talk."

He didn't seem so sure about that. He continued taking pictures while they took turns coming up with new and interesting vocations to which Travis could aspire. Her favorite was Travis Lockwood, Eating Challenge Champion. There was a hot wings competition at this little place near the station she was going to make sure he entered. She was about to mention it to him when a loud clicking noise went off by her ear. Summer sat up on her elbows. Just then, water shot out of the in-ground sprinkler, hitting her with a force she couldn't have expected.

They both jumped up as the entire field came to life, showering the dried-up grass and the two friends with shockingly cold water. Travis protected his camera and ran for the track. The old groundskeeper shouted at the younger man, who must have accidentally turned the system on. He was now oblivious because of the music being pumped into his ears.

Instead of running, Summer stood in the middle of the field and laughed. Once she got used to it, the cool water felt nice. She lifted her arms and tilted her face up to the sky. She closed her eyes and spun around as if dancing in the rain like when she was little. It was her mother's favorite thing to do. They'd strip off their socks and shoes and jump around in the wet grass while the heavens poured down. Their clothes would stick to their skin, and their hair would flatten and fall in their faces, but it was the best part of storm chasing.

Summer opened her eyes to find Travis standing on the track with his camera in hand. He took one more photo of her before bringing the camera down. The old groundskeeper finally figured out how to shut the sprinklers off and the water stopped its assault. Summer locked eyes with Travis, and her heart picked up the pace.

He moved toward her slowly, never breaking his stare. Summer let her gaze wander from the slightly damp T-shirt that stretched across his chest, to his narrow hips and back up to his clean-shaven, taut jawline. He stopped in front of her and placed a hand on her cheek. There was a strange uncertainty in his eyes.

"Did you know that one inch of rain falling over one square mile is somewhere around

17.4 million gallons of water?" Summer asked, wishing the wet ground would open up and swallow her whole.

"Why did you invite me here?" His tone had an edge to it.

Summer wanted to step back but was frozen. "I'm trying to help you."

Travis dropped his hand, releasing the imaginary hold he had on her. "Help me what?"

"Find what you love to do, so you can do it," she admitted. It sounded almost as strange as her weather facts. She was sure the next question would be why. Why did she want to help him?

Travis bent down to snatch up the camera bag that he'd left behind when he ran for the track. "Anything to get your thirty seconds back, right? If I leave KLVA, you'll get what you want. Sorry to disappoint you, Weather Girl. It looks like you're stuck with me."

His accusation was unexpected. He shoved his camera in the wet bag, then slung it over his shoulder. Summer watched as he strode away, wiping the water from her face. His mood changed faster than the weather around these parts, but unlike the weather, this she had never seen coming.

CHAPTER TEN

TRAVIS WAS IN trouble. Big trouble. He was falling. Falling for a blond-haired, blue-eyed weather girl. A girl with *heartbreaker* written all over her. It was pathetic, really, and he hated himself for letting it happen. That was why he'd lashed out at her on Saturday. It was easier that way. If he let himself believe for one second that she cared about him, he was a bigger fool than he'd been with Brooke.

He didn't know how to deal with this unexpected turn. When Ken hatched his plan for them to work together, Travis thought for sure they were so incompatible there would be no risk of getting involved. The best part about Summer was that she didn't like him. He wasn't even sure that had changed. She tolerated him. Now he didn't know what he wanted. Most of the time, he wanted to kiss her. Other times, he wanted to shake her... and then kiss her. Okay, maybe he wasn't as confused as he thought. His problem was, kissing Summer Raines wasn't going to make him what she wanted or needed.

Conner wasn't wrong when he'd teased him about not being good enough for her. Summer needed a guy who knew what he wanted out of life, the way she did. She needed a guy who took chances and didn't let fear get in his way. She needed a man with some confidence. If he couldn't figure out how to be what she needed, she would leave just like Brooke, and Travis wasn't up for that kind of heartache.

There was something else. Something he couldn't quite put his finger on when it came to Summer. He didn't know why, but he felt she always had one foot out the door. Something tethered her to Abilene, but it was only a matter of time before that woman broke free. He could tell by the way she pushed him to look for more out of his own life. Summer was born to run—literally and figuratively.

Travis's uncertainty accompanied him to the gym at the crack of dawn Monday morning to meet Conner. Lifting weights required focus that allowed him to shut out everything else. All he could think about was the burn of his muscles and the rep count.

"You sure you want to do that much weight?" Conner stood behind the bench press, ready to spot. "I thought you were supposed to increase the reps before you increase the weight."

Travis sat down on the bench. He was pushing himself, searching for that relief. He didn't need to be babied; he knew his limits. "It's fine. My shoulder can't take a hit from a three-hundred-pound lineman. You plannin' on tackling me?"

Conner frowned, unamused. "The last thing I need is to have to explain to Dad why you're back in the hospital, that's all I'm saying."

Travis lay back and gripped the bar with both hands. "I'm never playing ball again. So what's it matter?" Conner had nothing to say to that. No one ever did. Everyone was used to football and Travis being synonymous—like Summer and the weather. *Summer*. Thinking about Summer wasn't helping. He lifted the barbell, focusing on his breathing and form. He did twelve reps before setting it back down.

"You all right?" Conner asked from above him.

"I'm fine."

"You look…troubled."

"Troubled?"

"Remember when Mom got you that math tutor because algebra was kicking your butt? Every time she came over, you got this look on your face." Conner laughed and Travis scowled. "You have that look right now, buddy. Troubled."

Travis ignored him. "Again," he said, lifting the bar. One, two, three. Summer was worse than a quadratic equation. There was something about her that made Travis feel as if at any moment a storm would roll through and take her with it. Eight, nine, ten. Sweat began to drip down his temple. The muscles in his chest felt the burn. Eleven, twelve. He set the weights down.

"Is it the weather girl?" Conner asked. He was much smarter than he looked.

"No, this isn't about the weather girl. Don't talk about her." He picked up the bar again. It felt as if it had doubled in weight. He got six reps in before it became too much and Conner had to help him set it back down.

"So it's the weather girl," Conner said, ignoring his brother's demand.

Travis tried to lift the bar again, but Conner pushed down so it was impossible. Travis sat up in defeat. "I'm used to knowing exactly where I'm headed. Never had to think too much about anything, you know?"

Conner nodded. Travis couldn't have been much older than nine or ten when he'd told his brother he was going to play ball at UT. Not only that, but he'd be the first player to be drafted into the NFL from Sweetwater High since Sammy Baugh back in 1937. The future was predetermined. All Travis had to do was stay on course, never veer from the goal. He couldn't have imagined the road closing down on him. There were no detours, no alternative routes. He was lost without a map, and worse, without a new destination.

"What's Dad think?"

Travis tried not to laugh too loudly. It always came down to what their dad thought. No one in the family made a decision without running it by the old man first. "He thinks I'm a loser for not letting another doctor try to patch me up so I can get out there and play."

"That's harsh. I mean, they can't really patch you up—" Conner had that hopeful look in his eyes that was like a knife through Travis's chest "—can they?"

Travis got up from the bench and moved to another machine. He slid the pin between the weights and sat down. "No. No one can fix me." He didn't bother to look at Conner and the disappointment that was certain to be written all over his face.

"So, what's this have to do with Summer? Who, for the record, is hot in a smart-girl kind of way."

"You think she's smart?" Travis risked a glance in his brother's direction. Smart wasn't the way most people would describe the last couple women with whom he had had relationships. Not that he had a relationship with Summer.

Conner settled onto the hamstring curl machine. "Let's just say, when I jokingly asked if she made sure it wouldn't rain on homecoming, I got a five-minute lesson on clouds and how I could tell if rain was coming by which kind was in the sky. That woman knows more about clouds than I know about football. She's smart."

Travis smiled as he finished his set of leg presses. That sounded like Summer. "She's too smart to get mixed up with someone like me. That's what Summer has to do with this.

You ever want something you know you can't have?"

"Travis." Conner sounded as though he was scolding him for something he'd done wrong. "You could have that girl in a heartbeat. Don't you see the way she looks at you?"

"Like I annoy the hell out of her?"

Conner laughed and tossed a sweaty towel at Travis's head. "No, you idiot."

"Well, I am an idiot. I pretty much ruined everything on Saturday. If she liked me at all, she doesn't now."

"This isn't you, little brother. Where's your confidence? And don't say it got left on the field when you hurt your shoulder."

Travis shook his head. "I'm not who I was and it's only a matter of time before everyone realizes I'm nobody without football."

Conner's bulky shoulders sagged as he sighed. "You said yourself this woman doesn't even care about football. She likes you—not some football player. Whatever you did on Saturday, apologize. Women love men who can admit they were wrong. Trust me. I admit I'm wrong all the time. It's the only way Heidi lets me sleep in our bed most nights."

"You are obviously the last person I should

take advice from," Travis said, tossing the sweaty towel back at his brother.

Conner caught it with ease. "I see the way you look at her, too. Man up and apologize. Brooke moved on. It's time you did the same."

TRAVIS WENT HOME to shower and change for work. His house was quiet, unlike the gym. Quiet and lonely. As Travis finished shaving, he thought about getting a dog. Maybe some companionship was exactly what he needed. Summer had a dog.

He shook his head at himself in the mirror. Did all his thoughts have to lead back to Summer? Lately they did. He thought about her in the morning when he got up and noticed the sun shining as she'd predicted the night before. He thought about her when he saw a certain shade of blue or heard that song on the radio about being struck by lightning. The doorbell interrupted his latest Summer daydream. Throwing on his dress shirt, he buttoned it halfway before swinging the door open. His dad stood on his front porch with a white paper bag in one hand and a cup holder with two drinks in the other.

"Called you twice but you didn't pick up."

He handed the bag to Travis. "Brought you some lunch—I hope you didn't eat yet."

"I must have been in the shower," Travis said, backing up. "Smells good."

His dad stepped past him and checked out the new place. Back in Miami, Travis's house was filled with all the football paraphernalia of a star quarterback. His high school and college jerseys were mounted, framed and hung in the great room. *Sports Illustrated* covers and the *Austin Chronicle*'s front-page article about his NFL draft were proudly displayed. Trophies and awards covered the mantel. In this house, the only thing Travis could bear to look at was the Heisman Trophy. The rest of it was in storage, boxed up with everything else that didn't fit in his new life.

"Looks like you're settling in okay, huh?"

Travis knew it wasn't very impressive, but it was enough for now. Between workouts, appearances for the station and late nights in the studio, he wasn't home much anyway. Maybe a dog was a bad idea.

"Conner came by a few weeks ago and helped me get some pictures on the walls and such. Mom hung some curtains and bought some stuff to make it more homey."

His dad nodded, picking up one of the candles Olivia had placed on the end table. He lifted it to his nose and made a face. "Your mother loves buying things that make me want to sneeze." He set it down and headed for the dining room. "Picked up some sandwiches at that barbecue place you like in Merkel."

The old man was full of surprises. Travis ran back to his bedroom to finish dressing, then grabbed some napkins and forks from the kitchen, suddenly feeling more than a little famished. The two men dug into their lunches and didn't come up for air until all the food was gone. His dad asked if there were any brownies left from the box his mother sent home with him, giving Travis a reason to escape their painful silence. There had to be a reason his dad had come all this way to have lunch with his son, and something told him it wasn't to see where he was living.

"So," his dad started once all the food was gone and there was no way to avoid a conversation. Sam Lockwood was a salesman and rarely a man without something to say, but today he seemed at a loss for words. The room was so quiet Travis could hear the refrigerator humming in the kitchen and the air conditioner kick on.

"So," Travis repeated. His knee began to bounce under the table. It felt as if the temperature in the house went up ten degrees. Travis cursed himself for putting on his tie already. He loosened the knot and prepared himself for the plea his dad was surely here to make. He had to be here to plead his case about seeing the doctor again. It was the only logical explanation.

"Your mother agrees with you about the doctor." His father leaned forward with his elbows on the table. "She doesn't think you should see any more doctors."

Travis was more than surprised. He was sure his dad would have kept the whole doctor conversation to himself. Thank God for his mother. She was the only person who could tell Sam Lockwood he was wrong and get away with it.

"At least one of you sees it my way."

"I don't understand what harm talking to the man would do, but I understand you're ready to move on." His dad reached into the front pocket of his perfectly pressed white shirt and pulled out a business card. He slid it across the table. "Here's your plan B," he said as Travis examined the card with the University of Alabama logo staring back at him. "You call this guy. He wants you to come work as a quarterback coach. They got their eye on a kid coming out of Odessa. They think you can teach him what he needs to know to be their leader in a year or two. This is as close as you're gonna get to doing what you love."

Travis blinked, as if the words on the card would somehow change. Alabama? Quarterback coach? He flapped one end of the card against his hand. This was one scenario he hadn't considered. Travis Lockwood, Quarterback Coach.

"It's not the same as playing, but close enough," his dad continued. "If you work your way up, I could see you getting a head coaching job somewhere down the line. I suppose I saw that in your future after a long and successful career on the field. I think former quarterbacks make good coaches. This is a great opportunity."

Travis didn't know what to say. Coaching wasn't the same as playing, but he'd been coached by some of the best and had always been a fast learner. At the same time, coaching required a certain dedication to football Travis wasn't sure he had in him anymore. There was also something to be said for experience— Travis had none as a coach but plenty as a player. He would know exactly what this kid from Odessa was about to face.

"How long have you been working on this?"

His dad shrugged. "Couple weeks ago someone reached out to me. I told the guy I didn't think you'd be interested because I figured you'd jump at the chance to play if I could find someone who could fix you up." As soon as he met his gaze, the disappointment and defeat staring back at him made Travis want to look away. "Guess that's not the direction you're headed."

"I'll give him a call," Travis promised. There wasn't much more he could do to please a man who would never be pleased or proud ever again.

"Good." His dad nodded and stood up. "Gotta get going. I need to check on your brother."

"Well, thanks for bringing by lunch." The

conversation might have been uncomfortable, but the food was divine.

His dad told him it was nothing as he ran a hand over his sandy-blond crew cut. He stopped short of the front door. "Your weather girl say it was supposed to rain today?" he asked, tipping his chin in the direction of the red umbrella resting against the wall by the door.

Summer didn't live in Alabama. She lived here in Abilene. Why that mattered didn't make much sense, but it did matter. "No. No rain."

The creases in his father's forehead gave away his confusion, but he didn't ask any more questions about it. Travis watched him walk to his car and back out of the driveway. Once his dad was long gone, he pulled the business card out of his pocket and stared at the name and number for a moment. Sportscasting wasn't his dream job, he could admit that, but working at KLVA wasn't all that bad. Summer made things interesting, to say the least. Could he walk away without ever knowing if there was a chance something could happen between the two of them?

He tossed the card on his coffee table and

returned to his bedroom for his jacket. He stared himself down in his closet mirror. Alabama wanted him. There was little risk in calling the coach up and hearing what he had to say. Summer, on the other hand, was a huge risk. Putting his heart on the line scared him to death—just like the thought of jumping out of a hot-air balloon. Life wasn't interesting without a little bit of fear. Before he went with a sure thing, Travis knew he had to take a leap.

CHAPTER ELEVEN

MONDAYS WERE NO one's favorite. Monday was likely the most unpopular day of the week. Mondays were bad. This Monday was no exception. It was, however, worse than all those that came before it. This Monday, the world seemed to be working against Summer from the moment she got out of bed.

Garbage littered the kitchen floor, thanks to a neglected-feeling black Lab who had decided the best revenge was making his owner furious. In an attempt to make up with and tire out said dog, Summer decided to take Storm for a run. It was during this run that she somehow managed to trip over her own two feet, landing on and scraping her knee. This meant she would no longer be able to wear the dress she'd spent twenty minutes ironing earlier that morning. While cursing the concrete for being so hard and rough, she lost her grip on the leash and Storm took off between two neighbors' houses. Thirty minutes later, Summer cornered the naughty pup in a very unpleasant woman's backyard, where she was admonished for "letting" the dog trample the woman's marigolds.

The fun hadn't stopped there. Summer backed into the garbage can at the curb on her way to work and cracked a taillight, rode the elevator up with Rachel, who couldn't wait to tell Summer how frizzy her hair looked today, and bumped her bad knee on the corner of her desk when Richard barreled past her on his way to who knows where. She hadn't even seen Travis yet.

Things were bound to be uncomfortable after whatever it was that had happened on Saturday. He assumed her intentions were selfish, and the thought stung. The more she considered it, the more guilty she felt. She could see how he might think that was true. Maybe it was a little true. Maybe she did want him to go, but it wasn't about the thirty seconds anymore. It was these feelings he was stirring in her. Feelings that threatened to mess up her plans for an easy escape from Abilene when the right time came.

When he finally arrived at the station, there

was no stopping by her desk. No touching her stapler, playing with her paper clips, asking questions about whatever was on her screen. He went straight to his desk and stayed there. His eyes, however, wandered her way almost constantly. She resolved to talk to him as soon as she mustered up the courage.

"Summer!" Ken stood in his doorway, hand on his hip, not looking the least bit amused. The knot in Summer's stomach twisted tighter. "Come here, please," he said with an irritated tone that made the "please" sound anything but polite.

She eased out of her chair and avoided looking Travis's way, even though she could feel his eyes on her. Ken's door rattled as she closed it behind her. Ken wasn't a small man, but his large desk could dwarf a giant. He leaned back in his black leather chair, twirling a pen in his fingers. He motioned for her to sit down. Summer sat and crossed her legs, curious as to what was going on. Hopefully the red splotches on his neck had nothing to do with why he wanted to talk with her.

"What's the emergency, boss?" she asked with a smile, trying to keep things light.

Ken, not impressed by her flippant attitude, tossed his pen on the desk. "Can you explain to me why I have Alex Hayes from Texas Star Chevrolet, one of our biggest advertisers, calling me up and saying he heard you were making some not-so-flattering comments about their dealership?"

Summer sat a little straighter and leaned forward. "I've never said anything about Texas Star Chevrolet. I don't know why Mr. Hayes would say that."

"Maybe you made a comment while you were eating out or while you were buying your groceries. I don't know. All I know is that I thought I could count on you to watch what you say in public. You represent this station 24/7."

"I understand that. I'm always careful about what I do and say. As a general rule, I try not to talk poorly about anyone, including advertisers." She tried to remain calm, but it was a blow to have her character called into question.

"That's what I told Hayes. But he said he'd heard it from more than one person. He's not planning on pulling any of their advertising dollars right now, but he asked that I give you a stern warning. Should he hear you're out bad-mouthing them again, he'll have to take action." Ken sat forward, elbows on his desk, fingers steepled in front of his face. "Do *not* make him take action, Summer."

"Ken, I am telling you I have never said anything good, bad or indifferent about Texas Star. Ever. I can't stop something I'm not doing."

"Well, to make sure they know they have your full support, I'm taking ten seconds of the weather report for you to encourage people to buy their next Chevy from Alex Hayes and his team over there."

Summer launched out of her chair. "Ten seconds? I didn't say anything! I didn't do anything wrong!"

"It doesn't matter!" Ken shouted back. "All that matters is that Alex Hayes thinks you did. So you will make it better for a couple weeks by talking him up. You'll also ride on his float in the Rodeo Parade. End of story."

Having been properly scolded for something she didn't do, Summer wanted to spew everything she knew about blizzards in Alaska to anyone who would listen. No one in the newsroom seemed to notice she was on the verge of a breakdown—except for two people. Richard smiled snidely as he shoved a manila folder into his old, battered briefcase.

"Whatever you're doing to make him so mad, keep it up, Summer. Keep. It. Up," he said on his way to the elevators. Summer bit her tongue so hard it hurt. His arrogance was nearly intolerable. His newfound malice was unforgivable.

She glanced at the only other person paying her any mind. Travis nodded in the direction of the break room and started heading that way. She followed him and slammed the door. Travis perched on the edge of the long dining table. He was the epitome of calm and collected while Summer raged like a storm.

"Do you know that the temperature of lightning's return stroke can reach fifty thousand degrees Fahrenheit? That's hotter than the surface of the sun," she said, pacing in front of him. Lightning was only half as hot as her temper right now.

"What happened?" He reached out to stop her pacing. His hold on her arm was firm but gentle, and it made her stand still.

"Apparently, I've been bad-mouthing one of our biggest advertisers when I go grocery shopping. Apparently, I will be giving up ten seconds of every weather report to tell all of West Central Texas to buy their cars from Texas Star Chevrolet for the next couple weeks. Apparently, it doesn't matter if I have never even heard of this advertiser before, nor have I ever said a single word about them to anyone I have ever spoken to in my entire life! Apparently, Ken doesn't care about that. He only cares about the money. Apparently, defending my honor means nothing."

"I'm sorry Ken doesn't have your back." He took a deep breath. "And I'm sorry I yelled at you on Saturday."

Summer put some space between them and worked on regaining her composure. "I'm sorry you think I'm trying to get rid of you."

"I think we need to worry more about the person trying to get rid of you."

"It's Richard. My grandmother would say 'kill him with kindness,' but the means I'm considering don't seem very kind."

One corner of Travis's mouth shot up. "I can't tackle him, but you can kill him?"

Summer sat down on one of the plastic chairs and rested her head on folded arms. She was tired of these games. If Richard wanted her to quit, he wasn't going to get his wish.

Like a stubborn child, she would dig her heels in and stay to spite him. "All I want to do is talk about the weather. Is that so much to ask?"

"I don't think so." He sat down next to her. She could hear him tapping his fingers on the table. "Who knew there was this much drama behind the scenes? Everyone seems so friendly when you're watching the news. I never imagined there was a dirty underbelly of local TV news."

Summer laughed into her arms. Travis was funny when he wasn't biting her head off.

"I like it when you laugh," he said. "It's even better than that smile of yours."

Summer tried to swallow down the weather fact that begged to be blurted out. His compliment made the blood rush through her veins a little faster. It also made her want to run, for fear she might like it more than she should. Her heart and head were battling it out. Her heart beat for more as her head warned her not to take too much. Travis offered her another reason to stay in Abilene. The trick would be not letting her roots get too deep.

BY NEWS TIME, Summer had gone from angry to relaxed to panicked. Something was off.

She couldn't explain it; it was simply a feeling. Her gut told her something wasn't right. She tried to push it down, but the feeling confused her. It was as if a deadly storm was on its way. She watched the national radar and found nothing significant, nothing that would stir up this kind of apprehension. She made it through the five o'clock report without a problem, making her think she was perhaps unnecessarily paranoid. Richard was long gone, his day ending just as hers began. There was nothing to worry about, she told herself.

Travis attempted to distract her in between newscasts by taking her to dinner. He wasn't up for a chicken-wing challenge, but he dared to try their hottest hot sauce. Summer had to laugh when his ears turned bright red and the sweat began to bead on his forehead. She would never understand why someone would want to eat something that practically burned off taste buds.

It didn't take long for her thoughts to turn anxious. As Summer dug through her purse, unable to find her car keys as usual, this strange unease enveloped her.

"I'm going to buy you a Texas-size key chain so you never have to look for your keys again," Travis said, waiting patiently by the passenger door. She chuckled, but she was still bothered. "You okay?"

Summer stopped digging and looked up at the partly cloudy sky. "Maybe my internal radar is off. Based on how I've been feeling all day, the storm of the century should be headed our way."

Travis's eyes narrowed. "This is about the weather?"

"I'm being paranoid," she said, shaking her head. "Or maybe I need a vacation." A permanent vacation. One that allowed her to sleep in an igloo or kayak with penguins.

"A vacation?"

Summer pushed aside her wallet for the third time and finally uncovered her keys. Unlocking the car, she shook her head. "Ignore me. I don't know what I'm talking about anymore."

Travis pulled the seat belt across his broad chest. Summer tried to convince herself she didn't care that he probably had muscles in places she'd never seen muscles on a man before. She started up the car and backed out of the parking space. They'd only driven a block before flashing lights lit up behind them and a siren alerted her to the next bit of bad luck she'd have to deal with today. Summer pulled over and lifted her purse onto her lap so she could find her license.

Travis turned around and glared at the police car. "There was no way you were speeding." The officer reached the window as Summer rolled it down. Travis leaned over so far he practically climbed into the driver's seat. "There is no way she was speeding, sir."

"Travis Lockwood?" The officer removed his sunglasses to get a better look. Of course he recognized him. Summer was certain that every man in Abilene either played ball with Travis, had a child who played ball with Travis or watched him play at some point in his career.

"Yes, sir."

The officer narrowed his eyes and bent down to get a better look at the man in the passenger's seat. The navy blue uniform looked almost black against the man's pale skin, and seemed to match the dark hair on his head. "Well, well, well. How the mighty have fallen. You and all those Sweetwater boys used to think you were such hot stuff."

Travis scanned the man's face, trying to

place him. Summer guessed the bushy mustache was throwing him off. His eyes finally settled on the thin brass name tag pinned beneath the officer's badge. "Scott Rogers? You played QB for Duncanville, right?"

"That's right."

"You're a cop now, huh?" Travis seemed genuinely surprised.

"Aren't you observant?" the officer replied. "Maybe you weren't as dumb as we thought back in high school." Both Travis and Summer sat back, mouths agape. "So sorry to hear about your shoulder, Lockwood. That makes you, what? A nobody now?"

Summer's shoulders tensed. This was far from the usual response to meeting Travis. She was ready to snatch the booklet out of his hand and write her own ticket so they could get away from this guy. "I have a busted taillight. It happened this morning. I'll get it fixed as soon as I can, Officer. I promise."

Officer Rogers straightened up and slid his sunglasses back on. "I'd usually just give you a warning, but seeing as how you're friends with *the* Travis Lockwood, I think I'm going to have to cite you. Wouldn't want Mr. Big

Shot to think he and his friends can get away with breaking the law."

This snapped Travis out of the stupor the other insult had put him in. He leaned over Summer again, his jaw tight and his eyes fiery. "So you haven't changed a bit since high school. Still the same obnoxious jerk you were back then."

"Do I need to ask you to step out of the car?" The officer rose to the challenge. "Has either one of you been drinking tonight? Something that would make you think you can speak to an officer of the law like that?"

"Are you kidding me?" Travis nearly crawled out the window.

"Travis!" Summer pushed him back into his seat. "It's fine. Give me the ticket." She held her license out to the officer. He snatched it from her hand and returned to his car. Travis sank down into his seat. "I'm having a bad enough day as it is. Can you please try not getting me thrown into jail?" she snapped at him.

"Your bad day doesn't begin to compete with my bad year."

Officer Rogers came back with Summer's license and ticket and a satisfied grin. Luckily, Travis stared out his own window to avoid any more confrontation, seething but quiet. Putting her blinker on to get back on the road, she watched him sulk out of the corner of her eye. From the beginning, she'd been able to relate to his hatred of the sympathy people expressed whenever they spoke to him about his injury. It was similar to the way people had made her feel when her parents died. They'd say sorry while she imagined they were silently thanking God it wasn't them or their loved ones. What happened with Officer Rogers was different, though. Travis was the one feeling sorry for Travis, and there was nothing worse than inviting yourself to the pity party.

"It doesn't matter what that guy or anyone thinks," she said as she merged back into traffic. Travis said nothing in reply. "But for the record, I'm not sorry you hurt your shoulder. I'm glad it happened."

"Oh yeah?" He spoke to his window, not her. "Why's that?"

"Because it wasn't your dream." He glanced her way and then back out the window. "You deserve to dream, Travis."

He didn't say anything or even look back at

her, but his hand slid across the center console and covered hers as it rested on the gearshift. He gave it a little squeeze before pulling his back into his lap. She took that to mean he knew her words had absolutely nothing to do with her thirty seconds.

BACK AT THE STUDIO, Summer tried to regain some focus. She let go of her worries and prepared for her ten o'clock report. Rachel was in the makeup room when she came in for a touch-up. The row of lights above the eight-foot-wide mirror lit up her beautiful face. Rachel had the face of an angel. Unfortunately, looks could be deceiving.

"Word around the station is there's been a world of trouble for the Rain Princess lately. Let's hope you aren't distracted like last week. Those sloppy graphics were a disaster," Rachel said, swiping at the excess lipstick on her bottom lip.

"I wasn't distracted. There was a technical glitch."

"Is that what you're calling it? A glitch?" Rachel asked. Summer refused to be provoked, so she continued. "Maybe if you weren't so busy trying to get the attention of a certain sportscaster, you'd have less trouble."

"Travis has nothing to do with what happened. We're…friends."

Rachel laughed, but it didn't sound as though she thought anything was particularly funny. "Travis is friendly with a lot of women, isn't he?"

Summer locked eyes with her in the mirror. "What's that supposed to mean?"

"Well, he has quite a reputation." Rachel was a gossip, through and through. It was her business to know other people's business, so in some ways it made her good at her job. Gossiping about coworkers, however, was always a bad idea. "Let's just say I've heard some rather interesting information about our *friend* Travis."

Summer knew better than to let her get under her skin. Unfortunately, it was working. "Did you know the deadliest weather disaster in U.S. history was an unnamed hurricane that struck Galveston back in 1900?"

"Oh, Summer! Now, don't go gettin' all worked up. Just be smart." Rachel put away her makeup and smoothed down a stray hair. "If he's half the man the women in Sweetwatcr have reported him to be, you're in for a good time. But I heard he has a very short attention span. Don't expect to be his friend for very long, sugar." She gave Summer a little wink on her way out.

Blood boiling, Summer set down her lipstick. She put up with Rachel because for every nasty thing she said, she'd make up for it by doing something right for the community. Rachel had founded and was the head of a charity in Abilene that benefitted Alzheimer's research. Someone said her dad suffered from the terrible disease, but Rachel never discussed her family with coworkers. The good she did usually outweighed the bad. Usually. Tonight, she'd chosen the wrong time to get on Summer's nerves.

Summer hoped she'd make it through her weather report without calling Rachel a lying witch on the air. Everything went smoothly as she outlined the highs and lows for the day. Her graphics were all in order and she was confident she could wrap up hcr three minutes without any issues. Until she clicked to the seven-day outlook. The hair on the back of her neck stood on end. A second later, one of the studio lights swung down and crashed into the green screen, missing Summer's head by mere inches.

Complete chaos ensued. Sparks flew, crew members rushed to the scene and Travis had his arms around her before she even had time to process what had happened. They switched cameras and Rachel apologized to the viewing audience before they cut to commercial.

"Are you okay?" Travis pulled her aside, looking her up and down, searching for injuries.

"I'm fine. It missed me." Her voice was calm, but her body shook. Travis hugged her tightly as the shock began to wear off.

"Travis, we need you at the desk," the director said into their earpieces.

"Go," Summer said, giving him a shove toward the news desk. "I'm fine."

"Maybe you're fine, but I'm not. If that had hit you…"

His concern warmed her rapidly beating heart. "But it didn't."

He frowned and pushed her blond curls behind her ear, checking for a hidden injury. When he was completely satisfied she was unharmed, he went to do his job.

The production techs scratched their heads

over what had caused the light to fall, pointing fingers and questioning each other about who had been the last one to mess with the lighting above the green screen. One of the production assistants made sure Summer could report the seven-day outlook from the news desk at the end of the broadcast.

While she waited for her cue, she tried to process what had happened. What if that light had struck her? Was there a higher power here trying to convince her this job could be just as exciting as the one Ryan offered? Or was it telling her she needed to get out of here? The longer she thought about it, the more a frightening thought ran a chill up her spine. How could one of those lights come loose like that? She had had the bad feeling all evening. What if someone wanted to do her harm?

It was one thing to tamper with her maps. It was another to try to hurt her. Summer began to seriously worry she had an enemy on the set. One who had crossed the line tonight.

CHAPTER TWELVE

THE FIRST TIME someone messed with Summer's weather report, nothing was done. Travis heard that Richard denied doing anything to her graphics and that Ken had accepted that without question. The only consolation Travis was able to give Summer was that Richard seemed quite peeved when his fan didn't work the next morning. Fans tended not to work when their power cords were cut.

It was a childish prank, but Richard didn't do himself any favors with the way he treated people. Everything about him made Travis suspicious. He figured Richard had something to do with the other mishaps Summer was experiencing—the missed appointments, the trouble with the advertiser. But the crashing light put a new twist on things. A twist Travis didn't care for one bit. He tried to watch the old weatherman like a hawk. One wrong move and Travis wouldn't hesitate to take his head off.

Travis tried to be rational about it all. Maybe it was a coincidence that after Ken announced the new promo plans involving Summer and Travis, strange things started happening to the weather girl. Maybe she just had really bad luck. Maybe that light was loose for a completely innocent reason and just happened to fall while Summer was standing under it.

Maybe.

Maybe Richard was a spiteful son of a gun. Maybe his jealousy had gotten out of control. Maybe he had lost his mind and was willing to do something criminal to get back at Summer. The only thing Travis knew for sure was someone needed to be held accountable for what had happened in the studio. This could not be written off like the graphics fiasco. If Ken didn't get to the bottom of this, Travis would.

Summer was in Ken's office discussing the previous night's events. Travis waited outside the door, hearing nothing but muffled voices. He needed to see her, know she was all right.

Everything seemed to move in slow motion when Travis saw the light come crashing down, barely missing Summer. It could have done some serious damage. It scared him half to death. The resilient weather girl had handled the incident better than he had. She might have recited all the statistics related to Hurricane Katrina after the newscast, but she recovered quickly. Travis, on the other hand, still hadn't calmed down.

During his sleepless night, Travis wrestled with the feelings he could no longer control. Denying his attraction to her was pointless. He might be a nobody, but maybe being with Summer could inspire him to figure out who he should be.

Summer emerged, looking slightly perturbed.

"What did he say?" he asked, pushing off the wall and trailing her.

"He promises everything will be 'investigated thoroughly' and says I have nothing to worry about." The way she said it didn't sound convincing.

"That's it. I'm saying something." Travis turned, but Summer grabbed his hand to stop him. If he weren't so mad, he could have appreciated the opportunity to hold hands a little more.

"I've survived gale-force winds that could have blown me out of town and a lightning storm that looked like something out of a science-fiction movie. I can survive someone's lame attempts at ruining my weather reports."

"Hitting you with a studio light is not the same as ruining your weather report."

Summer tilted her head. "You know what I mean." She let go of his hand and headed for her desk. She glanced toward Richard's empty chair. "Ken thinks it was simply an accident. No reason to jump to conclusions that someone made it happen."

Travis sat on the edge of her desk. "Maybe it was an accident. But if it wasn't, I want someone's head. And I usually get what I want."

Summer gave him half a smile. "I'm sure you do." She pushed his leg. "Now get out of here. Some of us have work to do."

TRAVIS HADN'T REALIZED how much of his new job would be done outside the studio—speaking engagements, special appearances, station promotion. There were so many community functions to attend, Travis almost lost track. He was ready to hire an assistant to help him keep it all straight. Luckily, the station's intern was willing to do anything for anyone. If there was one thing Travis knew how to do, it was delegate.

Shannon was a godsend. The young woman could teach a class in organization. She knew how to upload appointments onto Travis's phone so it would beep and tell him where he needed to be and when. She made sure he had something to eat every day and even offered to help him with tasks that had nothing to do with work, like picking up a birthday card for his aunt. He felt guilty that he had little wisdom about the business to impart to her, but she didn't seem to mind.

"I talked to Chuck Handley over at the museum like you asked." Shannon pulled his attention away from the blond beauty who could somehow work without being distracted by recent events. "Everything's set. Here's a list of what he wants in return." She handed him a list of over a dozen items. Travis looked it over with a grin he couldn't contain.

"Perfect," he said. Everything was falling

into place as he hoped. Summer had helped him avoid failing at this job and he wanted to thank her. Austin offered up the perfect way to do just that.

"All you have to do is call him when you're ready and he'll meet you. I can put a reminder on your phone and link it to his contact number."

"You really are the best, Shannon. You know that, right?"

The girl giggled and turned as red as a can of Coca-Cola. "You know, I bet if you asked Ken, he'd let me come with you to Austin. I could help you guys out, make sure everything goes as planned. I'd love to see you in action outside the studio again."

True, Ken would probably give Travis whatever he wanted. The boss was ready to induct himself into the Broadcasting Hall of Fame after Travis and Summer successfully reported from their third high-school football game. Travis was gaining confidence and it showed in his reports. Ratings continued to rise and the advertisers were rolling in. KLVA was beating down Channel 4's door for the number-one spot; it was only a matter of time. Together, Travis and Summer made a great team. If Travis wanted that to continue off the air, there was no room for Shannon on this trip."Oh, come on. You don't want to work on the weekend if you don't have to," he said, gently trying to discourage her.

"I'm free that weekend, and working for you would barely be like working at all." Shannon was cute but not Travis's type. No, his type was blond, blue-eyed and strangely fascinated with the weather. Only one woman fit that bill. She happened to be the woman on her way to the break room, looking mighty worked up. Travis watched as Rachel stood and followed her, an obvious recipe for disaster.

Travis jumped up. "You want something from the Coke machine?"

Shannon blinked and took a step back to avoid being knocked over. She shook her head as he patted his pockets for change and took off.

As he approached, he could hear Rachel. "Has anyone explained to her that she is not his personal assistant? She's shameless. I mean, she gets in his face practically every chance she gets."

Travis found it entertaining that Rachel

would be so appalled by Shannon's fawning, considering the fact that she herself had been guilty of it on more than one occasion.

"Leave the poor girl alone," Summer said. "She's no different than everyone else who dotes on him around here."

"Well, I'm going to say something to Ken. That girl needs to be put in her place."

Someone needed to be put in her place, but it wasn't Shannon. Travis stepped into the room.

Both women startled, and Rachel instantly turned on the charm. Her hips swayed as she moved in his direction. "There's my favorite sports man. I was just telling Summer that I think you and I are due for another dinner together. You need to take me out for some Chinese tonight, sugar."

"Then I'm surprised Summer didn't tell you we already have plans. But thanks for thinking of me." Travis walked over to the Coke machine and slipped in a dollar. "You know who you should ask to dinner?" Both women were rendered speechless. "Shannon. You know, the intern? She would be thrilled if you gave her two minutes of your time."

"That's a fine idea," Rachel said as she

fluffed her hair with her hand, "but… Shoot, I just remembered I need to go over some things with Brian tonight. Maybe another time."

"Another time, then. I'll let Shannon know. She'll be so excited." Travis pushed the button for his drink and smiled. Rachel tried to smile, but it was more like a grimace. She hightailed it out of the break room, leaving a snickering Travis alone with Summer.

Summer sat at the long rectangular table, tearing a napkin into tiny pieces. "You know she's never going to take Shannon out to dinner, right?"

Travis twisted off the cap of his Coke. "I know, but she's starting to rub me the wrong way."

"She's jealous."

"Of Shannon?" He laughed. How could Rachel be so blind when his sights were so clearly set on Summer?

Summer pushed her chair back and rose to her feet, the napkin bits clenched in her fist. She tossed the confetti into the garbage and pulled open one of the cabinets. "Well, you two have been attached at the hip lately," she said, pulling out a coffee mug. "People are bound to assume things. You've always been very popular with the ladies."

Clearly Rachel wasn't the only one who couldn't see. Travis came up from behind, trapping her against the counter with his arms. She reacted immediately—her spine straightened into a rigid line while the rest of her quivered. Her breathing stopped for a second, and Travis couldn't wipe the smile from his face.

"I don't think she needs to be jealous of Shannon," he said softly in her ear. Summer swallowed hard. He swore he would tell her how he felt and see if she thought she felt the same. After she was almost decapitated the other night, he vowed to do it sooner than later. "Where am I taking you to dinner tonight?"

"I… We… I don't know if…" Unable to finish any of her sentences, she stopped trying altogether.

"It's just dinner. We've had dinner together several times."

Now she was breathing too fast. "Did you know that even though tornadoes can appear any time of day, most happen between three p.m. and nine p.m.?" she asked, still shaky.

"Can you feel those comin', too?" He stepped back, offering her an escape. The weather fact was enough to let him know she was more interested than she'd been letting on.

Summer turned around, her arms like a shield across her chest. "Some storms have a way of catching me off guard," she admitted.

"Have dinner with me tonight?"

Her eyes exposed her fear. She didn't trust him. Or maybe she didn't trust herself. Summer took a deep breath and let it out slow and easy. "Okay." This woman was nothing if not up for a challenge.

HIS FAVORITE WEATHER girl was waiting for him by the elevators after the five o'clock report. Travis held up a finger, letting her know he needed one more minute. His father was reading him the riot act on the phone.

"If you let this opportunity pass you by, there may not be another waiting for you. You have to show some interest."

Travis hadn't called the coach over at Alabama yet. Someone—Travis guessed his brother—was in big trouble for telling his father about his lack of follow-through. "I've been busy at work," he tried to explain.

"We're talking about getting you a real job. The right job. Don't make excuses. You never used to make excuses."

"I'm not even sure I want to be a quarterback co—" That was the wrong thing to say. Travis could hear his father put the phone down and curse loudly. After a good ten seconds, he picked it back up.

"Call Alabama, son," his dad said.

Travis mustered all the confidence he could find. He had a right to do what he wanted. And it was time to figure out what he wanted to do without input from his dad. "I'll consider it, but right now I'm going to put a hundred percent into the job I have." He looked back at Summer, who was chewing on her thumb nail while she waited for him. She was cute when she was nervous. "I'm really starting to like it here." Before his dad could say anything else, Travis said goodbye and hung up.

Summer needed to get back in time to reset some of her graphics, so they agreed on a little café within walking distance of the station. It wouldn't be long before this time of day would find the sun sinking lower in the sky, making the weather during the evening break more comfortable and mild. Cars and trucks filled with commuters clogged the street, but the sidewalk was nice and clear.

Travis watched Summer as she fixed her gaze on the ground in front of her. It was almost as though she was intentionally trying to avoid stepping on the cracks in the pavement. He began to wonder if she was a superstitious thrill-seeker. Cautiously reckless perhaps, he mused. She wore her hair up today, a few loose curls framing her pretty face. Summer was a natural beauty. She never wore too much makeup—eyes bluer than the ocean didn't need any help standing out. Her lips were always a soft pink and lightly glossed. He was going to kiss those lips someday.

As they walked, Travis tried to strike up a conversation. "So, if this weather keeps up, are we going to make it in the record books for the driest fall?"

Summer glanced up at him briefly. He could see her trying to hold back a smile.

"What? What did I say?" he asked, nudging her with his elbow.

Her smile broke free and spread across her face. She looked up, shielding her eyes from the sun. "You're really willing to talk to me about the weather?"

"Sure, why not?"

She shrugged and averted her eyes again. Travis couldn't wait to get to the restaurant so she could sit across from him and he could look into those eyes all dinner long. "Once you get me started, I might not be able to stop. I can talk about the weather all day."

Travis laughed. "I bet you can." He let his hand brush against hers, wondering what it would be like if she let him hold it the rest of the way. The contact caused her to lose her concentration and step on a crack. His ability to affect her made him a little smug.

Summer avoided his touch by lifting her hand to push some hair behind her ear. "When I was little, I used to wake up and run to the window to see what the weather was like outside. I needed to know. Didn't matter if it was Christmas morning or my birthday—the weather was the most important thing."

"But I thought you could feel it, you know, if it was going to rain and all?"

"I feel rain coming. Like with the rest of

you mere mortals, all other weather conditions are a complete mystery to me."

"Sounds like you fancy yourself something of a superhero, huh? The weather girl, here to save the day." He said it with affection, not mockingly. "I can't believe you don't work at some big weather research facility, investigating and protecting the innocent from the big, bad, evil storms. Why work here—" he held his arms out and spun in a circle"—where the weather is pretty much always like this?"

Summer stopped walking. "There's nothing wrong with working here. I like it in Abilene. My family is in Abilene. I don't know why I need to justify why I am happy to work in Abilene! As if working somewhere else would be so much better. Like storm chasing is—" She stopped talking and started moving again. She blew past Travis like a gale-force wind. He had no idea what he had said to upset her. Truthfully, he didn't want Summer to work anywhere but KLVA.

"Hey," Travis said, touching her arm as he jogged up next to her. "There's nothing wrong with wanting to work here. I like working in Abilene, too."

Summer shook her head and rubbed her

forehead as though she had a bad headache coming on. "I think I need some food. Hunger makes me cranky." She tried to give him a smile, but it didn't come off quite right. Something was weighing heavy on that mind of hers.

Merle's Café was stamped across a deep red awning on a corner building two blocks from the station. Two small wrought-iron tables with matching chairs sat outside as a makeshift patio. A wood placard covered in chalkboard paint sat just outside the door, welcoming people in with a drawing of a steaming cup of coffee and a list of the day's specials.

Travis held the door open for Summer, and she thanked him quietly as she brushed against him lightly.

The hostess recognized both of them and seated them immediately. Travis slid into the worn red vinyl booth and looked around. Merle's had a 1950s feel. Travis wondered if that was because it hadn't been updated since 1950. The late-evening sun cast its orange-yellow rays across the dingy black-and-white tiles on the floor. Aluminum signs advertising Coke for ten cents a bottle hung on the walls, along with pictures of down-town Abilene back in the day. What Merle's lacked in ambience, it made up for in food. The smells coming from the kitchen and the tables and booths nearby made Travis's mouth water. This was down-home cooking at its finest. Summer sure knew how to pick a place.

The waitress handed over the menus while going on and on about attending the State Championship game Travis had played in as a sophomore. It took a request for some ice water to get her to move on.

"So it sounds like sports reporting has become something you want to do now," Summer said, the menu blocking her beautiful blues from his.

"The better I get, the more I like it. Maybe ESPN will come knocking soon and I'll be off to New York or wherever their studio is."

The menu she was using as a shield tipped down just enough for her eyes to meet his. "Is that so?"

He shook his head, grinning. "Like you said, there's nothing wrong with working here in Abilene."

"Great. I'm never going to get my thirty seconds back. I'm not sure I'll survive."

"You'll survive." Travis loved that she didn't shy away from teasing him. The waitress arrived with their waters and took their orders. When they were alone and she had no menu to hide behind, Travis continued, with his dimples in full effect. "I think you've finally stopped hating me."

"I never hated you. I tried to hate you, but you're too likable."

He liked that answer. He liked that answer a lot. "I am, am I?"

"Less and less by the minute."

He wasn't buying it. "Admit it. You like me."

"I don't know. You never return the things you borrow, you drive a pretentious car. The list of reasons not to like you goes on and on."

"Your umbrella is sitting right by my front door. I never remember it because it hasn't rained in weeks."

"Don't make me come get it," she warned.

He laughed. "You aren't as scary as you used to be, Weather Girl."

Poor Summer looked so flustered he half expected to hear all about typhoons or the average number of lightning strikes in a Texas thunderstorm. Summer managed to keep the weather facts at bay.

"Country-fried steak with mashed potatoes, pork chops with the vegetable medley and an extra side of french fries," the waitress said as she set the plates in front of Travis. "And the half turkey sandwich on sourdough and a chicken noodle soup for the lady. Is there anything else I can get you?"

"Is there anything left back there?" Summer asked, staring wide-eyed at her dinner companion, who was already shoveling in a mouthful.

"What?" he mumbled around a bite of his pork.

"How is it humanly possible for one man to eat all of that?"

"I work hard, I play hard, I have an appetite. You should have seen me when I played ball. I could eat twice this much."

Her giggle was better than the food. Travis finished off one plate and started on the other.

"You're going to be five hundred pounds soon if you aren't careful," she said, shaking her head.

"You offering to help me work it off?"

Summer set her sandwich down. "If I remember correctly, the last time I took you running, you nearly passed out."

"I remember watching you get drenched by the sprinklers, loving every second of it. Like you were dancing in the rain. You looked beautiful." Seeing her like that had stirred feelings he wasn't ready to deal with then, but he was prepared to try now.

"Stop. What's gotten into you tonight?" The corner of her mouth twitched, dying to give in to a smile.

"You say stop, but you don't mean it," he said before popping a giant piece of broccoli into his mouth.

"I do. I mean it," she asserted, keeping her eyes everywhere but on him.

Travis set down his fork and slid out of his seat. Summer's brow furrowed until he planted himself next to her. He pushed some hair back so he could see her face. "Tell me there's nothing I can do to make something happen between me and you."

Summer's breathing changed, almost stopped. Her spoon fell into her soup. "There's nothing you can do," she said, her voice wavering.

Something was already happening. She could lie to herself, but not to him. Travis leaned in, his nose almost touching the shell of her ear as he brought his mouth closer. "Nothing? You haven't once wondered what it would be like to kiss me?"

He could feel the heat coming off her now. Her skin turned red. She swallowed hard and her teeth bit into her bottom lip. "Don't kiss me." It came out like a desperate plea. As if kissing her would break her in two.

"I won't. I promise." He sat back, giving her a reprieve, then went back to his own side. She watched him pick up his fork and fill his mouth with some french fries. Summer grabbed her water and drank until the ice cubes were all that was left.

She was going to kiss him. Not today, not tomorrow. But she was going to kiss him. Travis had no doubt. "I'll wait for you to kiss me. Someday soon, Summer Raines, you're going to want to kiss me."

CHAPTER THIRTEEN

IT WAS A beautiful day for football. At least according to Travis, who kept saying it. Repeatedly. The entire four-hour drive to Austin was spent in awkward silence or in conversation about the weather. Maybe he was trying to humor her. She couldn't be sure. Ever since he swore she was going to be the one to kiss him, all she could do was think about doing just that.

Every woman with working eyes probably thought about kissing Travis Lockwood. She glanced over at him in his worn-out jeans and faded Longhorns T-shirt. How he managed to pull off that ugly burnt orange color was beyond her. Maybe it was the spectacular view of his arms that distracted her from the color of his shirt. The large silver watch that wrapped itself around his wrist drew her eyes in. The tanned, muscular forearms kept them there. The tattoo inked on his biceps made her curious and a little breathless. Quarterbacks had nice arms—well, this particular former QB did anyway.

Summer didn't want a casual fling, though. Her heart wasn't built for it. Plus, she was spoiled. She wanted the real, lasting kind of love her parents had. True love existed and Summer wasn't about to settle for anything less. She certainly wasn't going to let Travis treat her like some kind of trophy.

Not that she believed what Rachel had said about him. Travis never came off like some sort of womanizer. Truthfully, she was more afraid they would be like her grandparents, who loved each other dearly but weren't always on the same page. Her grandmother was a little bit more rebellious, while Big D liked to stay within the lines. They didn't agree on everything, and Summer was fairly certain her grandmother occasionally picked fights because she thought they were fun.

At the same time, Summer couldn't count the moments she had witnessed between the two of them that made her heart swell. There were just too many. Big D liked to dance with his wife in the kitchen after they worked side by side on the dinner dishes. Her grand-

mother loved peach pie but made apple because it was her husband's favorite. They held
hands when they walked to and from church
and they never argued before bed. Their love
was undeniable, but it involved a lot of compromise.

What Summer wanted was more like the
life her parents shared. Everyone said Gavin
and Gracie were a match made in heaven.
They never fought or argued. They loved the
same things and shared the same passions,
but there was nothing they were more passionate about than each other. She still remembered the way they looked at each other,
the smiles they thought were just for them.
Their love was in every look, touch and word.
They were true partners, even in death. It was
probably better that way. Summer couldn't really imagine either of them without the other.
It just wasn't right.

Then there was the timing. Timing was everything. Just like with Ryan's job offer, Travis was proposing something Summer wasn't
ready for, but being with him was tempting
for sure. Thinking about it all caused Summer's brain to fill with useless information
about high pressure and jet streams.

"Beautiful day for football," Travis said as they sped along the highway.

"So you've said." Fourteen times, to be exact.

"You aren't feeling any rain coming, are you?"

Summer shook her head. "No rain. Clear skies all day and all night."

"Good." Travis nodded. "That's real good."

They followed behind the station van in Travis's car. Greg, the camera guy, was quite the lead foot. Summer was glad Travis was behind the wheel in case they got pulled over. The slick sports car made her feel uncomfortable—it was too fancy, too swanky for someone like her.

Summer was a simple, down-home kind of girl. Something told her the woman who used to ride shotgun was not. There had been someone else. She'd broken down and searched Travis on Google, and found the article about his engagement and subsequent breakup. She saw pictures of him and a petite brunette with big green eyes. His former fiancée was glamorous and sophisticated. Nothing like Summer.

"Stop thinking so hard. It makes your forehead wrinkle," Travis said, giving her knee a squeeze. Summer covered her forehead with her hand. Of course he would be worried about a woman having wrinkles. He laughed. "I'm kidding. What is going on in that pretty head of yours?"

She blew out the air in her lungs. The man made her second-guess herself more than Ryan did. As if being unsure of her career choice wasn't bad enough, now she had to wonder if she was getting in over her head with a guy. Summer hated not knowing how big the risk was. "Nervous about being back in Austin?"

Travis shook his head. "My four years at UT were some of my best. It's hard to explain, but there's something about playing college ball that's different than anything else. There's this whole other vibe. I don't know." He seemed embarrassed and a little wistful. "Some of my best memories are of being on that field."

"Good. I'm glad you can think of it that way."

"Just because I can't play doesn't mean I can't look back fondly at the times I could."

Summer was happy to hear him talk like that. If their trip to Sweetwater was any indication of how things were going to go, there was a good chance people would make him feel as if he let them down today. She hated that because as much as she wanted to deny it, she cared about him. She cared about Travis and his feelings, even if he drove a car that made her feel out of place. Even if he was once engaged to a woman who looked like a supermodel. Travis was kind and decent, and he and his fragile sense of self-worth mattered to her.

They arrived in Austin several hours before kickoff time. After checking in at the hotel, they headed to campus to put together some prerecorded clips before the live shot for the five o'clock news. They made a stop at Travis's old fraternity house. Summer felt more popular than she had been when she was actually in college. Travis looked none too pleased when he had to remove more than one arm from around her shoulders. Needless to say, they didn't stay long.

The alumni tailgate tents weren't much better. Ken had been right again—Travis received a hero's welcome. Coaches, players, athletic directors and highfalutin alumni all treated him like Texas royalty. Summer could see how easy it would be to let this kind of attention go to someone's head. To his credit, Travis handled himself with grace and humility.

Watching Travis closely, Summer noticed how his eyes changed and his smile faltered a little bit every time someone offered up an "I'm sorry" or "Such a shame about your shoulder." Over and over, it was as if he were at his own wake. The man couldn't play football, but that was far from being dead. She was ready to scream at the next person who even thought about offering up some kind of condolence.

The news crew was granted full access to the field before the game started. The turf under their feet was thick and lush. Summer crouched down and ran her fingers through the artificial grass. It was nice, but not like the real thing. Nothing ever compared to what Mother Nature could do. A shadow fell over her.

"When I was here we had natural grass. This is state-of-the-art turf. UT is moving up in the world," Travis said, smiling down at her. His large frame blocked the sun, making him glow at the edges. He really was a beautiful creature. Broad but narrow in all the right places, and that smile shone almost brighter than the sun.

Summer stood to her full height but still had to look up. He was a titan of a man, large and looming but not really dangerous. He never came across as anything but warm and inviting. Summer could feel herself being pulled in, and was tired of resisting. "See, I like it real," she said. "Real is always better than fake."

Travis's hand came up, his fingers brushing against her cheek and leaving her breathless. "I don't doubt that about you for a second. I've never met anyone as real as you."

It was an unusual compliment, but one Summer took to heart. What he saw was what he got, and it felt good to know he was still interested. It was difficult to deny that she was interested in the real Travis, too.

The production assistant reminded them there was work to do and Travis dropped his hand. Summer took a deep breath and tried to remember not to let herself get swept away. She told him there would be no kissing, and she meant it.

They filmed a couple segments during

which Travis showed her how to make the Longhorns symbol with her fingers and taught her the words to the school fight song. The two of them teamed up in a two-against-one scrimmage against the Long-horns' mascot, Bevo, for the cameras. The very real longhorn bull was held fast by two wranglers and some rope, but that didn't stop Summer from being concerned that the giant animal would run her down without a second thought. Ken hadn't mentioned she'd be risk-ing her life this weekend.

She ended up dropping three passes be-fore she finally managed to catch one. Tra-vis laughed when she spiked the ball in the end zone and did a knee-knocking touchdown dance. In the end, it was the most fun Sum-mer had had at work, ever, and it had nothing to do with the weather at all.

Once the game started, Austin was alive with football fever. Summer had been over-whelmed by the noise and activity that sur-rounded the high-school game they attended, but that was nothing compared to this. DKR-Texas Memorial Stadium was larger than life and filled with more UT orange than she had ever seen. The band was phenomenal and

Summer felt that energy Travis was trying to describe on their way down. For someone who had never understood or cared about the game before, Summer found herself having fun. Maybe she liked football, or maybe she was losing her mind. Whenever Travis was around, the latter was a distinct possibility.

Summer was definitely falling in love with the pageantry of the sport, the way the boys burst out of the tunnel and ran onto the field, fueled by the cheers and screams of the crowd. She loved the band and their spectacular halftime show. The constant energy and spirit of the dolled-up cheerleaders was impressive. UT came out on top and there was no doubt the campus would be celebrating late into the night.

THE GAME WAS long over when Summer and Travis did their final live report via satellite at ten. After they cut, Ken called them up and congratulated them on pure perfection. Summer noticed the pride on Travis's face. He had come far from that first news report. His confidence was up and it showed in the way he spoke and carried himself. Gone were the nerves and sweaty brow, replaced by the dimples and down-home charm. Summer's thirty seconds were officially gone for good.

By the time they were done, the parking lot was dark and empty. Summer had overheard Travis turn down several requests to meet up after the game. He said he had plans. She couldn't help wondering what those plans were, and if they included her.

"So, I have this great idea," he said as they walked to his car.

Their pleasant day together had caused her guard to drop. A tingle of excitement ran through her. "I love great ideas."

"I sort of want to take you to a movie."

Summer fought a smile. "Your great idea is you sort of want to take me to a movie?"

Travis rolled his eyes—at her and at himself. "This is the best idea I have ever had. I absolutely want to take you to a movie, but I have to warn you, we're going to be the only ones in the theater."

"Why's that?" Summer asked, her interest piqued. She didn't know what to think.

"Because this is not your average, boring Hollywood movie." He waggled his eyebrows. He was enjoying keeping her in the dark more than he should.

"What's that mean?"

His eyes lit up like those of a child with a secret too big to keep. "You'll see," he said, tugging at the tie he had to wear for the broadcast before getting in the car.

There was nothing Summer liked more than a thrill. They made a quick stop for refreshments at a nearby 7-Eleven. Travis bought her Sno-Caps and two boxes of candy for himself. He grabbed some licorice as well before checking out. It was a good thing the man worked out. He ate more calories in a day than Summer ate in a week.

"Is it possible that I've seen this movie before?" she asked while they sat in the 7-Eleven parking lot.

Travis was texting with some mystery person. "Unlikely."

"Does it have anything to do with football?"

"Nope," he answered, staring at the newest message.

"Was it made before or after I was born?" Maybe it was an oldie but a goodie.

"It's current." Satisfied with whatever the message said, Travis started up the car and pulled onto the road.

"I don't scare easy. If you're hoping I'm going to cuddle up with you because it's some sort of horror flick, you're sorely mistaken."

His smile grew bigger. "It's not a horror movie."

Another thought crossed her mind. "It's not…" She couldn't bring herself to say it. "Would you watch it with your mother?"

Travis chuckled. "Stop worrying. It's PG and I would totally watch it in the company of my mother. You will not have to cover your eyes or run out of the theater screaming, I promise."

Summer relaxed back into her seat. He wasn't telling. Patience was a virtue. She'd have to wait it out, but her head still spun. It was obvious he had planned this evening well in advance. If he was trying to show her he was the real deal, he was doing a good job. There was no doubt he could have gone to a number of postgame parties and been surrounded by beautiful women who would have hung on his every word. The fact that he chose to take Summer on a mystery movie date warmed her heart.

"Is it a cartoon?" she asked, going to the opposite extreme.

"I'm not tellin' you, so stop asking!" He laughed. She liked it when he laughed. Hopefully this movie was funny, so she could hear it some more.

THE BOB BULLOCK Texas State History Museum was closed. Who watched movies in a museum anyway? A nice man, who Summer assumed was the mystery texter, showed up a few minutes after they arrived. He was armed with a ton of UT paraphernalia that Travis quickly signed. It became clear that this was his payment for the special treatment they were now going to receive. The man led them to a theater inside the humongous museum. Travis offered her one of his Twizzlers while they waited for the movie to start.

"Can I get a hint?" she asked, taking a bite of the strawberry licorice.

"You're going to love it. I promise." Travis's smile was so big that Summer almost leaned over and kissed it off his face. When the film began, she gasped. *Wild Texas Weather* was a twenty-two-minute slice of heaven with special effects like simulated wind, rain, lightning and fog that made them feel as if they were there inside the storms.

No one watching could ever call Texas weather boring. Everything about Texas weather was extreme, from its tornadoes to its hurricanes to its temperatures. Summer was overwhelmed with emotion as the film came to an end. In less than half an hour, Travis had done something incredible. He had reminded her that she lived in one of the most fascinating weather states in the country. They didn't have igloos or penguins, but they had severe floods and dusty haboobs. Texas had blizzards and scorching droughts, hail the size of a baseball and lightning storms that were prettier than any fireworks show.

"I can't believe you did this for me." The tremor in her voice and the tears in her eyes should have embarrassed her, but she was having a moment and Travis always made it okay.

"What?"

She shook her head. She didn't even know how to explain it. He had proved this was no game. Maybe Travis had been trying to prove that all along. No man had ever indulged her as much as he did when she went off on weather tangents. He listened and asked questions when most people fled, plugging their ears. Travis made her crazy, but he never treated her like she was.

"You snuck us into a museum in the middle of the night to watch a movie about Texas weather. You reminded me why I love this place, why I love my job. Not only that, but you chose to do this for me instead of running around campus with all those people who love you."

Travis grabbed her hand and gave it a gentle squeeze. "I don't want to be anywhere but with you."

"Why?" She swiped at a tear as it fell. It didn't make sense.

"What does it take to get you to understand? I like you, Summer. I can't believe you don't realize how amazing you are. You don't compromise yourself for anyone. You're so smart, and you retain crazy amounts of information in your head. You're beautiful but barely notice because there isn't an ounce of vanity in you. And you have the softest-looking lips I have ever seen on a woman and—"

Before he could finish his sentence, Summer leaned forward and placed those soft lips over his. Timing be damned.

She knew he was going to be a good kisser. She had hoped for excellent. She got phenomenal. One big hand cradled her cheek while the other wrapped around the back of her neck, pulling her closer and deepening the kiss. She might have initiated it, but he was in control. She liked it. She liked it a lot.

She pulled back first, but not before he pressed one more kiss to her lips. "Please tell me we can do that again," he said, sitting back in his seat.

Summer touched her own mouth, which still tingled from the contact. "I hope so," she replied. "But can we watch the movie one more time?"

Travis laughed out loud but nodded. "We can watch it all night long."

He had no idea what he was promising.

CHAPTER FOURTEEN

"I SHOULD GO inside," Summer said for the twentieth time. She kept saying it, but never actually got out of the car. Not that he minded. He was waiting for the perfect moment to kiss her goodbye. He'd have to initiate this time, but he couldn't help being smug that she had kissed him first, as he had predicted.

"Thanks for driving," she said.

"You're welcome." He reached out and squeezed her hand, afraid they were getting close to really saying goodbye.

His thumbs brushed the soft skin on the back of her hand as he tried to remind himself it would be wrong to kidnap her from her grandparents' driveway.

"I should go," she said again. He didn't want her to go. He wanted to keep her forever.

"So you've said," he teased. He could tell she didn't want to leave yet. "Can I call you later?"

She grinned. "I'd like that."

He was leaning in for that goodbye kiss when a knock on the car window caused them both to jump. Travis's heart stopped for a second. An older woman with the same eyes as Summer looked apologetic as Travis tried to catch his breath. Summer reached back and grabbed her overnight bag from the backseat.

"Thanks again."

"Anytime."

Pushing the door open, she made introductions. "Mimi, this is Travis. Travis, this is my grandmother, Sarah."

"Pleasure to meet you, ma'am." He nodded and gave a little wave, trying to play it cool, but all he could do was smile like a fool.

"Don't call me ma'am, call me Mimi. And saying hello to an old woman in the driveway isn't meeting her. Turn that car off and come on inside. Summer missed church and we held lunch. Least she can do is let me get to know you properly."

"Mimi…" Summer looked hesitant. A nervous hand gripped the strap of her bag so tight the knuckles turned white. Wary eyes flitted between Travis and her grandmother.

"He just drove four hours. I'm sure he has better things to do than hang out with us."

"Well, you got something better to do, Travis?" Mimi asked, hand on hip. Summer's spunk was definitely inherited.

"No, as a matter of fact, I don't believe I have anything to do." He shut off the car and got out. Spending more time with Summer was the only thing he wanted or needed to do today.

Summer smiled, but there was worry in her eyes. "Are you sure? Please don't let her—"

He wondered if she was asking because she was really concerned about taking him away from something or if she wasn't comfortable with him meeting her family. They had crossed a major bridge last night, but he feared seeing that look in her eye, the one that was always searching for an escape.

"I'm all good," he assured her with a wink. He slid the strap off her shoulder and carried her bag to the house. Mimi tipped her head and smiled her approval. If he could win the grandma over, he'd feel a bit more confident. When Mimi opened the door, a black Labrador bolted out and headed straight for Summer, tail wagging.

"There's my boy." Summer knelt down and gave her dog the attention he craved. "Was he good for y'all?" she asked her grandmother, who was halfway inside the house.

"Oh, you know Big D spoils that animal rotten!"

The friendly dog realized Travis was an unknown and quickly positioned himself between the man and his owner. He gave the stranger a good sniff, checking for trouble. "Hey there, big guy." Travis petted his head.

"Storm, Travis. Travis, Storm."

He liked the name right away. It was so very Summer. "Nice to meet you, Storm." Now that Travis was no longer a threat, the dog had no time for him. He was much more interested in Summer's affection. Travis could completely relate. The dog followed them up onto the porch and through the front door. Inside the small, cozy house waited one more obstacle, however. Summer's grandfather eased out of his faded blue recliner. When he stood, he was eye to eye with Travis, who was almost six foot four.

"Travis, my grandfather, David. Big D, this is my friend Travis."

"*Kissing* friend," Mimi added, arching her

brow. Summer scowled at her grandmother, making the old man shake his head. Travis bit his tongue and chose not to remind Mimi there had been no kissing thanks to her.

David Raines was tall and thin, with gentle eyes. His shoulders were narrow and his pants were belted tight. "For heaven's sake, didn't you embarrass the girl enough when she was growing up?" he asked his wife as he stuck out his hand for a firm shake. "Nice to meet you, Travis. Don't you listen to anything that one has to say about anything. And please don't hold any of it against Summer."

"Never, sir."

"Oh, come on. Let an old woman have some fun." She grabbed Travis by the arm. "Help me in the kitchen while Big D gets the scoop. My granddaughter never tells me anything."

"Shocking," Travis said with a laugh. Summer mouthed an unnecessary sorry. He liked Mimi. She reminded him of his own grandmother, who had a generous spirit and no filter.

"Joining us for lunch earns you some major points. Shows you aren't only interested in what was happening in that fancy car before I came outside." She handed him some plates and opened the silverware drawer. The kitchen smelled mouthwatering. Ham, apple pie and homemade bread. Mimi was a keeper.

"Summer is more than a kissing friend," he assured her. The last thing he wanted was for these people to think his intentions were anything less than honorable toward their granddaughter. "I have nothing but respect for her."

"I like that, too," Mimi said, her hands full of forks and knives. She set them on the plates. "She had fun yesterday, I could tell. We watched both reports. I couldn't believe you got that girl to play some football." She placed napkins on top of silverware.

Travis smiled, remembering the look on Summer's face when she finally caught the ball. "I think she's been holding out on me. I bet she was the star on her Powder Puff team in high school."

Mimi froze and then burst into a fit of laughter. Doubled over, she hugged her slightly round middle and tried to catch her breath. "Oh, you are too much. Summer's only ever been a dance-in-the-rain kind of girl."

Imagining that beautiful woman dancing

in the rain made him smile. "Maybe I've converted her, then."

"If anyone can get her to like football, my money is on you." Mimi laughed, motioning for him to follow her to the dining room. Together, they set the small, round table for four.

"Summer says she comes over here every Sunday. It's nice you guys are so close."

"My granddaughter loves two things—the weather and her family. And we adore her. She's my only reason for getting out of bed some days." Mimi smacked Travis's hand when he put the fork on the wrong side of the plate. "Didn't your mother ever teach you how to set a table?"

"Football was my only chore," he sheepishly admitted.

"Good thing you're cute. Buys you some time to learn."

Travis finished setting the table and they returned to the kitchen, where Mimi loaded his arms with all the fixings for lunch. "Can I ask you something?" Travis lowered his voice and glanced at the door.

"You can ask me anything. Can't promise I'll answer," Mimi replied, looking intrigued.

"I like your granddaughter. I like her a lot."

Fear caused him to check the door one more time. It would be just his luck that Summer would overhear him talking like this. "What are the chances I'm going to get my heart broken here?"

Mimi stopped her busywork. She cocked her head to the side and gave him her full attention. "Now, what makes you ask that?"

"She's been fighting against liking me from the moment she met me, even though I swear I'm a nice guy."

Mimi inhaled deeply, nodding, then shaking her head as she exhaled. She returned to the task at hand. "I'm sure you're a real nice guy. I like you, so I'm going to give you some advice," she said, rummaging through the refrigerator for the butter. She straightened and turned toward him. "Do you know why Summer obsesses about the weather?"

Travis had never considered the "why." Summer and the weather went together like peanut butter and jelly or spaghetti and meatballs or... Boy, he really needed to eat. "She seems connected to it. You know with the 'feelings' and everything."

"Summer fixates on the weather because there's safety there. She can chart and collect data. She can look at her radar screen. Add to that her 'feelings' and you have someone who thinks she can always predict what's coming." Mimi's face was serious and a bit too somber. "But you and I know life doesn't always work like that. Things happen that we can't control. There are storms we can't predict that wreak havoc on our lives and the lives of the people we love. That scares Summer more than she'll ever admit. Every daring thing that girl does is calculated and controlled. If she doesn't know what's going to happen, she won't take the risk."

So she was scared, just as he was. Somehow it felt better, knowing he wasn't alone. He knew all about fearing the risk of a broken heart.

"You're a man most women could see themselves settling down with. That makes you a risk because that girl is just like her daddy. Like I said, Summer loves two things—her family and the weather. Her daddy took his family with him to chase storms. Summer ended up here and chooses us over that life. She doesn't know I know she's waiting for the day she doesn't have to choose." Mimi put a hand on his arm and gave it a squeeze. "Be worth it and everything will work itself out."

Be worth it. The woman had basically told him Summer didn't want to be tied down. Settling down with someone wasn't in her grand scheme. That made her just as much his risk as he was hers. *Be worth it.* Could he even be worth choosing?

Mimi announced lunch was ready and Summer, Big D and Storm all answered the call. Summer's nerves were evident. Travis's smile meant to reassure and earned him one from her in return. He held out her chair so she could sit. Everything became crystal clear when she was near—she was worth the risk, she was worth any risk.

"Please tell me she was nice," she said, taking her seat.

His hand fell on her shoulder. "She's amazing. Like you," he whispered. Her endless blue-sky eyes looked up, full of unnecessary modesty. "No worries."

"No worries," she parroted back as he took his seat next to her.

Lunch was as delicious as it smelled. Travis ate like a king. Summer's grandparents made him feel more at home than he sometimes felt at his own parents' place. They asked him questions that had nothing to do with football. Instead, they focused on subjects like his family, growing up in Sweetwater and his take on various issues affecting the local community. They wanted to know if he attended church regularly and if he'd read any good books lately. He wished he was more interesting and thought about stopping at a bookstore on the way home.

They had plenty of questions for Summer, too. They wanted to hear all about their trip to Austin and what she thought about football now that she had experienced it close up. Big D and Mimi's love for their granddaughter was evident in every look and word, even when they were teasing her. Watching the three of them banter back and forth made Travis's heart happy.

Big D and Mimi shared a look when Summer told them her favorite thing about Austin was the museum. Mimi smiled at Travis as if to say, "Well done, young man." The grandmother was officially won over, as was the dog at his feet, who was enjoying a bite of ham that had "accidentally" dropped to the floor. "I think Travis should join us for lunch every Sunday. He could come to church, too," Mimi said as she stood to clear the table.

"Mimi…" Summer's cheeks turned pink.

"What? You tell me you don't want that boy sitting next to you every week," the old woman challenged.

Summer hid her face in her hands. "Did you know that 1941 was the wettest year in Texas history? Over forty-two and a half inches fell."

Mimi chuckled. "That means she wants you to come back," she said to Travis before taking some dishes to the kitchen. Summer jumped up and grabbed a load of dirty plates, brushing away Travis's hand as he reached out to help.

Big D sat back in his chair at the head of the table. He gave his belly a pat and then tossed some scraps on the floor for Storm. He was a spoiler, indeed. "Dealing with their crazy is worth it in the end. I can attest to that."

Travis laughed through his nose. He might not know if he was worth the risk, but there was no doubt Summer was. "She'd have to be a whole lot crazier to keep me away."

Big D nodded. "Good answer, son."

Summer and Mimi returned, the elder appearing properly admonished. Travis got up to help them finish clearing the table despite their objections. He wanted to be invited back. He wanted to be invited back every Sunday. It wasn't something he could have considered if he was still playing football. For the first time since it happened, his injury seemed more like a blessing than a curse.

AFTER SOME OF the best apple pie in the world and his third glass of milk, Travis followed Summer to the family room. The fireplace mantel was covered in photographs. Pictures of Big D and Mimi with less wrinkles. Two girls and one boy huddled around them, dressed in their 1970s Sunday best. Big D with a mustache. Mimi holding a grandbaby. And a curly-haired blond standing with her parents in front of something that looked like a tank. It was the same picture Summer had on her desk. Young Summer was built like her grandfather, skinny and tall, but perfect.

"Where's the rest of the family?" Travis asked, pointing at one of the frames that looked as though it had everyone in it.

Summer smiled at the photo, her fingers

touching the faces of her mom and dad. "My aunt Ginny lives outside Dallas with her husband. They have three boys, all live in or around the Dallas-Fort Worth area. Aunt Sue lives in Ohio. She never had any kids. She and her husband, my uncle John, own a restaurant up there. That keeps them super-busy, I suppose. I don't think they've been down here to visit in a couple years."

Travis pointed to the more familiar image. "You have this picture on your desk."

Summer took that particular photo down, her fondness for her family evident in her expression. "That was our storm-chasing van. My dad reinforced the exterior with these ridiculous panels. This thing was souped up. He had all this equipment in there that would be completely outdated now, but back then, it was some cutting-edge stuff."

"You had storm-chasing days, did you?"

"Oh, I was quite the adventurer when I was a kid. We used to travel wherever the exciting weather took us." She was wistful for a moment. "I saw my first tornado when I was five. I remember thinking it didn't look right. It wasn't like the one in *The Wizard of Oz*."

"Your first tornado? How many tornadoes have you seen?"

"Twelve." She set the picture down. The subject changed her whole demeanor. Summer was brought to life by this kind of stuff. "It would have been more, but they didn't always take me on the chase. Too dangerous, they'd say. It's also not exactly easy to catch a tornado. Most of your time is spent driving around under clear skies, tracking where one is most likely to occur. They don't appear as often as the movies would like you to believe."

She was absolutely fascinating. Travis wanted to know everything. He wanted to see the world through her eyes. "So you spent your childhood in Tornado Alley?"

"Oh no," Summer said with a laugh. "My parents did that for a little while, then moved on to other storms."

"What other kinds of storms did you chase?"

"Hurricanes. Those are easier. You have a lot of warning before they hit land. We once went up to Toronto and studied steam devils off Lake Ontario. Got caught in this huge ice storm in Quebec one winter. It was bad. But if you want ice, Texas storms can really do the job. There's a picture of me somewhere, holding hail bigger than a baseball—like in the movie last night." She turned and headed for a big bookcase, her fingers dancing over the spines of photo albums.

"So your grandparents took you in after your parents died?" Travis asked.

Summer found what she was looking for and pulled the dark evergreen album off the shelf. "My aunt Ginny halfheartedly offered to take me in, but with three teenaged boys, we knew they kind of had their hands full. Plus Mimi cried so hard when Big D brought it up, he never mentioned it again."

"She loves you, that's clear."

"Not as much as I love her," Summer said with a smile that quickly faded. "Mimi was devastated when my dad died. She didn't get out of bed for a month after the funeral. Big D did his best to take care of her and me until she pulled out of it." Travis couldn't picture the woman in the other room being so lifeless. She radiated life, just like her granddaughter. "We've kind of been taking care of each other ever since. I owe them so much, I feel like I can never repay it all."

Summer flipped through the photo album. Travis took it away from her, setting it on the coffee table so he could take her in his arms. She didn't resist, and rested her head on his chest. Even though her loss was a decade old, his need to comfort her was overwhelming.

"That had to be a dark time for all of you."

"It was, but things worked out in the end." Summer smiled up at him. Travis leaned down, ready for that kiss he'd been denied in the car.

"Dog needs to go outside to do his business. I take it you two aren't interested." Big D's timing was as bad as his wife's.

"I got him, Big D." She stepped away from Travis and snatched the leash from her grandfather's hand.

"I'll go with you," Travis offered.

"Good idea," Big D said, sitting down on his recliner and grabbing a well-worn book from his side table. "Looks like you two need some fresh air."

Travis nodded and tried not to laugh as Summer turned as red as a ruby. She got the leash on Storm and headed outside.

Summer was speed-walking down the driveway. Travis grabbed her arm, stopped

her escape and slid his hand down to enve-
lope hers. "Don't be embarrassed," he said.

"We're lucky it was Big D who walked in.
Mimi would have taken pictures," she said,
making him laugh harder.

"I think I love Mimi." He could see why
Mimi and Big D were worth it to Summer.
The two of them meant the world to their
granddaughter.

"That figures. She has a way about her."
Summer shook her head. "I can tell she likes
you a whole lot, but don't get any crazy ideas
about trying to steal her away from Big D,
though. He's a lot tougher than he looks."

Travis only had ideas about one of the
Raines women. Summer was the one and
only. He could only hope he was worth the
risk.

CHAPTER FIFTEEN

MONDAY. SUMMER HATED Mondays. But she'd gone to bed hopeful this one would be much better than the last, considering she was now kissing friends with Travis. However, as she began to wake, Summer's body tingled. It told her something in the atmosphere was brewing this morning. Something big. She needed to get up even though her bed was soft and inviting, begging her to stay in it just a little bit longer. Summer often wondered if this was what it was like for Peter Parker when trouble was near. Superpowers were such a burden sometimes.

She dragged herself out of bed and shuffled into the den. She turned on the TV, switching the channel to KLVA. Richard had to be seeing something on the radar. Her laptop booted up while she went to make some coffee and let Storm out. Rain had blown in overnight and was currently pelting the house raucously.

Her oversize couch wasn't her bed, but was almost as comfortable. Summer settled in and brought up the National Weather Service website. She clicked on the radar, watched and zoomed into Abilene. Her tired eyes widened as she made sense of what she saw. She scrambled to her feet in search of her phone. She needed to call Ken.

Running to her bedroom, she yanked her dresser open and pulled out a change of clothes. Her heart was racing at an impossible speed. She closed her eyes, feeling twelve years old again. She remembered her parents fluttering around her, talking too fast when they saw something on the radar. The excitement rolled off them in waves. So many things had to come together to unleash a tornado, and when that happened it was like magic instead of science.

This time it was her storm, not theirs. This time she would lead the chase.

There was no time to do her hair and makeup. She pulled her hair into a ponytail and called the station. When she finally got Ken, she unloaded on him in a rush. "My feeling is telling me I need a camera crew to meet me north of the air force base. You need to send them now. Have them call us on this number when they get west of 83. Can you get Richard? I need to talk to Richard." She held the phone to her ear with her shoulder as she put on her shoes.

Richard came on the line. "Summer?"

"Tornado." That one word was all it took. Ken dispatched a team before Summer finished telling Richard what she'd seen on the radar. She could hear Ken repeating the word *tornado* over and over again as if he couldn't believe it was true.

"Summer," Richard said before they hung up, his voice not full of its usual venom. "Be safe."

THE SKY WAS overcast, the clouds so heavy they couldn't help raining down. Lightning flashed angrily as the rain pounded on Summer's car, the visibility near zero. She had one more stop to make before she went looking for that storm.

Travis answered the door in nothing but his pajama bottoms. "Get dressed, grab your camera and meet me in the car in no more than five minutes."

Travis rubbed his eyes. His brain seemed

to only now take in the fact that Summer was standing on his front porch in the rain. He pulled her inside. "How about we stay inside this morning? I'll make breakfast."

As tempting as that offer was, Summer wriggled out of his arms. "There's a tornado coming. I can feel it."

Tornadoes were better than a gallon of coffee. Travis was wide-awake in an instant. "Tornado? For real? I thought you couldn't feel those."

Summer spotted her red umbrella perched beside the door. She reached in and snatched it. Opening it up, she smiled. "Are you really going to question me right now, or are you gonna come chasing with me?"

Travis was in the car in fewer than five minutes. Summer had him drive so she could watch the radar from her phone. Travis was fueled by pure adrenaline. He bounced in his seat, and his hands gripped the steering wheel for dear life. They drove just outside the city, toward the more rural west.

"Pull into that field up there." She pointed and searched the sky for signs.

"What do we do now?" Travis asked as he

parked. The car shook slightly from the force of the howling wind.

"We wait," she said. She set his camera bag in his lap and smiled. "And then we take pictures of a tornado."

Storm chasing had become a wild game anyone could play these days. The National Weather Service had issued a tornado warning for these parts overnight, but Texas didn't see much action like this in the fall. Storm chasers were all farther east this time of year. But nobody had bothered to tell this particular supercell that it was out of season. It was primed for tornado activity.

Summer called the station. The producer patched her through so she could report over the phone. When they went to commercial, she spoke to Richard. "I'm telling you, this shear looks good."

"Updafts?" Richard asked.

"There are a couple up ahead. I don't know if the camera crew is going to get here in time." A dark anvil cloud approached, high and wide, the most dangerous type. Soon, they were enveloped in a swirl of hail and debris. It hit the car in a rage Summer hadn't witnessed in years. Then she saw the cloud drop, and the sky began to rotate. "We got one! Get those sirens going!" she shouted into her phone. She smacked Travis's arm. "Take a picture of that!"

As if it were reaching down to touch the ground with a spindly finger, the cloud whirled itself into a funnel. Travis lifted his camera out of his lap and captured the fledgling tornado as it grew bigger and stronger, tearing at the soil and vegetation where its point met the earth. Its roar was deafening. They were just west of a small mobile home park, and the wind monster was headed in that direction. Summer could only pray she had given people enough time to find shelter.

"Let me drive," she said, climbing over Travis as he slid to the passenger side. He continued to take pictures as the tornado skipped across the field, taking down everything in its path. Wire fences, telephone poles, trees, nothing stood a chance against it. Summer followed the twister, careful to keep her distance in case it suddenly shifted direction. Sirens rang out over the din of the merciless storm. They watched as it ran over the park like Godzilla, destroying whatever it touched.

The gray, spinning mass ate the homes up and spit them out.

Travis took pictures of it all, documenting each disaster as it occurred. Summer watched in awe as the tornado thinned out and slowly retracted upwarded, until it was completely gone.

"It's over," she whispered. Her body thrummed with an energy she'd forgotten. It was a feeling she hadn't realized she missed until now.

Summer and Travis eventually met up with the camera crew and filmed the damage. Thanks to their immediate sighting, the warning went out and provided the mobile-home residents with some notice. Although there was enormous property damage, there were only minor injuries.

The two of them stayed on the scene most of the day, documenting the destruction and helping in any way they could. It was amazing how something that lasted a few minutes could wreak such havoc. Travis took pictures of it all—a teddy bear buried under a pile of debris, a toilet sitting in the middle of a field, a heap of wood, shredded like mulch, that earlier in the morning had been the side of a barn.

When it was time for them to get cleaned up before work, Summer and Travis climbed into her car, still feeling the high from the chase. They drove in silence, both lost in their own thoughts. She walked him to his door, holding her umbrella over their heads—the clouds still sent a drizzling rain down to earth.

She was still in a fog when Travis wrapped his arms around her and kissed her dizzy. He broke away first and shook his head. "That was…"

"I know," she answered, lost in the moment. Her feelings for Travis mixed with the thrill of the chase were a potent combination. Travis appeared to feel exactly the same. He rested his head against her shoulder. Each of them breathed heavily and clung to the other.

"That was amazing," Travis said in between breaths.

"I know." It was a rush that couldn't be put into words. Mother Nature was a force to be reckoned with. It was beautiful and frightening at the same time. Witnessing the sheer power of it made a person feel small but alive.

"Your heart is beating so fast," Travis said.

Maybe it was the tornado, maybe it was being in his arms. Summer couldn't be sure, but she went with the safest choice. "Storms do that to me."

"Storms, huh?" She could feel him smiling against her shirt. "Go clean up, Weather Girl. You have a big report to give tonight." One soft, sweet kiss on the cheek and he let her go.

Back home, Summer started the shower and sent a text to Ryan. She was gloating a little, but she didn't care. She found a tornado on her first try. It didn't usually work that way. She got lucky.

He texted back right away. Like mother, like daughter. Your mom spotted one on her first chase.

Summer smiled wider. Knowing that about her mom made her feel more connected to her in some way. She was her parents' daughter. The little ache that still existed in her heart reawakened. They would have been proud of her for following her instincts because this was what she was born to do.

Her phone rang; Ryan wanted a detailed account. "Tell me all about it, start to finish, and don't leave anything out."

Summer talked so fast she was sure he couldn't make out half of what she was saying. She told him about waking up and looking at the radar. She explained the conditions and her race to get right where all the pieces of the complicated weather puzzle came together in perfect harmony. She told him about getting the warning out and the damage done. She told him everything, and he listened to it all with rapt attention.

"Sounds like quite an adventure. I wonder how you'll ever manage going back into a studio after that."

He knew exactly what to say to knock her off the cloud she was on. "Ryan…"

"Don't say it! Don't say a word, Summer. We are not going to discuss this job that is absolutely perfect for you. I don't want to hear you try to rationalize away the feeling you got today. I want you to relish it. I want you to remember this feeling so when I call you next week, you'll tell me exactly what I want to hear."

"You don't play fair," she complained. Ryan's laughter on the other end of the phone line was infectious.

"What I want to know is, did you get any pictures of this thing?" he asked.

Oh, did she have pictures!

SUMMER LOVED HER JOB. In fact, things at work were so much better since the tornado. She and Richard had shared that moment, and he finally realized they could be partners instead of enemies. He was actually being nice to her. And interestingly enough, all of Summer's other troubles at the office disappeared. No glitches, no lights falling on her head, no phone calls from angry advertisers.

A great job, a loving family and a man who had real boyfriend potential made Abilene the place to be. At least that was what she told herself when she was awake. But when Summer slept, she dreamed about wild tornadoes and lightning storms that lit up the sky. Dreams that wooed her as no lover ever could. She fantasized about hosting a show that allowed her to visit tropical wonderlands and frozen tundra. Almost four weeks had passed since Ryan offered Summer the chance to leave her life in Abilene behind. Saying no was going to be as difficult as saying yes. It was breaking her heart in two.

Distractions helped keep Ryan's deadline from creeping into her thoughts. As long as she was busy, Summer didn't have time to think about silly things like her future. Mimi and Big D always needed something done at their place, which was why she was in their backyard getting sunburned right now. The fence out back had some new slats that needed to be painted. The grass had grown an extra inch thanks to the rain they got on Monday. It tickled her ankles and made painting the bottom of the fence more difficult. She'd have to come back before Sunday and mow it.

The manual labor was great. It helped free her mind of her current worries. Unfortunately, Mimi had no idea what Summer was avoiding.

"Did you talk to Ryan about your big tornado chase?" Mimi asked from the shaded lounger on the patio. She fanned herself with a magazine as she watched her granddaughter slave away in the sun.

Summer glanced back at her over her shoulder. "As soon as I got home."

"I bet he was impressed."

"He travels around the world. He goes where volcanoes are erupting and tsunamis have hit. He roams around the Sahara and takes pictures of penguins in Antarctica. He sees things I only talk about when I'm nervous. One tornado isn't very impressive to someone like him." She tried to hide the longing she felt as she spoke. She loved Abilene. She loved her grandparents. There was also a distinct possibility she could be falling in love with Travis.

"Your daddy would have been there right beside him," Mimi said wistfully.

"Mom, too. Ryan said Mom saw a tornado the first time she led a chase. He said I remind him of her."

Mimi sighed. "You are so much like both of them," she said with a hint of woe.

Summer's heart clenched. She set the paintbrush down and removed her floppy hat so she could wipe the sweat from her brow. Her parents would have taken Ryan's job offer without a second thought. Were they alive, they would have encouraged her to take it. But they weren't here. They had left her. They had left Mimi and Big D without a son and daughter-in-law. They left Summer here. This was where she belonged.

"I talked to Ryan this week, too." Big D's

voice startled her and Summer spun around. He had been snoozing in his chair when she got here, but now he handed her a towel to wipe the smudges of paint off her hands.

"You did?"

Big D gave her a look that made her very uneasy. He knew something she wasn't ready for him to know. He knew something she did not want Mimi to know ever. "I wanted to make sure he saw your report. Then we talked about that new show he's producing."

Summer felt her stomach drop. She swallowed hard and begged him with her eyes not to say any more. "Did you know the tallest tsunami ever recorded was seventeen hundred feet? It was a megatsunami. Back in 1958."

Mimi straightened up in her chair. "What new show? And why are you gettin' all worked up over there?"

Summer decided downplaying the whole thing was the best idea. "He's got an idea for a new show and he asked me to consider working for him, but I have a job—a life— here in Abilene."

"He offered you a job?" Mimi frowned, her shoulders slumped. All the wind had been taken out of her sails. "Would you have to leave Texas?"

This was not the conversation Summer wanted to have and not when she wanted to have it. Big D must have known all along that something was up. Summer shrugged. "I don't know. Maybe." Big D cleared his throat and looked at her pointedly. "Fine. Yes, I'd have to leave Texas," she relented.

Mimi said nothing but stared at Big D, who seemed to be communicating with her wordlessly. When their silent conversation ended, Mimi stood up and headed for the back door.

"I'm not taking it! I'm not leaving," Summer called after her. Mimi went inside without a word. Summer felt the guilt expand in her chest, but it quickly turned to anger that she directed at her grandfather. "Why did you do that? Why upset her for no reason?"

"Why are you so afraid of upsetting her even a little bit?" he asked calmly.

Summer began to pace and fidget. "I'm not afraid of upsetting her. I just don't see why we should worry her about something that isn't going to happen."

Big D relaxed into the lounger his wife had

vacated as Summer's agitation grew. "Why isn't it going to happen?"

"I'm not leaving. Why would I leave?" Her voice began to rise.

"Why wouldn't you leave?"

She stopped pacing and stared at the old man. He was a picture of serenity while she was a frazzled mess. How could he not understand? Why was he doing this? "Because my life is here," she said, attempting to sound confident and sure.

"What if you could have a life out there? Out on the road, chasing storms and doing what comes natural?"

Summer felt her resolve beginning to crumble. What if she could? It was the question that had been haunting her. She could go. She could see things and do things she only dreamed about. But leaving would have its consequences. "Did you know on average there are six hundred weather-related fatalities a year?"

Big D smiled, but there was sadness in his eyes. "You aren't going to die if you take this job, and neither is your grandmother. It's about time you both figured that out."

CHAPTER SIXTEEN

LIKE MOST EVERY day, Travis stared at Summer from his desk. She was working with Richard on some special tornado report. The two of them were suddenly best buddies, which was much better than bitter enemies. Still, Travis didn't trust him. Amazingly, Summer's luck had turned around the second she and Richard became allies. Coincidence? Travis didn't think so.

They looked busy, so Travis didn't interrupt. When he wasn't staring at her from across the newsroom, he was usually sitting on the corner of her desk. He wanted to bother her, to go over and grab one of her pens so she'd have to reach across him to try to take it back. He wanted to make her laugh and help rid her of those worry lines he could see on her forehead.

He took a minute to glance around the busy newsroom. Everyone was hard at work, preparing and researching. They all had such purpose. His phone buzzed in his pocket. The name on the screen caused him to hit Decline. Sam Lockwood was not happy with his son these days. Travis knew he was calling to berate him about not following up with the guy from Alabama. Alabama was so far away from Abilene, and Abilene was where Travis wanted to be.

His focus shifted back to the main reason he had for sticking around. He caught Summer staring in his direction. Unnecessarily embarrassed, she looked away. She had her hair pinned up, so she couldn't hide behind it today. He watched as her cheeks flushed with color. Now he really wanted to go over there. He could only imagine what fun weather fact she'd be sure to share in this state of mind.

This moment more than any clarified how very different his life was from a year ago. A year ago, he thought he was in love with a woman who loved spending his money more than she loved him. The fancy house in Miami, the fast car in his garage and the endorsements that put his face in magazines were things he thought he needed. Back then, he felt confident about who he was even if it wasn't exactly who he wanted to be.

With Summer, everything was different. He had none of those material things anymore, except for the car—which she clearly didn't like. He lived in a modest house. No company wanted a has-been to sell its product. KLVA paid well, but not as well as the NFL, not even close. Summer didn't care about the money or the fame, though. She was learning to love football for the game itself, and it had nothing to do with being part of the Travis Lockwood empire. There was no empire. There was only a man who was lost and trying to find his way.

Summer wanted to help him find his way. She was full of patience and understanding. She encouraged him to think for himself, pointing out the worthwhile qualities he tended to overlook in himself. She was strong and brave, beautiful and bold. When he looked at Summer, he knew—he was in love with her.

He knew it when they kissed on his doorstep after the tornado. Witnessing the sheer power of nature was intense, but nothing came close to the feeling he experienced when he held Summer in his arms. It had to be love because there was nothing in the world that could compete with it, and supposedly, love conquered all.

"Travis, sugar, can you do me a favor?" Rachel and her plunging neckline eclipsed his view of Summer.

He had to stop and think about it, his Southern manners hindered by the recent unearthing of Rachel's mean streak. As much as he wanted to say no, Travis decided to be a gentleman. "What can I do for you?"

"I need your opinion on something. Can you come into the studio with me?" She held a hand out and wiggled her fingers as if he was going to take it. Travis stood up and shoved his own hands deep in his pockets. Rachel lowered her arm to her side, looking none too happy about being left hanging.

"I only have a minute or so," he said, adding to her dismay. "I have some things to do before the newscast." Namely, talking to Summer.

"Come on, now. You know all you need to do is ask, and all those silly little production assistants will do anything you want." Rachel's walk was something out of a Mari-

lyn Monroe movie. She sashayed all the way
from the newsroom to the studio. There was
no one else there, not even the tech guys. Rachel sat down behind the news desk. "Does
this color look all right against the backdrop?" she asked, all wide-eyed and innocent.

Travis knew he shouldn't have indulged
her. She was wasting her time. There was
never going to be room in his life for Rachel
and her games. "You know better than anyone what looks good and what doesn't. I don't
think you asked me to come in here to talk
about your clothing choices."

She smiled and fluttered her eyelashes,
playing it up as if there was a hint of embarrassment in being caught. "You got me. I
didn't ask you to come in here to talk about
that. I came here to offer you something instead." Her eyes pleaded along with her
words. The usual cool confidence she displayed began to dissolve. "The Rodeo Parade
is this weekend, and I know we'll both be
there. Afterward, I'm hosting a charity dinner. Last year at this event, we brought in
over three thousand dollars for Alzheimer's
research. I'm sure we can top it this year with

your help. Ken thinks it would be a wonderful idea if you were to come…as my date."

As much as he wanted to help a good cause, being Rachel's date was not happening. Before Travis could turn her down properly, a loud crash sounded behind him. One of the production techs stood next to a freestanding floodlight as it lay on the floor, shattered glass scattered around it. Travis was about to ask him if he was okay when Rachel unleashed on the poor guy.

"You're going to get yourself fired, Pete! Didn't I tell you to stay clear of here? You scared me half to death. Is that what you want? You want to scare me to death?"

Confused by her outburst, Travis went over to help Pete with the broken light. "I don't need your help, Lockwood," the man said with a sneer. "Y'all need to get out of here so I can clean up this mess before the newscast."

He didn't have to tell Travis twice. He headed for the doors while Rachel hung back to continue her tirade. He figured he'd get out of "date night" with Rachel by going straight to Ken. Why his boss thought having him escort Rachel anywhere was a good idea was beyond him. Travis rapped on Ken's door.

"Come on in!"

Travis pushed open the door and slipped in, closing it quickly behind him before Rachel returned from the studio. "About this weekend," Travis started.

"What about it?" Ken glanced up from his computer. He was obviously in no mood for beating around the bush.

"I can't be Rachel's date to the charity dinner thing. I know you think it's a good idea, but I have to decline."

Ken's eyebrows pushed together. "What in the world are you talking about?"

"Rachel's charity dinner. I can't be her date."

"Okay…" Ken stretched the word out as though he was waiting for Travis to say more.

"Okay. Great. I'm glad you understand." Travis bolted from the room before Ken could change his mind. It was a good thing Ken didn't think it was one of his brilliant ideas, like putting Travis and Summer together. When Ken thought his idea was ratings gold, there was no talking him out of it. Travis had no complaints about being paired with Summer, though. In fact, someday he needed to thank Ken properly for that.

Summer was alone at her desk when he caught her eye this time. She looked as though she needed to be distracted. Travis took his spot on the corner of her desk. "Hello, Weather Girl."

"I see you and Rachel needed a little one-on-one time," she said, completely unable to hide the hint of jealousy in her tone. It was music to his ears.

"I guess I need to write a big check to her charity this weekend."

"That's nice of you," Summer said, giving him her full attention. "She's really increased awareness in the community and started some great programs that support caregivers—not just in Abilene, but all over West Central Texas."

Travis could feel his eyebrows pinch together. "First, you and Richard mended all your fences and now you're singing Rachel's praises? Is the world coming to an end or something?"

Summer put her hand on his knee. "Don't forget I also started liking you, which means we might see some snow around these parts next July."

She was so strange, and he loved it. He

loved her. He pulled on one of her curls. "I might need you to remind me just how much you like me. Maybe you can show me this weekend?"

"Maybe," she said with a smile. "But right now I need to work, so go bother someone else." She pushed his leg until he stood up.

He left her to her charts and graphs, feeling better than he had in a long time. The weather girl was the only one he wanted to bother. Indefinitely.

KLVA SENT OUT a crew to film the entire West Central Texas Rodeo Parade on Saturday. Brian, Rachel, Travis and Summer were expected to represent the station. The women were going to ride on the Texas Star Chevrolet float while the two men rode horses alongside it. The sky was a cloudless blue and the fall sun was still hot, causing the sweat to drip off Travis's forehead. He took the cowboy hat off his head and wiped his brow with the sleeve of his ridiculous plaid shirt.

"Howdy, Cowboy," Summer said, sneaking up behind him. "Look at you, all decked out in your jeans and plaid. The hat is a nice touch for the rodeo."

He set the hat back on his head and tipped the brim in her direction. "Texas forever."

"Forever." She smiled and warmed him better than the sun ever could.

One of the production techs lingered nearby. Travis still had a hard time remembering some of the crew members' names, but he recognized him as the guy from the other day.

"Hi, Pete," Summer said with a wave. She knew everyone's name.

He looked at her funny, as if he hadn't expected her to acknowledge him. He was a scrawny character with long, skinny arms and legs. His jet-black hair was pulled back in a ponytail.

"Summer." He nodded in their direction. "Travis."

"Pete," Travis said with a nod of his own. He remembered how Rachel had yelled at the poor guy. Pete hung out near them, his eyes flicking in their direction one too many times for Travis's liking. Finally, he headed over to the equipment van, giving Travis and Summer some much-needed privacy. "Is it me, or is Pete a little creepy?" Travis whispered.

"He's quiet. Be nice," Summer said, swatting his chest. "He also has it bad for Rachel. It makes me sad for him."

"I'm sad for him, too. Carrying a torch for Rachel is pretty much the worst way to waste your life away." His arms circled Summer's waist. "If he was holding out for you, that would make sense. Not that I would ever let him or anyone have a chance."

She stood on tiptoes kissed him on the cheek. "You are so cute in that hat."

"Well, I'll have to remember that." He winked and let her go.

She bit down on her bottom lip and backed away. "I'm going to talk to Ken. I'll see you over by the float?"

"I'll be the good-lookin' cowboy on the horse."

Her smile illuminated her whole face. "No doubt."

Travis grinned all the way over to the horse trailer. He loved that woman and he was going to tell her tonight. With Shannon's help, he'd gotten ahold of Hank, the bungee-jumping hot-air balloon guy. If he was going to be worth it, Travis needed to show Summer he could face his fears before asking her to face hers. Nothing said "I love you" like jumping out of a hot-air balloon.

Rachel and Brian were both hanging out by the horses. "There you are. I was wondering where my favorite sports man was hiding," Rachel said, moving toward him. Her jeans looked painted on, they were so tight. "You ready for our big date tonight?"

Travis's mouth fell open. He'd figured Ken had let her know he wasn't required to make an appearance tonight. The two of them hadn't talked since she asked him. "Ken said it was fine if I didn't attend. I thought you knew."

Undeterred, Rachel invaded his personal space. Her finger ran the length of his chest. "Now, I don't mind a little playing hard to get, but I'll have you know, I'm not used to being the one doing the chasing." Travis backed away. "Oh, come on. It's for charity."

He kept his voice low so as not to embarrass her in front of everyone else. "I'm not playing any games with you, Rachel. I'll happily write you a check for your charity, but the only person I have a personal interest in around here is Summer. The sooner you get that, the better." He stepped around her and shook hands with the man who owned the horses.

Brian and his horse got along great. Travis and his? Not so much. After two attempts at getting the stubborn mare to move, Travis gave up. The owner must have expected trouble and had another horse for Travis to try. While he saddled that one up, Travis sat on the street curb, watching everyone prepare for the parade. Around the corner, hundreds of people were lined up along the streets of downtown Abilene, sitting in their fold-up chairs or in the back of their pickup trucks. Kids waited impatiently for the parade to begin, driving their parents crazy.

Travis took off his hat, the heat getting to him. He wiped his brow as two feet entered his peripheral vision. He looked up, setting the hat back down on his head. "What's going on, Pete?"

Pete seemed a bit on edge. "You can't have them both, you know."

Travis's eyebrows disappeared under his hat. "Both?" Then it clicked. He shook his head. "Oh, I'm not riding them both. That first one was too difficult, so I'm giving the second one a go."

Pete's expression went from angry to horrified. "Is that how you treat them? If one gives you some trouble, you go after the other?"

Travis held his palms up. "Well, I can't ride them both at the same time, now, can I?"

Pete's eyes managed to go wider. "You… You are… You are the reason I hated every football player in my high school! Didn't your mother teach you how to treat a woman?"

"A woman?" Travis got to his feet. He had a good half a foot on Pete, who took a step back. "What are you talking about?"

"Summer and Rachel! What are *you* talking about?"

Travis laughed so hard he couldn't speak for a couple seconds. "Good Lord! I thought we were talking about the horses. That's funny." He wiped his eyes, still chuckling at their misunderstanding.

"I saw you with Rachel right after I saw you with Summer. You better stay away from my Rachel," Pete warned.

This time, the lights really came on. "Oh, Pete. Trust me, Summer's the only woman for me. Rachel's all yours. Although I will say, I think you can do a lot better."

Pete pointed a long, dirty finger in Travis's

face. "I saw you, Lockwood. I saw you standing too close. I saw you whisper in her ear. Once I help her with Summer, she'll be mine. You better not get any ideas." He started to take off, but Travis grabbed the back of his shirt and halted his retreat.

"What did you say? Exactly how would you help Rachel with Summer?"

"I didn't say nothing! Let go of me!" Pete struggled to get loose, but he was no match for the stronger, younger man. "Let go of me."

"What did you do?" Travis spun Pete around so he could look him in the eye. "Tell me what you did to help her with Summer. Come on, Pete. Summer thinks you're a nice guy." She was wrong, and Travis was ready to make him pay for that.

It didn't take more than that to get him to sing like a canary. "Rachel said Summer was trying to take her job. I found her crying at her desk one night. Do you know what it does to me to see that angel cry?" Pete asked.

Travis could feel himself losing control. All along he'd blamed Richard, when the real culprit was right here. His grip on Pete's shoulders tightened. "You rigged that light to fall, didn't you?"

"I was only going to try to get her fired, but that didn't work. I thought I could scare her enough to make her leave on her own. I swear I wasn't trying to hurt her, just scare her away."

Rage engulfed Travis and narrowed his vision. All this time, it had been Pete and Rachel who were trying to hurt Summer. He heard his voice rising as he shook the smaller man. "We're going to get rid of someone, all right."

"Travis!" Summer crossed the street in a panic. "What are you doing? Let him go! People are going to wonder if you've lost your mind!"

He did as she said. "I hope her kindness makes you feel like the spineless creep you are. She's protecting you when you went out of your way to do her harm."

Summer latched on to Travis's arm and pulled him away from a cowering Pete. "What are you talking about?"

"This is the guy who's behind all your trouble at the station. Rachel made him think you were trying to take her job. Pete's the one who was making your life miserable, not Richard," Travis explained.

"Pete?" Summer's eyes pleaded with him to tell her it wasn't true. The coward looked away, unable to give her what she wanted. "How could you do that?" she asked, completely stunned. Again, no answer came.

Travis dragged Pete over to Ken and the rest of the crew by the van. He told Ken everything and demanded action. There was no time to settle the issue, however. The parade was beginning and Travis and Summer needed to be in it. Ken wouldn't hear another word until the parade was over. Frustrated, Travis mounted his horse and followed Summer back to the float.

"You okay?" he asked as she got herself situated. He could see she was anything but.

Summer glanced over at Rachel, who was oblivious of everything that had gone on a few moments ago. She turned back to Travis. "Did you know that around twenty-four thousand people die by lightning strikes around the world each year?"

"Summer..."

"I'm fine. I'm completely fine." She was lying. Before Travis could do anything about the vengeful look in her eye, the parade started and the float began to move. He rode alongside, watching Summer fume as she probably asked God to send some lightning Rachel's way. He had to remind himself she could only predict the weather, not control it.

The high-school band in front of them began to play. Their green and gold uniforms looked uncomfortable in this heat, but they weren't the ones Travis was worried about overheating. Summer was so furious she could barely put on a smile and wave to the crowd. The heat she was feeling had nothing to do with the weather. The Texas Star Chevy float was covered in red, white and blue tissue paper, streamers and glittery paper stars. Luckily for Rachel, a car with KLVA license plates and the words WIN ME painted across the windshield sat in the middle, separating her from Summer. A big Texas flag and the dealership's logo were the backdrop.

Travis had a difficult time concentrating on the cheering crowd as Summer and Rachel both moved to the front of the float. He tapped his heels against the sides of his horse, encouraging the beast to speed up. He watched as Summer said something to Rachel, causing the woman's public persona to slip a little. Rachel frowned and stared back at Summer. More words were exchanged, heated words he couldn't make out over the music of the marching band.

"Summer!" Travis attempted to get her attention, but it was too late. Summer said something that sent Rachel into a fit. She pushed Summer so hard she almost fell backward off the float. Stuck on his horse, Travis was helpless, his heart thumping relentlessly in his chest. If anything happened to her, he'd never forgive himself. Summer stood her ground, and the two women screamed and gesticulated as the crowd looked on in complete shock and horror.

Travis stopped his horse and handed the reins to the nearest bystander. He ran up to the truck pulling the float, banging on the window and telling the driver to stop. He turned to go break up the fight.

"I knew you were crazy!" Rachel was yelling.

"I'm crazy? You're paranoid and completely delusional!" Summer shouted back.

Rachel let out something like a battle cry and ran at Summer full steam ahead. Summer waited until the last moment before stepping to her left, and Rachel's momentum carried her right off the side of the float and into a pile of steaming horse manure. Travis wanted to laugh at the beauty of justice being served, but Summer didn't look as though she found any of it very funny.

Ken jumped up on the float and grabbed Summer before Travis could. Rachel popped up, ready to kill. Or cry. Travis couldn't be sure, so he decided to put himself between the two women. Ken led Summer away from the onlookers and their camera phones. Everyone from the station followed.

Back at the van, Summer was full of uncontrollable fury. Her hair was a wild mess of curls on top of her head as her body shook with anger. Travis put his hand on her shoulder, hoping to provide what little comfort he had to offer in front of their coworkers.

"I want her fired!" Rachel screamed as she held her hand under her nose. The fresh horse manure staining her jeans smelled horrible.

"Me?" Summer asked, wide-eyed with shock. "You attacked *me!*"

"She pushed me off the float. You all saw!"

"You convinced Pete to make a light fall on my head! You told him I was trying to take your job so he would mess with my reports and get me fired!"

Rachel's laughter enraged Summer further. "She's lost it, Ken. If you don't get rid of her, you will cost this station every advertiser I have ever brought you."

Travis had heard enough. "Pete told us what he did, Rachel. He said you encouraged him."

"I never asked him to do anything. I'll admit I've felt threatened by her transparent attempts to upstage me. Maybe he felt bad for me and acted on those feelings. But I swear to you, Ken, I never asked him to do it."

"You aren't going to buy her lies, right?" Travis asked Ken, who was unusually quiet. There was no possible way anyone could believe her.

"I…" Ken shook his head. "I don't know what to believe. Do you know what an incident like this is going to do to our reputation?"

"She knocked me off the float! You have to fire her. You have to!" Rachel demanded.

Travis stared Ken down, daring him to fire Summer. If he did that, he'd be out a weather girl *and* a sportscaster. There was no way

Travis would work for Ken if he gave Summer the boot.

"Forget it," Summer said before Ken could reply. "I quit." Without another word, she stormed off, leaving Travis behind. It felt like a life-changing hit, similar to the one he'd taken in Chicago. Only worse. Because Summer mattered more than football ever did.

CHAPTER SEVENTEEN

"I SHOULD CALL Ken." Summer was in panic mode. Travis had driven her home and now all she could do was pace her living room floor. The heels of her boots click-clacked on the wood floor. She tried to take a deep breath, but it felt as if the walls were closing in.

Had she really quit? Rachel had made her so angry. Ken's lack of support hadn't helped. She said she quit, but she said it without thinking about what it really meant. She'd considered the job with Ryan over the past couple days, finally deciding staying in Abilene was the best option. After much deliberation and soul searching, it was Travis who convinced her to stay. He didn't even know he was doing it. And now everything was ruined.

"I'm sure he'd understand you got caught up in the heat of the moment," he said.

She stopped pacing and cast a furtive

glance in his direction. He had his head bowed and elbows resting on his knees, one leg bouncing anxiously. His patience was waning. She'd done nothing but fret for the last half hour. He was ready for her to rectify the situation, to call Ken. Travis had no idea what she had really done by quitting—the door she had opened or how badly she wanted to run. He couldn't hear the wind calling her name the way she did.

"Did you know that we hit triple digits nineteen days in June and twenty-seven in July?"

Sidestepping her weather nonsense, he tried to reassure her. "You have a job. You just need to call Ken and tell him you want to keep it."

The pacing resumed, as did the chewing on her thumbnail. Summer had more than one job. She could call Ryan just as easily as she could call Ken. Another quick glance at Travis and it felt as if her world were splitting down the middle. "I can't leave."

"Why would you leave?" Travis rose to his feet, wrapping his arms around her. "I want you to relax." He was her shelter from the storm, the one place she knew she was safe.

A knock on the door pushed all thoughts of relaxation from Summer's mind and sent Storm into a tizzy. Rachel had threatened to have Summer arrested for assault when she climbed out of the pile of manure. The last thing Summer needed was for the police to come for her. There had to be plenty of witnesses who could verify it was Rachel's own fault.

Hesitantly, she opened the door to find Mimi and Big D with worry written all over their faces. Mimi hugged her granddaughter tightly. "We were waiting at the end of the parade route, thinking you were comin' any minute, when we heard there was some sort of fight. Imagine our surprise when they said it involved the Channel 6 weather girl!"

"I'm sorry. I left so fast I didn't think about you being in the crowd."

"What happened?" Big D asked, petting Storm while waiting patiently for his hug.

Summer let go of her grandmother and sought comfort in his arms. "It was Rachel. She instigated all the trouble I've been having at the station. She told one of the techs I was trying to steal her job. How ridiculous is that?"

"Never liked that girl," Big D mumbled as they made their way into the house. "Something was off with that smile of hers."

"So you pushed her off the float?" Mimi laughed.

"More like she fell," Summer said sheepishly. "And I quit." Mimi fell silent. She and Big D exchanged a look. Summer knew that look. "But I'm going to call Ken and beg for my job back."

"Sometimes our hearts know what we want before our minds catch on." Big D put a gentle hand on her cheek. "Maybe it's not Ken you should be calling."

She should have known he would say that. For some reason, he was bound and determined to ship her off to New York on the next available flight. "Can we not do this right now?"

"Ryan chose you for a reason," Big D continued.

"Ryan will have no trouble finding someone else for that job," Summer argued.

Big D's voice rose just a bit. "You're braver than this, Summer."

"I need a moment with my granddaughter," Mimi interrupted. "Alone."

Big D nodded and reached out to give Mimi's hand a squeeze. "Come help me walk this beast," he said to Travis, whose eyebrows were furrowed in confusion. "I better get out of here before I get myself in trouble." He took the leash off the hook by the door and attached it to Storm's collar. Travis followed them out without a word.

"I'm not going anywhere, Mimi," Summer said, attempting to ease at least one mind. They sat on Summer's sky-blue couch. Mimi, with her bright yellow sundress and her white-blond hair pulled up in a bun, looked like an unhappy sun.

"Because of me?"

"Because of a lot of reasons," Summer replied.

"But mostly because of me." It was a statement, not a question.

"Because of me." Summer pressed a hand over her heart. "Everyone I love is here. You, Big D." Travis. She thought it but didn't say it. She'd been thinking it all week long. She was in love with him. She wasn't sure how or when it happened, but it had. "Even Mom and Dad are here."

Mimi shook her head. "Your daddy and

mama aren't here. I might have put their bones in Texas soil, but their souls are still in the whispers of the wind."

There was no arguing with that. "Well, you and Big D are reason enough, then."

Mimi's eyes welled with tears. It was too much for Summer. Her gaze dropped to her lap, but Mimi's voice was thick with the same emotion. "You're like my pretty little caged bird, convinced you don't want to fly when it was what God put you on this earth to do." Mimi lifted her chin. "Listen to me, sweet girl. I've selfishly kept you here since your daddy died. It's about time I let you go and let you live your life for you."

Summer swiped at her own tears before they fell. Fear and doubt overwhelmed her. She was terrified of making the wrong decision, but she knew one needed to be made. It was like being asked to choose between divorcing parents. How did someone choose one love over another?

"Summer, we love you," Mimi said, taking hold of her hands. "We want you to be happy. Tell me this job with Ryan won't make you happy."

"It will and it won't." She couldn't ignore

the way her heart ached when she imagined telling Travis about the other job. It would have been hard enough to leave her grandparents, but Summer had to go and fall in love with a man who had broken down all of her walls so effortlessly.

"Any of this indecision have to do with that mighty fine looking man who's walking your dog with Big D right now?"

Summer shrugged, unable to speak around the lump in her throat. Maybe it had more to do with Travis than she wanted to admit.

Mimi nodded as one side of her mouth smiled. "He'd probably go with you if you asked. Something tells me that boy would follow you anywhere. The way he looks at you reminds me of the way your mama used to look at your dad, and we know how that worked out."

That was impossible. How could she ever ask Travis to give up everything to follow her dreams? The man deserved to figure out what his own dreams were first. "Maybe I'm too afraid to do any of this," she admitted. "Maybe Big D is wrong. Maybe I'm not brave enough."

"Try," Mimi said softly. "Try it and see.

We'll all survive here. You won't be gone forever."

Mimi always led with her heart. She did what felt right. Big D thought things through, did what he knew was best. Both of them were telling her to take this leap.

After a few minutes had passed, the front door opened and Storm came racing in, tongue out and tail wagging. Big D and Travis followed behind him. Travis's blue-gray eyes were definitely overcast.

"Everything okay in here?" Big D asked.

The two women nodded and tightened their hold on each other's hands.

"We should let you and Travis work this out," Big D said, holding a hand out for his wife. He tapped the toe of his shoe against Summer's foot. "We're glad you're all right. No more fights on moving vehicles, though."

Summer managed a small smile. "Promise."

Mimi gave her a hug before taking her husband's hand. She walked over to where a solemn Travis stood. She squeezed his arm and whispered something in his ear. His head lifted, his eyes saying all the things he was holding back. Mimi gave him another reassuring pat on the shoulder and headed for the door.

Travis's stare burned her skin as Summer said goodbye and saw her grandparents out. She leaned back against the front door after shutting it. Not sure what to say, she waited for him to speak first. His silence enveloped her like a scratchy wool blanket. It didn't take long for the weather facts to flow freely.

"Did you know that a small thunderstorm can hold as much as thirty-three million gallons of water?"

He finally looked away, his gaze dropping to the floor in front of him. "That's a lot."

"There was once a storm that hit Dell City with hurricane-strength winds. Destroyed an airport hangar."

"Scary," he replied without his usual interest.

"At any particular time there can be almost two thousand thunderstorms occurring in our atmosphere. Luckily, they aren't all that extreme and most aren't deadly."

"Who's Ryan?"

She swallowed hard. It was the easiest question he could have asked, but still hard. Her mouth went dry. Hearing Ryan's name made her want to call him. And if she called him, she would accept his job offer. That terrified her. "He's a friend of my parents."

The clench of his jaw made her nervous. "Your grandfather said he's a television producer."

"He's that, too." Summer pushed off the door and headed back into the living room. She resumed her pacing in front of the small fireplace.

"He offered you a job." He wasn't asking.

Feeling cowardly, she used the excuse her grandmother had just told her was no longer valid. "Yes, but it means leaving Mimi and Big D." *And you.* "It requires lots of travel and I'd be based out of New York."

"What kind of job is it?"

Summer didn't want to talk about it, knowing there was no way to downplay how good the opportunity was. "I don't know. He wants me to track storms as well as visit places that have experienced some of the wildest weather in history."

"It's like This Day in Weather History, only a whole hour instead of thirty seconds, and on location instead of in the studio?"

It wasn't like that. It was a thousand times

better than her little idea. "It doesn't matter because I'm all my grandparents really have. My aunts don't visit, don't help."

"It sounded to me like they want you to take the position."

"What they want isn't as important as what I want."

"This job that's supposedly perfect for you, isn't what you want?" he challenged.

What she wanted was the courage to tell him she was in love with him and would stay if he felt the same, but the words were lodged in her throat. There was a part of her that hoped he'd come out and say it first, that he'd profess his own love and ask her to stay.

Instead, Travis threw his thumb over his shoulder. Her silence spoke all the wrong things to him. "I'm going to head out. You have a phone call to make and I need to… I have to… There are some things I should…" He couldn't finish, but didn't have to. Summer knew he was running away.

"I'm sorry I told Ken I quit," she managed to choke out as he made his way to the door.

Travis's hand stilled on the doorknob, but he didn't turn around. "I'll call you later." He pulled open the door and slipped out without a goodbye. But that was exactly how it felt—like goodbye.

SLEEP ELUDED SUMMER that night. She tossed and turned, overthinking all the things she had and hadn't done that day. She'd gotten into an actual fight. She'd quit her job. In a moment of passionate hate, she had done the one thing she was sure she wouldn't be able to muster up the courage to do.

She hadn't told Travis how she felt about him. Instead, she'd come clean with him about Ryan's offer. And he'd left her to make a decision—a decision she still had to make.

She hadn't called Ryan or Ken, although Ken had called her more than once. She'd let his calls go to voice mail and prayed the next time the phone rang it would be Travis. Travis didn't call.

She flipped onto her back, staring at the ceiling fan as it spun around slowly. The nights were cooler this time of year. Summer had the windows open and the air-conditioning off. Tonight's low was predicted to dip down to sixty-three. That was average. Tomorrow's high was eighty-seven. That was slightly above normal. The sun and heat were getting old; they needed some rain. The storms that came with the tornado didn't produce much precipitation. West Central Texas still suffered from drought.

Summer recited the highs and lows for the week over and over in her head, hoping it would lull her to sleep. When that failed miserably, she thought about how different things were when she'd woken up this morning. She was looking forward to seeing Travis at the parade and couldn't wait to wrap her arms around him and sneak a sniff of his cologne. He smelled better than any man she knew.

Rolling over on her stomach, Summer hid her head under her pillow. She should have told him she loved him. Travis probably thought the job with Ryan was a done deal. He probably thought their relationship was over before it even began. He was wrong, though. She owed it to him and to herself to tell him how she really felt. As Big D said, she was braver than this.

Summer climbed out of bed and checked the clock. It was after midnight, but that wasn't going to stop her from taking a leap of faith. She grabbed her phone off the dresser and typed out a text she figured Travis would read when he got up. It was a simple invitation to go running in the morning. She'd miss church and lunch with her grandparents, but it was worth it. She hit Send and crawled back into bed, proud of herself for having some sort of plan. It was right when sleep began to find her that her phone beeped with Travis's reply.

Meet me at Red Bud @ 8.

RED BUD PARK was quiet and uncrowded, so different from the last time they'd been there. Summer twirled Storm's favorite toy and tossed it for him to chase. The dog returned with his slobbery rope in his mouth and dropped it at Travis's feet, as if he knew who had the better throwing arm. She tried not to let it hurt her feelings, which wasn't so hard once Travis picked it up and threw it a good sixty yards.

"I see what everybody's been going on about. That's some arm," Summer said as they watched Storm run like lightning. Her hand shielded her eyes from the sun.

"I could throw a football a lot farther than

that slimy thing." He wiped his hand on his shorts.

The plan was to run together, but the black Lab was the only one getting any exercise at the moment. With the exception of their awkward greeting when he arrived, Travis hadn't said much. He didn't ask her if she had called Ken or Ryan. He didn't even comment on the weather. Still, it looked as though he had something to say.

Storm returned and lay down a few feet away. The poor dog was out of breath, his tongue hanging out of his mouth. He kept his toy out of Summer's and Travis's reach, in need of a breather. Summer began to stretch her legs. She needed to run until her muscles burned and her chest ached. Anything to distract her from the tension that floated around and in between them, filling all the empty spaces like a dense fog.

"I came here last night," Travis finally said. "Hank, the hot-air balloon guy, met me."

Summer's head snapped up. "How did that happen?"

He stopped and cleared his throat. His jaw clenched a couple times before he was able to continue. "I was going to surprise you last night, but I guess things got messed up."

The guilt felt like a ten-pound rock in her stomach. She hadn't meant to ruin his plans. "Did you jump?"

"I had him take me up and hook me to the cord. I stood there for the longest time, trying to convince myself that I could do it. It was seriously the scariest thing I have ever done."

"But you did it," she said proudly. "Next time we'll have to do it together." Summer sat down in the grass and looked up at him. He was a hulk of a man, but his face was soft and gentle. He wore running shorts and a sleeveless UT T-shirt. His arms made him the kind of man who should always wear shirts without sleeves. If Ken really wanted to get to number one, he needed to buy Travis some sleeveless suits.

"I did it. I jumped and screamed and thought I was going to die."

Summer laughed. How she wished he had invited her along to see that. "It is truly terrifying. I'm scared every time I go up."

Travis shook his head. "I have a picture of you standing in that balloon basket right before you jumped." He looked into the sky as if she were still up there. "There was this complete calm about you. I remember how alive and energized you were after the fact, but before you jumped, you were cool as a cucumber. You're truly one of the bravest people I know."

His compliment made her smile, but she felt ashamed, and she ducked her head. She didn't feel very brave lately. Even Big D saw through her. She'd been living in this limbo, refusing to make the tough decisions, avoiding the emotions that were making themselves crystal clear. "Jumping out of a balloon doesn't make me brave. And just because I looked calm doesn't mean I wasn't scared."

Travis cleared his throat and ran a hand through his hair. "I need to tell you something," he began. "I was waiting for the right time to do it, but I don't know what the right time is anymore."

Summer looked back up, concerned. "You know you can tell me anything."

"I've been lost and afraid for a really long time now. Afraid of failing. Afraid of making the wrong decisions. Before my injury, I thought I was infallible. Afterward, I felt I had failed everyone who ever believed in me."

"That's not true. That might be how you felt, but I can't believe that's how everyone saw it."

"Trust me, there are people I have most definitely failed. But you, I don't want to fail you."

He could never fail her. She wanted to say that, but her anxiety pushed the most recent weather facts out of her mouth. "Did you know New York City averages about twenty-two and a half inches of snow a year?"

Travis let out a breathy laugh and held out a hand to help her to her feet. He didn't let go once she stood up. "That's a lot of snow."

"Not really. Not in comparison to Rochester or Ithaca. Those nor'easters are brutal, dumping almost a hundred inches of snow some winters."

"We sure are spoiled here in Texas." He brushed her cheek with the back of his fingers. This was why she loved him. He understood her better than anyone. He never let her weirdness get in the way. He took her hand in both of his. "You changed how I look at myself. You made me believe I should ask for more from life than what I already had. You challenged me to see the world in a different

way and not let the fear keep me from trying something new. You were exactly what I
never knew I needed."

The way he looked at her seemed to mirror
the way she felt about him. In his eyes, she
could see he respected and cared about her.
There was also something bigger, something
she felt in the center of her chest.

There was love.

He was in love with her as she hoped. Just
as she was in love with him. Summer's stomach did a flip-flop and she could feel her heart
in her chest. Love did that. It made your heart
double, triple in size and press against your
ribs. It made you feel alive as nothing else
could. She couldn't let him say it first. If he
said it first, he'd think she was just reacting
to him when she said it back. She was the one
who was supposed to make the declarations
this morning.

Travis kept talking while Summer silently
fretted. "I need you to know I appreciate that
you liked me even when I didn't like myself."

"I don't like you," she interjected impul-
sively. Travis frowned, making her smile. Just
like when she stood in that balloon basket,
this calm before the storm took over. She was

ready to take the leap. "I love you. I'm in love with you, and I want to stay here with you. I'm not taking the other job."

Instead of kissing her and professing his own feelings, Travis let go of her hand and took a step back. "Summer," he groaned. "Why are you doing this to me?" That couldn't be good. He turned his back to her and clawed at his hair. "You have to take that job."

"I don't," she asserted, tugging on his arm to make him face her. "I thought about it and I want to see where this relationship goes. I won't be able to do that thousands of miles away. I love you, Travis. I'm staying in Abilene."

His hands slipped from the top of his head to cover his face. "I'm not."

"What?" Summer's oversize heart began to beat double time. "What are you talking about?"

He dropped his hands to his sides. Gone was the love and respect she thought she'd seen in his eyes moments ago. Now there was only a pain that made her chest ache. She stared down at his feet and tried to stop herself from bursting into tears.

"I'm taking a coaching job in Alabama. I can't be the reason you don't follow your dream. We both have to move on, Summer. It's the best thing for both of us."

"Alabama?" It was the only thing that registered. He'd taken a job in Alabama. She should have known better. She was a fool. A complete fool for believing he could be in love with her. He wasn't here to tell her he loved her. He was here to finish off that goodbye.

The worst thing about the way love caused your heart to expand was that it hurt that much more when that stupid, overinflated organ split down the middle. It was a lesson Summer wouldn't soon forget.

CHAPTER EIGHTEEN

THE UNIVERSITY OF Alabama's campus was beautiful, rich in history and traditional architecture. Travis took a tour of the Quad, which used to host the football games back in the early days. Now the Crimson Tide's facilities were some of the most impressive in all of college football. The entire coaching staff was welcoming, and the offer they put on the table was hard to refuse.

Travis loosened his tie as he looked out the window of his hotel room. This was the job his father was telling him to take, the one that was supposed to be perfect for him and what was left of his skill set. Even Summer had once said he was an excellent motivator.

Summer.

She had moved to New York two weeks ago, and nothing was the same. Not the station, not Abilene—not Texas, for that matter. Alabama offered Travis the chance to get away from everything that reminded him of her. It was a clean slate. A fresh start. Yet, as Travis listened to the head coach and all of the assistants go on and on about their program, as he stood in the middle of the huge stadium, he realized something important. He didn't want to coach football quarterbacks. He didn't want to be part of the football machine at all. The kid coming from Odessa deserved a coach whose heart was in it one hundred percent. Travis wasn't even in it half that much.

He turned down the offer with a "thank you, but no, thank you." Travis decided he needed to stop doing what made his old man happy and figure out what made *him* happy.

Travis rested his head on the window's cool glass. What did make him happy? Summer. Summer made him the happiest he'd ever been, and his heart was with her, not here in Tuscaloosa. She loved him and he let her go without telling her he loved her back. He did love her. With everything he had, he loved her.

Travis flopped down on the bed. He had messed up. Staring up at the ceiling, he imagined calling Summer up and telling her this was all a big mistake. He didn't mean to tell her to go; he meant to tell her he loved her, too, and that she should stay. They could get married, have a family, go to church and eat lunch at her grandparents' house every Sunday. Their children could go to school with Conner's kids, grow up friends and cousins. His mom could teach Summer how to make red velvet cupcakes and they could go running every morning so he didn't get a cupcake belly. It would be a good life, one filled with love, family and lots of blue sky.

Only one problem—Summer had the chance at an exceptional life. She could chase storms and live a new adventure every day. She could not only talk about the weather, but also experience it, live it. Travis had let her go because that was what she deserved. This new show was made for her. She might have been reluctant to leave Abilene, but he believed it was what she truly wanted. The right thing was to tell her to go, to force her to take the risk and chase the rainbow.

He sat up and rubbed his eyes with the heels of his hands. The worst part was, he had thought he'd found where he belonged at the same time he'd realized Summer belonged somewhere else. Sportscasting felt less right without Summer in the studio. He was back to square one. Lost and unsure of himself.

He grabbed his wallet off the dresser and slipped it in his pocket. He needed some food in his stomach, and to fill the void inside him. As if that was possible. Summer was gone, and it was only a matter of time before she met some dashing storm chaser who swept her off her feet. They'd run away together to study floods in Europe and Travis would be left in Texas under a permanent rain cloud. His future sure wasn't looking too bright.

Travis went straight to his parents' house when he returned to Texas. He had Conner pick him up from the airport and tag along for moral support. He needed to be honest with his dad once and for all. The brothers found their mother weeding the flower beds. She looked over her shoulder when she heard the car pull up. Rising to her feet, she adjusted the wide-brimmed hat on her head.

"Well, this is a surprise! I thought you were still in Tuscaloosa."

Travis shut the car door and opened his arms for a hug. "Just got back."

She squeezed him tight before stepping back to take a good look at her son. Placing a hand on his cheek, she looked him square in the eye. He hoped she wouldn't see the anxiety he felt. He tried smiling to throw her off. The wrinkle between her eyebrows deepened as she attempted to get a read on him. Giving up, she moved on to greet Conner. "Come inside," she said, hooking arms with Travis. "Your dad has been waiting to hear all about the new job."

Conner gave him a little push when his feet seemed to forget how to move. He'd thought jumping out of that hot-air balloon was scary. Facing his father's wrath was quickly becoming much more terrifying.

"Sam! Your boys are here!" Olivia took off her hat and set it on the coatrack by the door. Pulling off her work gloves and dropping them in a basket, she offered her sons something to drink. Conner was quick to help, chasing after their mom and giving Travis a thumbs-up as their dad came down the stairs.

"Finally!" Sam threw his arm around his son's shoulders and led him into the family room. "Your phone broken? I left a message, your mother left a dozen. How'd it go?"

Travis took a deep breath. He'd practiced what he was going to say in the car with his brother, but all those words were lost in his dad's presence. "The interviews went well. They have a stellar program over there. I was very impressed with everything."

"So when do you start?" His dad's smile was big and broad. There was that long-lost pride in his eyes. Travis hated to do it, but he had to wipe it all away.

"I didn't take it," he confessed. Sam Lockwood stared at his son in utter disbelief. "I don't want to be a quarterback coach. I don't really want to be a football coach at all."

Sitting down on the overstuffed couch, his dad held his head in his hands. "I can't believe you."

"I appreciate everything you did to get me the interview, I just—"

"You just what, Travis? You just gave up? You don't want to be a coach? What in the world do you want to be, then?" His father's voice rose with every question, causing his mother to come out of the kitchen, where Conner had been attempting to detain her.

"Why in the world are you yelling at him?"

"Because your son has lost his mind! He doesn't care about his own happiness."

"That's not true," Travis said, standing up for himself. "I didn't take the job because I do care. I'm miserable. I've been miserable. And I'd be more miserable if I did something the rest of my life that I didn't love."

"So what is it that you love to do? Because I thought it was football," his dad said through clenched teeth.

"I don't know," he admitted. His mom put her hand on his arm and squeezed. "But I want to figure it out."

"And you can't do that at Alabama?"

"It's not fair to the team for me to be there and not be completely committed."

"That's a good point," his mother chimed in. She took the seat next to his dad. "I'm sure you'll figure out what you want soon enough."

"All that time, all that money, all those years…wasted." His father's head fell back into his hands and he spoke to the floor.

Conner came up behind Travis and put his hand on his brother's shoulder. "It wasn't wasted. Travis was an incredible football player. He deserved all the time and attention he got. But let's be real, Dad. Did he ever have a choice? I played three sports growing up. Mom even took me to karate classes for a week until I decided it wasn't for me. I got to hang out with my friends and be a normal kid. Travis had football. All year. All the time. When he wasn't playing, he was training. I think this is his chance to see what else he's good at."

Travis could feel the tension leave his body. His brother said it better than he ever could. That was exactly what he was asking for—for his family to support him in finding what other gifts he had to share with the world.

"All that's ever mattered to me and your dad is that you boys are happy," his mom said as she rubbed her husband's back. "If Travis isn't happy coaching, then that's not what we want for him. Right, honey?"

"I thought that football was what he wanted," his dad mumbled.

"I never thought there was another option."

His dad looked up, their eyes connecting for the first time since he broke the news. Finally, Travis saw something other than disgust. There was even a hint of understanding. "No one played football like you, son. But your mother's right. Your happiness is what matters. Maybe I just need to step back and let you figure this out."

"I don't want you to think I don't appreciate everything you've done for me, Dad. I haven't been very fair to you. I depended on you instead of trusting myself and then blamed you when I wasn't perfectly content."

"You never needed me as much as you thought you did," his dad said with a faint smile.

If that was true, maybe there was hope for Travis yet. Though he wasn't confident it would happen anytime soon, Travis was beginning to believe he would find his own way.

"Any word from Summer? Does she know you aren't going to Alabama?" his mom asked, changing the subject and bringing back the tightness in his shoulders.

"We're not really on speaking terms, Mom."

"Maybe you should do something about that," she said, getting up off the couch and returning to the kitchen to get those drinks. "That woman seemed to make you happy."

True but irrelevant. Summer was gone because he'd told her to go. There was no taking that back.

EXERCISE WAS THE only thing that helped keep Travis's mind off Summer. Red Bud Park probably wasn't conducive to a Summer-free run, but it was where Conner offered to meet Travis on a Saturday. The sun was hiding behind some early-morning cloud cover. Cumulus clouds to be exact. Summer had taught Travis a thing or two about clouds. Maybe she'd be proud of him for remembering.

Travis rubbed the spot in the center of his chest that had begun to ache. This was a bad idea.

"You're gonna have to take it easy on me. I can't run more than four miles," Conner said as they stretched out. "And none of that interval sprinting stuff. We go one pace the whole time."

"Remind me, why did I want you to come running with me again?" Travis pondered aloud as he started to jog away.

Conner was quick to catch up. "Because no one else can stand to be around you while you wallow."

"I am not wallowing."

"Travis. This is worse than when you broke off your engagement. You are living in Wallow City. Wallowing is your middle name. If they were going to name a Gatorade flavor after you, it would be Wallow."

Travis gave his brother a good shove, causing Conner to veer off the pavement and into the grass. "At least my socks match."

Conner looked down at his feet. He had one white and one black sock on. He shook his head at himself. "Having a baby in the house does some crazy stuff to your head, man. Crazy stuff."

Travis laughed, but that phantom ache in his chest was back. Travis was jealous. It was a first for sure. Conner didn't know how good he had it. Travis would happily wear mismatched socks if it meant having the woman he loved at his side and a baby to dote upon.

He ran faster to force his brain to focus on something other than what he didn't have. Conner couldn't keep up, but something else could. A four-legged beast came racing by with a leash trailing behind. The dark-as-night furball looked awfully familiar.

"Storm!" Travis shouted, and sure enough,

the runaway dog stopped dead in his tracks. Storm took a good look at Travis, cocking his head to the side. Once he realized who he was dealing with, he took off into some bushes only to reemerge with a stick, ready to play with the man who could throw really far.

"What are you doing out here on your own? Huh, boy?" Travis grabbed Storm's leash, scanning the area for the disappointed dog's owner. Storm wanted to run.

"You know this big guy?" Conner asked, giving Storm a pat on the head.

"Yeah, he's—" Travis stopped when he saw Summer's grandfather coming their way. Of course it wouldn't be Summer. She lived in New York. But part of him had thought for a second that maybe, just maybe, she was here. Travis brought Storm over to Big D. "Mr. Raines, how are you, sir?"

"Well, look at that. Maybe this mutt knows exactly what he's doing. Good to see you, son." The old man stuck out his hand and Travis gave it a shake before handing over the leash.

"It's good to see you, too, sir."

"I learned today that you don't take Storm for a walk. He takes you. I couldn't keep up."

Travis laughed. "Summer once told me she should have named him Lightning instead of Storm. He's pretty fast."

Big D bent down and scratched the dog behind the ear. "You got to slow down for this old man. I'm not like your mama."

The pain in Travis's chest continued to make itself known, making it hard to breathe. He needed to get away. Coming to this park was the worst idea Conner ever had. "Well, it was good to see you, sir. Say hello to your wife for me."

"Can't do that," the older man said. Travis stopped his retreat. "Sarah won't be happy with a secondhand hello. If I get to see how you're doing, she's gonna need to see how you're doing, as well. You'll come over for lunch tomorrow. Eleven o'clock. Don't be late. She won't be happy if you're late, either."

"Sir," Travis began.

"Eleven sharp. You don't want to see that woman unhappy," Big D warned.

"Eleven o'clock," Travis said with a nod. He ran back to Conner, unsure of what just happened. Having lunch with Summer's grandparents did not sound like the best way to get over her. Travis didn't hear a word Conner said the entire run. He was lost in his head, wondering which would be worse—making Mimi mad, or spending the day doing nothing but thinking about Summer. In the end, he decided it was in his best interest to stay on Mimi's good side. He'd be thinking about Summer all day anyway, no matter who he was with.

"I'VE NOTICED YOU'VE lost some weight these last few weeks. If TV adds ten pounds, I figured you'd show up lookin' like a toothpick, so I made some stuff that'll stick to your ribs," Mimi said as Travis helped her set the large dining-room table.

"I appreciate that, ma'am."

The old woman gave him the crook eye. "What'd I tell you about calling me ma'am?"

Travis set down the silverware as he'd been shown the last time he had lunch there. "I look forward to eating everything you're cookin', Mimi."

"That's better. Now, what's going on with that job in Alabama."

Telling Mimi meant it would get back to Summer for sure. Travis wondered how Summer would take the news. "I ended up turning down the job, actually. I may not know what I want to do, but at least I know what I don't want."

"You don't know what you want to do?"

"Not yet."

"Hmm." Mimi seemed unconvinced.

"I'm a young man. I have plenty of time to figure it out." He inhaled deeply through his nose. "And thankfully, I can figure it out while eating your apple pie."

Mimi shook her head at his attempt to keep things light. Once they finished setting the table, she went back to work in the kitchen and told Travis to go relax. Big D shared the Sunday paper with him while they waited for lunch. Summer's grandparents seemed to be holding up pretty well, considering their granddaughter was on another continent. Although Mimi did seem very happy to have someone else to cook for besides her husband.

"I was flipping through some old albums yesterday. Found one of Summer and her parents when they visited the Mojave Desert. Summer was only six, I think," Big D said from behind his paper.

Travis lowered his own paper. "Oh yeah? What were they doing in the desert?"

Big D pointed a finger toward the bookcase. "It's red. Bottom shelf. They were lookin' at volcanic craters and lava tubes."

"Wow, I didn't know there was stuff like that out there." He got up and grabbed the album, flipping pages before he even sat back down. "She was so cute," Travis said, holding up a picture of a young Summer posing for the camera. Big D dropped his paper and squinted to get a good look.

"Still is."

Travis sighed. "Yeah, she is." He looked at the photos and asked Big D questions, only getting some of the answers he was looking for—the old man only knew what he'd been told about the trip. Travis could only imagine what kind of stories Summer would soon be able to tell. Someday the albums would be full of grown-up Summer in all the amazing places she'd visited around the world.

"Lunch is ready!" Mimi called.

The three of them gathered around the table and dug into Mimi's chili and corn bread. Meals like this made Travis want to come back every Sunday, chest pain be damned.

"Summer called from Finland a couple days ago," Mimi said. "She said she took some pictures of the Northern Lights, but they didn't turn out too well. She thinks she needs a better camera."

Travis finished his bite of corn bread. "She's got that pocket-size point-and-shoot. She needs to upgrade to a DSLR. They make some reasonably priced entry-level ones, which are pretty easy to use. She doesn't need to get one with too many advanced features like mine."

"Yours has advanced features?" Mimi asked.

"I went all out when I bought it. I had a basic APS-C-format camera when I was in college, but when I was drafted to Miami, I treated myself to a full-frame digital SLR. Those are best in low light and at higher sensitivities. I did a lot of my sightseeing after games, so…" Mimi and Big D were both staring at him. "What?"

The two of them exchanged a look, and Big D said, "Maybe you could suggest one since you're so knowledgeable."

"So knowledgeable," Mimi added.

Travis dug his spoon into his bowl. "Sure. I can do that."

"That would be good of you," Mimi said.

"It'd be nice if she could chronicle her adventures like her mama and daddy did."

"We were looking at pictures of Gavin and Grace's trip to the Mojave Desert," Big D said to Mimi.

"That was one of Gavin's favorite places. He sure did love the heat. It's not as exciting as seeing a tornado, of course," Mimi said, looking at Travis again.

"Nothing beats seeing a tornado," he said without a doubt. "The sheer power of it—it's just amazing."

"You should see what a hurricane can do," Mimi said. "Or a tsunami."

"I'm sure it's incredible."

"The world is full of incredible things," Big D added.

Travis nodded, taking another bite of corn bread. The food was so good he hoped Mimi would pack him up some leftovers. Mimi's intense gaze was becoming too much, though. It was as if she was waiting for him to say something. But he had no clue what that could be. "You all right, Mimi?" he asked as she rubbed her forehead with her hand.

"I know they say you can lead a horse to

water, but you can't make him drink, but, boy, you are killing me. Come on, drink!"

Travis picked up his water glass and took a sip. Mimi's head fell into her hands while Big D chuckled. "What? What am I missing here?" Travis asked, more than confused.

Mimi sat up and took a deep breath. "I've been trying to bite my tongue. I know your daddy made all the decisions for you when you were little, and even when you were grown enough to make them yourself. I knew it would take some time to figure it out, but my goodness! You let other people tell you what to do for so long you don't even see your choices anymore!"

"What choices?" Now Travis just felt foolish. He was trying to know himself better, but he didn't trust his own instincts.

"Why didn't you take that job in Alabama?" Mimi asked.

That was easy. "I don't want to be a football coach. I enjoy a good game, but I don't want to eat, drink and breathe it. To be a good coach, football has to be your life."

"Good answer." Mimi smiled. "You were right when you said it's good to know what you don't want. That's important. But what you *do* want is key here."

Travis knew that. Didn't she know he'd been working on it? No one wanted to figure out what would make Travis happy more than Travis. "I don't know," he admitted, staring down at his bowl of chili instead of looking Summer's grandparents in the eye.

"You do, son," Big D said.

Mimi agreed. "You sure do."

Travis let out a big sigh and looked up. "What? What do I want?"

Mimi shook her head. "We aren't going to tell you!" She pursed her lips and thought long and hard. Then she snapped her fingers. "I got it. Pretend the world is ending tomorrow. What would you do if you only had one day left live?"

Without thinking, Travis gave his most honest answer. "I'd fly to New York and tell Summer I love her."

"I knew you knew," Mimi said proudly.

His frustration all spilled over. He threw his hands up. "I knew long before she left that I love your granddaughter. Whole lotta good that's done me."

"Let me tell you what I see," Mimi said.

"I see a man who not only loves my granddaughter, but loves her weather stories almost as much as she does. You come over here and could look at photo albums for hours. You listen to every random fact that girl has ever uttered in your presence. The experience you shared with her, finding that tornado, is one you will never forget. Right?"

Travis nodded. Chasing that tornado was life-changing.

Mimi continued. "I see a man who knows things like what kind of camera would take photos in low light or whatever it was you were trying to explain earlier. And I see someone who misses Summer more than I do, and I miss that girl something fierce."

"I miss her more than anything."

"So what are you doing here?" Mimi asked. "Not that we wouldn't mind feeding you every Sunday, but you should be with her. You should be the one taking the pictures with her. You should be a part of her adventures. You two are so much like Grace and Gavin, I don't know how you can't see it."

Travis laughed. "You think I should be a storm chaser?"

"Don't you?" Big D asked.

Travis sat back and scratched his head while he thought about it. It did make some sense. It made a lot of sense. It made more sense than sportscasting or football. He leaned forward, his elbows on the table. "I would kill to be a storm chaser."

Mimi leaned back and looked up at the ceiling. "Finally!"

"But I can't just show up on Summer's doorstep and ask for a job."

"Why not?" Mimi's eyebrows pushed together.

"What if she wants nothing to do with me?" All his doubts resurfaced. "What if I'm not good at it? What if my photos aren't as good as you think they are? What if—"

"Travis." Mimi interrupted his laundry list of fears. "What did I tell you the first time I met you?"

"Be worth it and everything will work out in the end." Those words had haunted him ever since. "That's the problem. What if I'm not worth it?"

Mimi shook her head. "You were worth the risk. You proved that by letting her go. A lesser man would have been selfish, would have fed her fear and told her to stay. Trust me when I say she'll be worth it, too. Take the risk, Travis. Take it."

An overwhelming feeling of possibility swelled inside Travis. It was as if all the stars had aligned and pointed him right to Summer. She was worth all the risks in the world, and he would take them all. His smile was so big it felt as if it were going to split his face in two. The answer had been so simple. Mimi's frustration made so much more sense.

He dived back into his chili. No man started his new life on an empty stomach. Summer's grandparents watched with their eyes wide as he shoveled the food into his mouth. Wiping his lips with his napkin, he kept on smiling. "Can I finish my lunch first?"

CHAPTER NINETEEN

GETTING AROUND NEW YORK CITY when it rained was a nightmare. It didn't help that the temperatures this time of year started dipping into the forties and rarely got over sixty, while the wind was anything but light and breezy. Summer held the collar of her jacket closed and hid under her new blue umbrella. The old red one was still trapped at Travis's house, and after everything that had happened, she couldn't bring herself to retrieve it from him before she left. New city, new job, new umbrella.

She never thought she'd miss sunny and ninety so much. The good thing was, she wasn't supposed to spend a lot of time here. Ryan and his production team were already busy planning the next excursion. They had returned from Finland fewer than forty-eight hours ago. Summer hoped for a warmer locale for the next adventure.

Not that Summer's Finnish experience

hadn't been memorable. She viewed the Northern Lights from a heated glass igloo and convinced the crew to go snowshoeing, dog sledding and snowmobiling with her. The trip was even more exhilarating than she'd imagined it would be all those months ago, when Ryan used it as his first lure.

Holding tightly to the handle of her new umbrella, she waited at a crowded street corner for the light to change. The rain gathered in shallow puddles on the pavement. Summer couldn't wait to get back to her apartment and into her warmest pajamas. It was early in the afternoon, but the jet lag was having its way with her internal clock. All she wanted to do was snuggle under her quilt and eat something other than seafood. She'd had enough of that in Finland. The rain brought with it the smell of the ocean and it made her stomach turn.

The walk sign lit up and the crowd of people around her moved as if they were one entity. People in New York moved much faster than people in Texas. No one took a leisurely stroll. Not even on the nice days. They didn't like anyone who couldn't keep up, either. Summer crossed the street, keeping her head down and her eyes on the concrete so she wouldn't step in anything that would make her feet any wetter than they already were.

The old graystone apartment building she called home wasn't fancy like Ryan's place in Manhattan. There was no doorman or swanky lobby, but it was in a decent Brooklyn neighborhood and had everything she needed close by, including the barbecue restaurant that made a pulled pork sandwich that smelled like home. That sandwich was the only reason she ventured outside on a day like this. She held the bag of food against her chest.

The neighborhood had *almost* everything. Some things she needed were over seventeen hundred miles away in Abilene. One in particular she wished she could stop needing so much. Travis broke her heart, and yet she still had these…feelings. Feelings that overwhelmed her and made her cry late at night. As much as she loved this new job, it wasn't the same kind of love she felt for that stupid man. But he didn't love her. Nor did he need or want her. He wanted to coach football at the University of Alabama.

It was humiliating, really. She'd handed him her heart and he'd immediately given it back, apologizing for not being able to accept it. She still couldn't believe she'd read the signs so wrong, but she couldn't be mad at him for not telling her about the Alabama job earlier. Hadn't she done the same thing? The only difference between the two of them was that she would have picked him over the job.

Summer pushed all thoughts of Travis from her mind as she entered her building's breezeway. Closing up her umbrella, she rested it against the wall under the row of mailboxes and began digging through her purse for her keys. Those darn things managed to find the deepest, darkest corner of her purse every time. It took real talent to move things around in there to find them. Just as she won the hide-and-seek game those keys loved to play, a prickly feeling on her neck made her feel she had eyes on her.

Summer peeked over her shoulder through the glass door, but she didn't see anyone on the street paying her any attention. The passersby were all hidden under their umbrellas. Black umbrellas, umbrellas with polka dots, even one rainbow umbrella. Directly across the street a single red umbrella shielded some-one from view. No one was looking back at her, but it wasn't the first time today she'd felt as if someone was watching.

Hoping to not have to come down here again, she unlocked her mailbox, got her mail—nothing more than junk, from the look of it—and unlocked the security door with her hands full. Thankfully, an older gentle-man was there to hold the door for her. She smiled and thanked him.

"No problem, young lady," he said as he ducked out into the rain. He reminded her of Big D and her heart ached a little more.

Before she pressed the button for the el-evator, the chime rang and the silver doors slid open. Summer smiled at her neighbors as they stepped off, but no one smiled back. New York City wasn't like Abilene in that re-spect, either. There were some friendly folk in the big city, like the man who held the door for her, but most people tended to keep to themselves.

Safe and sound in the empty elevator, she took a deep breath, feeling the full weight of her tiredness. She needed to eat and sleep. Her phone rang inside her purse. Juggling her things once more, she pulled it out and answered before it went to voice mail.

Ryan didn't even give her a chance to say hello. "I think I forgot to tell you we need you to come in and help with a couple interviews. Can you be here in an hour?"

Summer leaned against the back wall of the elevator. Her exhaustion seemed to triple at the thought of going back outside and trekking to Discovery's Manhattan offices. "An interview for what exactly?"

"I'm hiring you an assistant."

"Seriously?" There had been some talk of an assistant when they were in Finland—someone who could help her with details she didn't always have time to focus on. But she figured a new hire had to be approved by someone before it would really happen. Although an assistant would be fabulous right now, Summer lacked the motivation to go to work.

Ryan ignored her frustration. "We need your input, obviously."

"Can't we do it later in the week?"

"Today, Summer. Come on. Do you want me to send a car to get you?"

The elevator opened on Summer's floor,

and she managed to drag herself into the hall. Where Ryan's energy came from, she'd never know. Regardless, this interview was happening with or without her. If this person was going to be working as her assistant, she had to go. "Can you give me an hour and a half? I haven't showered or eaten today."

"Someone will be there to get you in ninety minutes." She didn't argue.

Entering her empty apartment, Summer was struck by how much she missed being greeted by Storm when she came home. Big D and Mimi were taking good care of him. There was no doubt he was living the good life, eating table scraps and running free in their backyard. For all the worrying she did about everyone else, she'd never considered how alone she was going to feel. The tiny apartment cost as much as her house back in Texas but wasn't nearly half the size. The sparsely furnished space didn't exactly scream *home,* but Summer viewed the road as her home now anyway.

Instead of changing into pajamas, she quickly ate her lunch, showered and attempted to dress respectably. These interviewees better be worth the effort. And no one better be named Rachel because that would not bode well for the prospective assistant's employment. The buzzer rang, alerting her to her car's arrival. She grabbed her purse and dashed out the door.

Outside, a man stood by a black town car, holding a red umbrella. For a second, Summer's heart stopped. She couldn't see his face, but he was built like a certain former sportscaster she knew and frustratingly still loved. She froze until he lifted the umbrella. His dark hair and square jaw clearly did not belong to Travis. She shook her head at her misguided hope. Travis wasn't in New York. He was back in Abilene, most likely planning his move to Alabama. She'd done what she'd set out to do, encouraging him to follow a new dream. He had—it just didn't include her.

THE DISCOVERY OFFICES were on the Lower East Side. Summer made her way to the production office, where she was meeting Ryan. She got into an empty elevator and texted him that she'd be there in a minute. The doors began to close, only to be stopped by a loosely wrapped red umbrella. Summer's eyes shot up, that tingle on the back of her neck returning with a vengeance. The doors opened and a harried-looking woman entered, scowling at her.

"Didn't you hear me ask you to hold the elevator?" she snapped.

Summer dropped her phone into her purse, embarrassed to be one of those people, the ones too busy on their smartphones to notice the world around them. "I am so sorry. I didn't."

The woman harrumphed and pressed the button to her floor. Good thing she wasn't going to the same place as Summer. The last thing she needed was another hostile working environment.

Ryan had a conference room set up for the interviews and was seated at the head of the table with a huge cup of coffee in front of him. Maybe that was his secret—massive amounts of caffeine. Summer was willing to try anything. She set her bag down and sat next to her mentor and boss.

"Is there coffee somewhere around here?"

"There's a vending machine down the hall and to your right," Ryan replied, not looking up from the papers in front of him. A strange smile played on his lips.

"Are those the résumés?" she asked. Leaning forward, she tried to get a look at what was so entertaining.

He quickly pulled the papers into a stack and slid them over to her. "Are you getting some coffee or should we get started?"

Summer slumped slightly in her seat. Coffee sounded good. Getting up and walking down the hall to get some did not. "Let's start. I have no energy to go get coffee."

Ryan laughed and got up. "Just think. Once you have an assistant, you won't have to get up and get your own coffee ever again."

"Hallelujah." She pulled out a small notepad with some questions she'd jotted down on the ride over while Ryan fetched the first candidate. She looked over the first résumé. The applicant was lucky her name was Gretchen. She had some experience working retail and as a receptionist. Nothing in television.

Gretchen followed Ryan into the room, wearing a white suit that made her look more like a nurse than a personal assistant. She was slim, with bleach-blond hair. A flashy neon scarf was tied around her neck, matching the shocking blue mascara that painted her eyelashes. Summer couldn't help staring. Gretchen wanted to work for Summer because she thought it was a good stepping stone to becoming an assistant to movie stars, her ultimate goal. Summer had to give her points for being honest, but there was no way Gretchen was going to work for her.

Next, there was Avery. Avery was a twenty-two-year-old bundle of energy with a laugh reminiscent of Woody Woodpecker. She was sweet as could be, but was also not getting the job.

Kyle was an avid fan of reality television and could name every winner of *Survivor*— in order. He'd considered going to school to study television production but decided he'd just jump in and get his feet wet this way. Of course, if this didn't pan out, he planned to reapply to be a contestant on every reality TV show, as he had done each year since he turned eighteen. Kyle seemed destined to be in front of the camera rather than working behind the scenes.

Sylvia was not a fan of rain, something she repeatedly stated throughout the interview. When Ryan asked her if she knew their show focused on extreme weather, she got up and left of her own accord. At least she saved them from having to call her later to tell her she didn't get the job.

There was Nigel, the retired schoolteacher who was looking to start a new chapter in his life, and Veronica, former assistant to seventeen different people in the past five years. No one fit. Summer was beyond tired and began to feel more like a zombie. After Veronica, she decided the only way she would survive the remaining interviews was to get that coffee.

She was pushing her quarters into the machine when something made the hairs on the back of her neck stand up again. She felt someone come up behind her, but before she could turn around, his voice took her by surprise.

"Did you know that the Empire State Building gets hit by lightning about a hundred times a year?"

She closed her eyes. It couldn't be. She spun around and opened them. Travis's cheeks and the tip of his nose were pink from the cold, but his eyes were the bluest she'd ever seen. Summer blinked and blinked again, afraid he was nothing more than a figment of her exhausted imagination. "What are you doing here?"

He smiled. There was something different about it. There was something different about *him,* but Summer couldn't put her finger on it. His hair was longer, almost as long and shaggy as it had been the first time she laid eyes on him. His dimples were the same. She didn't have time to think any further. His nose was cold but his lips were warm. He pressed them to hers and she didn't want the moment to end.

"I missed you, Weather Girl," he said when he pulled back.

No one had called her that in so long it almost hurt to hear the nickname. At the same time, it made her want to kiss him again. He was here. Not just in New York but in the Discovery Network's building. "No, really. What are you doing here?"

"Would it freak you out more if I said I was here to return your umbrella, or that I came because I love you?" Sure enough, in his hand was her red umbrella. But it was the second option that left her spinning.

"You love me?" The thrill shifted to unexpected anger. "You *love* me?" How dare he say that now, after he'd broken her heart and sent her away? How dare he say it, when he was moving to Alabama and she was here? There was no future for them, so why tell her now?

Fueled by her hurt, she took off down the hallway back to the conference room. She sat in her seat and picked up her pen. Her hands were shaking so badly Ryan put a hand on her shoulder.

"What's wrong?"

Summer had no words to explain what had happened. She could still feel the softness of Travis's lips on hers and smell that familiar cologne. Travis was here and he loved her. He loved her and she'd run away, leaving him by the vending machines probably as hurt and confused as she felt.

"I have to go," she said, fumbling with her things.

Ryan's grip on her tightened. "Hold on there. We only have one more person to interview."

"I don't care who you hire. I have to go." Summer flung her purse over her shoulder and stood up. She had to find Travis and figure out what was going on. She feared she'd chased him away and was never going to find him again.

"I think you're going to want to stay for this one." Ryan motioned for someone at the door to come in.

Travis, looking quite chagrined, walked in with a cup of coffee in hand. Summer fell back into her chair. He set the paper cup in front of her. "You forgot this," he said quietly.

"Look at that," Ryan said. "He already knows how to bring you coffee. I think we have a winner here."

Summer tore her eyes from Travis to find a very smug Ryan looking back. He had known what he was doing all along. Her whole body was shaking now. "Can Travis and I have a minute alone, please?"

"It's your assistant position to fill. I'll leave this interview to you." Ryan popped up and grabbed his jacket off the back of his chair. "Wait till you see this guy's references. David Raines had some very nice things to say about him when I talked to him the other day."

Big D. Summer had been set up by her own family—and not by the usual suspect. Mimi was the meddler, not her husband. They were both getting a very stern talking-to when this was all over.

Ryan stopped and shook Travis's hand, quickly introducing himself. "I'm looking forward to seeing you again, Travis," he said on his way out.

All those other interviews were for show. There was only one person truly up for this job.

"I can't believe we managed to surprise you. I thought for sure Mimi would blow it," Travis said, taking a seat across from her.

She probably would have laughed if she could get over her shock and simultaneous relief. "Why are you here? I thought you were going to Alabama."

Travis smirked—the same look she'd taken note of earlier was back. "I'm here because this is where I belong."

"What does that mean? You belong here?" She didn't dare to hope. She hadn't asked him to come to New York with her because he was going to Alabama.

"I didn't take the job in Alabama, because that was what my dad wanted, not what I wanted. I told you I was taking it so you wouldn't give this job up. I thought I could make it work, but I would've been living a lie. I'm not a coach. I don't want to be a coach."

"What do you want?" The words came out in a rush. Summer gripped her armrest. The way he looked at her had her pinned in her seat.

He let out a laugh that could be mistaken for a breath if you didn't know him. "That's been the magic question for a while, hasn't it?"

It had. From the moment she met him, he was trying to figure out who he was and what he wanted. Was it possible he finally had an answer? "Well?"

"Did you know that when you see a rainbow, the sun is always behind you and the rain in front?"

Summer covered her face with both hands. "Oh no, I did it. I cursed you with random weather factitis." She peeked through her fingers. "There's no cure. I am so sorry."

"It comes in handy when the conversation gets tough." Leave it to him to see the bright side of her quirk. "I may have looked a few things up so I could impress you and Ryan today. I really want this job."

Summer dropped her hands. "What about your job at the station?"

"I quit. Turned in my resignation to Ken about a week ago. My last day was yesterday." He seemed so calm for a guy in a strange city with no job. He was unemployed and here because he loved her. This was too much to process on so little sleep. She picked up the coffee and took a sip in hopes the caffeine would help her make sense of all this.

As she set the cup down, her shaky hands came back. "Ken must have flipped."

"I guess you could say it didn't go over well. I feel bad. If it weren't for Ken, I might never have met you," he said. Hope bloomed in her chest. There was no stopping it. "We should send him a gift. What says 'thanks for introducing me to the love of my life and sorry for bailing on you'?"

"The love of your life?"

"That's what my heart tells me when I listen closely." Travis stood up and walked around the long conference table.

"Is that all it says?" she asked.

He swallowed hard and shook his head as he pulled her to her feet. He took her hand and placed it over his own heart. "It also told me to come here and follow you around forever and ever."

Summer could feel his heart beating like hers. "For sure?"

He nodded and leaned down to kiss her again. "With a little help from Mimi and Big D, I realized I want to do this with you. I don't care if I have to lug equipment around or pick up your dry cleaning. I need to be here—or wherever you are. Always."

She could feel tears sliding down her cheeks. "I want you here. Always."

He kissed her tears away and pushed the hair from her eyes. "I love you, Weather Girl."

One side of her mouth quirked into a lopsided grin. His smile was full and wide. He wrapped his arms around her waist. "I still love you, too," she confessed.

"You do?"

She nodded, rubbing her nose against his.

Travis held her face in his hands and looked down on her with a reverence she felt in her soul. "More than El Niño and cumulonimbus clouds?"

Summer's fingers slid through the hair at the nape of his neck, pulling him closer. "The fact that you even know there are such things as cumulonimbus clouds makes me love you a million times more than any weather event known to man."

"So does that mean I got the job?"

There were no doubts. As sure as she knew when it was going to rain, she knew Travis was the only one for her. "You are most definitely hired."

CHAPTER TWENTY

One year later...

"WE HAVE SOME exciting news here at Channel 6. Two former members of our KLVA family had a very exciting day today. Local football legend Travis Lockwood and Abilene's favorite former weather girl, Summer Raines, spent the rainiest day in city history doing something not even Mother Nature could stop from happening." Christina Wilson, the new nightly anchorwoman, sat at the news desk alone but smiled brightly. "Brian Sanchez is our man on the scene tonight."

The control room switched to a shot of Abilene Southern Baptist Church. The pale stone building looked darker as the rain came down and puddles covered the sidewalk in front of it. Brian's voice played over the video of the flooded parking lot and a pile of umbrellas in a corner of the church entryway.

Water dripped from a huge swell in the ceiling in what looked like a bridal room.

"Abilene has not seen this much rain in a twenty-four hour period since May 11, 1928, when a record 6.24 inches of rain fell. Given the drought our area has endured for the past decade, it's hard to believe we were once the precipitation capital of Edwards Plateau. Today we attempted to regain our title. Luckily, a little—or maybe I should say a lot of—rain can't stop true love."

The Irving Berlin song "Love and the Weather" played in the background. A shot inside the church sanctuary revealed a young man and woman holding hands and looking very much in love. She wore white lace that stopped just below her knees and he wore a dark gray tuxedo better than anyone else could. The pastor announced them husband and wife and told the man he could kiss his bride. The groom didn't hesitate. He took her face in his capable hands and kissed her with all he had as the guests cheered.

"In spite of flooded streets and the threat of quarter-size hail, Summer and Travis couldn't pass up the opportunity to say 'I do' on this day in weather history," Brian's voice said over the shot.

"There's nothing Summer loves more in the world than the weather and Travis." The name Sarah Raines flashed on the screen as the proud grandmother spoke to the camera. "So it makes sense for her to get married on the rainiest day this city's ever seen."

Brian continued while old footage of Travis and Summer reporting from football games played. "The couple met while working here at KLVA. Summer told me today that she will forever be grateful to station manager Ken Collins, who brought the two of them together."

Sam Lockwood, father of the groom, was interviewed next. "If you told me a few years ago that my son would be traveling the world as a storm chaser instead of a quarterback, I would have said you were crazy. But Summer and this show of theirs make Travis happier than he ever was playing ball, and that means the world to me and his mother."

A clip ran of the newlywed storm chasers standing on the shores of Bermuda with waves crashing on the rocks nearby, just before Hurricane Owen hit the island. "Like

Mr. Lockwood mentioned, you can catch the happy couple every weekend in some even wilder weather conditions. Their show, 'The Weather Girl,' airs Sunday nights on the Discovery Channel."

Chief Meteorologist Richard Mitchell smiled as he was interviewed. "Should've known the rain wouldn't want to miss this wedding. Good thing Summer is never caught in the rain unprepared."

The next shot showed the wedding couple coming out of the church protected by a bright red umbrella. They stopped, standing in ankle-deep water, and kissed in the rain. She was wearing pink and purple rubber boots and carried a bridal bouquet of roses and calla lilies. Barefoot, the groom had his pant legs rolled up to his knees.

Brian came on, live via satellite. "Believe me, it was wet out there. There wasn't a dry eye or a dry anything in the house today." Behind him, the wedding guests crowded the dance floor. Tables draped in winter white were cleared except for the centerpieces— pink rain buckets filled with flowers and covered by red parasols. "Here at the reception, we're finally warm and dry. I heard someone say they think we should go outside and dance in the rain, but I think I'll stay right here."

"Good idea, Brian." Christina was still smiling. "All of us here at Channel 6 say congratulations, Summer and Travis. We wish you a lifetime of love and happiness and hope it's nothing but blue skies from here on out."

* * * * *

LARGER-PRINT BOOKS!

GET 2 FREE
LARGER-PRINT NOVELS
PLUS 2 FREE
MYSTERY GIFTS

Love Inspired

Larger-print novels are now available...

LILPDIR13R

ReaderService.com

Manage your account online!

- Review your order history
- Manage your payments
- Update your address

---

*We've designed
the Harlequin® Reader Service
website just for you.*

Enjoy all the features!

- Reader excerpts from any series
- Respond to mailings and
  special monthly offers
- Discover new series available to you
- Browse the Bonus Bucks catalog
- Share your feedback

Visit us at:
ReaderService.com